Praise for Dragon Island

"An adventure tale that's witty, suspenseful, and full of heart... Manas' thriller feels a lot like a good action movie: witty, snappy, tense, and energetic... many readers are sure to enjoy this Jurassic Park-flavored romp."
— *Kirkus Reviews*

""Epic, intelligent and cinematic... a worthy addition to the canon of great monster thrillers."
— *BestThrillers.com*

"Manas delivers a brisk, cinematic science thriller in Dragon Island, fusing paleontology, military secrecy, and creature-driven suspense into an adventure that moves with blockbuster efficiency."
— *Booklife Reviews*

"J.B. Manas delivers pure adrenaline in *Dragon Island*. Think *Jurassic Park* meets military conspiracy—prehistoric terror, modern secrets, and a cover-up that could cost them everything. Cinematic, fast-paced, and impossible to put down."
— *National Bestselling Author Veronica Wolff*

Dragon Island

ISBN-13 (Paperback): 979-8-9862591-4-7

ISBN-13 (eBook): 979-8-9862591-5-4

Published by Somerton Press | Philadelphia, PA

Dragon Island

J.B. Manas

SOMERTON
PRESS

Somerton Press

Contents

"The pervasiveness of dragon myths in the folk legends of many cultures is probably no accident."
- Carl Sagan*

* The Dragons of Eden, New York: Random House, 1977

Chapter One

Inferno

The first thing Raymond "Toro" Cortez noticed was the abrupt silence of the birds. He'd been focused on his gardening, but the shift in sound was strange. Usually, the rainforest beckoned him with beautiful melodies—the constant buzz of hummingbird wings, the riotous screech of the parrots—but now he heard nothing, as if the birds had sensed trouble and left town.

He rose and dropped his shovel. The yucca plants would have to wait. He lifted his straw hat and wiped the sweat from his forehead as he gazed into the shadowy depths of the silent forest to his left, just beyond his bamboo cabin. He shielded his eyes from the sun as he looked upward to scour the trees for any signs of fluttering.

Then he saw something: a flock of green Amazons flying silently toward the sea. That was odd in itself. What were they fleeing?

Toro had first heard about Isla Lagarta about thirty years ago from the locals in San Juan. They said it was a tiny island in an archipelago near Vieques, about eight miles from Puerto Rico's eastern coast. He'd been looking for something remote and quiet where he could do a bit of farming. According to them, much of the island's terrain was ancient volcanic rock, and the rest was mainly used for livestock pasture and some minor agriculture. It sounded perfect to him. After the horrors of Vietnam, and then a couple decades driving a taxi in

New York City—until that, too, turned violent—he needed a little peace. And here he'd gotten it in spades. He was in his forties then. Now he was seventy-three, and he wouldn't trade his current life for all the gold in Fort Knox. He liked to joke that the island was so tranquil, even Hurricane Maria skipped over it.

These days, the locals called it *la pequeña milagro*—the little miracle. Still, with most of the island's rainwater seeping straight into underground rock, save for the seasonal waterfalls fed by heavy rain or hidden springs, they were dependent upon fresh water coming in from San Juan via Vieques, so it hadn't exactly been a bed of roses—especially since the shipments were often late. But it beat New York and it definitely beat Vietnam.

Just as Toro reached for his shovel again, the winds picked up. An unusual noise drifted from the distance, like the whistling of a giant tea kettle. But as he strained his ears, the sound twisted into something more sinister—like a chorus of terrified children wailing in unison. It swelled until it echoed throughout the volcanic hills of Isla Lagarta. Before he knew it, the whistling had morphed into screeching, then erupted into violent howling—like the bellow of a great beast.

The trees began bending in the strengthening wind, and the noise grew deafening. He clapped his hands over his ears and hunched over, his heart pounding. What was that bizarre noise? A hurricane? A tornado? The weather didn't seem right for either. The sound was horrifying, unlike anything he had ever heard.

He glanced up. In the distance, a handful of people seemed to be running in his direction. At first, there were just a few villagers, but then more appeared behind them—many more. Within seconds, throngs were rushing toward him, likely headed for the cliffs that led down to the sea. He couldn't imagine what they were fleeing, but even the birds had sensed it.

The haunting howl grew thunderous, and a strong gust carried a pungent smoke. Beneath it, he caught the unmistakable tang of rotten eggs. Sulfur. For a moment, he wondered if a volcano had erupted, but the smoke lacked that familiar dry rock and metal scent. A gas leak wouldn't make that sound. A forest fire seemed unlikely; the village behind him had few trees. And besides, forest fires didn't smell like sulfur.

He didn't have to wait long for an answer. A tremendous shadow ascended over the fleeing horde, caused by something gargantuan flying just behind them. The object was much too massive to be a plane, though he couldn't exactly see *what* it was in the glare of the sun. Enormous bursts of fire rained down upon the masses and erupted with a vengeance over wide swaths of land. He knew napalm. This wasn't napalm.

The angel of death—or whatever it was—circled back toward the village, perhaps to torch anything it missed.

Toro's eyes burned as he squinted through the red haze. Charred bodies covered the ground in the distance, and the incoming stench of death assaulted his senses—a stench he tried so many years to forget, even avoiding campfires. His stomach heaved. Up ahead, one man, fully ablaze, ran toward him screaming until he dissolved mid-step into a pile of ash.

The massive entity looped around again. It was heading his way.

Those who'd survived the first blast continued running. He doubted they'd make it to the cliff, and even if they did, it was a long jump to the sea. Remembering his training, he instinctively tossed his hat aside and frantically pulled his t-shirt over his head. He grabbed the shovel and began digging as fast as he could. If he could manage to burrow himself into the ground, he stood a chance. For a moment, he was back in Nam, digging as fast as he could to avoid enemy fire, burrowing like a rat in the jungle.

As he repeatedly jabbed the shovel into the ground and tossed the soil, he kept an eye on the strange weapon of destruction in the sky. Whatever it was, it was getting closer.

Dig, Toro, dig. That thing'll be here any second.

The muscles in his arms burned as he tried to pry up as much soil as he could with each hoist. Occasionally, he'd hit rock and he'd need to shift a few feet, which wasn't doing him any favors.

The bloodcurdling roars continued as the skies filled with the suffocating inferno. Despite the scorching blast of intense heat, a cold sweat ran down his spine. He had trouble breathing as the dry heat filled his nostrils.

The entity was nearly upon him now.

He dug frantically, sweat stinging his eyes. The hole was barely big enough—but it would have to suffice.

He peered through the smoke and that's when he spotted a dark-haired young girl. She wasn't running with the others. She was standing in the middle of the field, frozen in place and facing the coming doom. She was only about eleven or twelve.

Now he had a choice to make . . . an impossible one. He could either climb into the temporary grave he'd worked so hard to finish, or rush to try to save the girl.

The bringer-of-destruction was almost upon them now, and as he gazed up at the strange sight, he thought he might very well be hallucinating. This wasn't any type of machine. No chance. It was some sort of living creature, with tremendous wings that moved with the wind. Or more likely, it was generating the wind.

He looked up to see the giant mouth opening, deadly jaws filled with rows of sharp teeth.

He had to decide fast. Dive into his hole and pray? Or try, likely in vain, to save the girl. It was a gamble with death written all over it.

In that moment, the hole behind him felt like a grave—and the girl, the only reason to live. Before he could think, his feet were already moving.

Chapter Two

Vikki

"Where do you think the dragon went?"

Dr. Vikki Barnes smiled at the third grader's wide-eyed question. She'd expected the topic to come up eventually—but not right in the middle of showing them a once-in-a-lifetime exhibit.

"You mean the Photoshop-o-saurus?" she said, earning a ripple of laughter from the kids and chaperones. Weekdays were always busy at the Academy of Natural Sciences, but today seemed to have a special electricity, probably thanks to the dragon.

"Whatever was on that video," she added, looking around at the other students, "I'm sure we'll all find out soon. But from a scientific perspective, it's highly unlikely it was a real dragon—almost impossible. So, kids, you can put your mind at ease."

The boy's hopeful grin didn't fade. "But I'm hoping it is!"

"Well, I'm sorry to disappoint anyone, but there's probably going to be some other explanation." She had an idea it would be an uphill battle trying to get kids excited about Devonian Fish when a so-called dragon was all over the news.

She glanced around at the restless school group. She knew that most of them just wanted to get to the giant dinosaurs, the taxidermy-stuffed lions, and then lunch and the gift shop. Still, she liked the challenge of trying to pique their interest.

"Are there any questions *not* related to the dragon I can answer?" she said. "The grown-ups can ask, too."

They all looked hesitant to speak.

"Just think about what we're looking at here," she said. "Right here in Philadelphia. Co-discovered by our own Ted Daeschler before he retired."

She pointed to the nearly intact fossil that was found in the Canadian Arctic, and the fully reproduced creature next to it.

"*Tiktaalik* was a 375-million-year-old fish with gills," she added, "but a head like a crocodile. Plus, its fins had bones for walking, not to mention it has wrist bones, a neck, and shoulders."

"What would a fish need with that?" said a freckle-faced boy from the middle of the group.

"That's exactly the right question," she said, pointing at him. "But this isn't just a fish. It's a missing link that helps us piece together how fish evolved to grow limbs. Keep in mind, this was a few hundred million years before dinosaurs even existed!"

That seemed to get at least some of the kids' attention, as a few mouthed, "Wow!" to one another.

She glanced around at the rest of the dazed faces. "Guys, during the Devonian Period, this was the very first life to make it from the sea onto land. That's why we call it the *Life Onto Land* exhibit. Isn't that cool?"

"Why do they call it the Devonian Period?" asked one of the teachers, a Latina woman in her sixties.

Vikki's phone buzzed but she ignored it.

"Great question! It's because the red-colored rocks from that period when North America and Europe collided were first studied in Devon, England. If it's easier to remember, we also call it the *Age of Fishes*."

"Wait, America and Europe collided?" said an older red-headed boy in the front.

"Land is always moving, but it takes a really long time. The Mid-Atlantic Ridge that separates our continents drifts apart just two centimeters a year. That's less than an inch! But multiply that over a 200-million-year period and that just so happens to be the width of the Atlantic Ocean."

"Oooooh, that's sick," he said. She still couldn't get used to today's slang.

"Hey, if the fish grew limbs, did they turn into dinosaurs?" asked an older Black girl in the back, likely a fifth grader.

"Another great question!" said Vikki. "Think of evolution as a tree. All land vertebrates—that means they have a spinal column—evolved from fish. Some branches of fish became amphibians, and some became reptiles. Some branches of reptiles became dinosaurs, and eventually, some even became mammals—like you and me. In other words, this exhibit is the story of how amphibians began, reptiles began, dinosaurs began, and *you* began!"

"So, we came from reptiles? Sick!" said the red-headed boy again as he flicked his tongue like a snake to his friend, the two of them giggling.

Vikki's phone buzzed again. She glanced at it quickly to see if it was anything urgent.

It was a text from Caroline upstairs: *Need you in the office ASAP. Visitor.* Weird. She wasn't expecting a visitor. She never got visitors.

"What about birds?" asked a tall, squeaky-voiced, teen boy in the middle of the group. "Did they evolve from pterodactyls?"

"Actually no. Birds evolved from a group of dinosaurs called therapods, which had arms and walked on two feet. You probably know the most famous therapod, the T-Rex. But only the smaller theropods, raptors, became birds. Pterosaurs were flying reptiles, a different species entirely."

"When you say raptors, do you mean velociraptors?" said the girl in the back.

"Yes, and other raptors, too. But the bigger question we always ask about evolution is why. Why did some fish grow limbs? Why did some dinosaurs grow wings? Species always evolve for a reason. Something always causes it."

"So why *did* fish grow limbs?" said the squeaky-voiced boy.

"Well at first it was a way to survive in shallow waters, and then they evolved even more to be able to live on land."

"How about wings?" said the boy.

"Pretty similar," she said. "The smaller dinosaurs walked on two feet and needed to jump to escape predators. And over time, their arms grew into wings to be able to jump better—from tree to tree for example. And as those dinosaurs grew smaller and lighter, they could fly."

"Is that why they had feathers?" asked one of the male teachers, a stocky bald guy.

"Well, not at first. Only some dinosaurs had feathers, and they had them long before they could fly. They may have helped them stay warm or attract a mate. But then the feathers evolved to help them fly, too."

"Thanks," he said. "I've been teaching the kids about ornithology."

"Well, you may be interested to know that one of the greatest ornithologists ever worked right here in this museum. Do you know what his name was?"

He shook his head.

"It was James Bond. In fact, Ian Fleming read his book, *Birds of the West Indies*, and liked the name so much, he named his spy after him!"

The teacher's mouth dropped, and he whispered something to his students.

"About the dragon," said an Asian girl in the back. "Is it possible it was a pterosaur?"

Vikki smiled. "Not a chance. Plus, pterosaurs didn't breathe fire, nor did any other species we know of."

"Plus, there'd be dragon fossils everywhere," said the Latina teacher, trying to calm the kids down.

"Well, not everything fossilizes," said Vikki. "We paleontologists really only have a very small data set to work with. But still, there's no scientific evidence that dragons ever existed, or even *could* exist, at least not like in the myths."

Vikki's phone buzzed again. She didn't even bother looking.

Since nobody else had their hand raised, she took advantage of the few seconds of silence. "Well, we're about out of time and I have to get ready for another group this afternoon, but thank you all so much for coming! I hope you learned a lot."

After the kids applauded and the teachers thanked her, she turned to head back upstairs to the offices. Most visitors didn't realize the museum only took up about a third of the building. The bulk of the action happened behind the scenes—the research, the offices, the storage, and so on.

She hesitated at the stairwell, glancing at the old expedition photos on the wall. Most days, she hurried past them. Today, she lingered a second too long before forcing herself upstairs. The travel-restricted life wasn't how she'd pictured her career. She'd once dreamed of wild places and new discoveries, but now she kept her feet firmly on museum floors. Some dreams, she'd learned, were safer left behind.

Meanwhile, she was dying to know who her visitor was.

She glanced down at her phone to check her latest text.

Her jaw dropped.

Chapter Three

Missing Persons

"Dad!?" said Vikki. "What are you doing here?"

Dr. Jim Barnes was seated in the chair opposite her desk, grinning, clearly enjoying her surprise.

"Well, that's a nice greeting," he said, smirking. "I just got in last night."

How's the Army Science Advisor gig going out there?" It seemed like forever since he took the job at the Hartford Research Institute in Santa Fe. "Usually, I have to come out to see you."

"Sorry about that. Well, I'm here now."

She bent down to hug him—there really was nothing like a father's hug. "I'm just amazed to see you here. Is everything okay?"

"I'm fine, but I'm more interested in hearing about you. Are you dating anyone?"

She could feel her muscles tightening. "You didn't fly all the way from Santa Fe to ask me that."

He reclined in his chair and shook his head as he smiled. "I'm just interested in your well-being, Vik."

"I'm doing fine. Are *you* dating anyone?"

"Nothing serious yet, but I . . . did kind of meet someone." He sounded like a teen afraid to admit to his parents he crashed their car. "I think you'd like her."

That was just great. He found someone, and here she was, going on blind dates with narcissists and pig-headed morons, and that was when they showed up at all—though she had a date tomorrow that sounded promising. She wasn't about to mention it or he'd ask her a zillion questions. Oh well, score one for Dad. Still, she wanted him to be happy.

She realized she was clenching her jaw and forced a slight smile. She took a seat behind her desk and straightened a messy pile of notes that he was probably going to make a comment about. He was always a neat freak.

"Is that why you're here?" she said. "Are you getting engaged or something?" She was hoping she didn't sound passive aggressive.

"What? No, I'm here on business, actually." He seemed relieved at her calm response.

"In Philly? I didn't know HRI had an Army science division here."

"No, I mean *here* here. Visiting you."

"I don't get it."

He leaned forward as if to tell her some big secret. "I assume you saw that dragon video."

"Oh . . .my . . .God. Not you too!"

His face grew surprisingly alarmed. "Who else contacted you about it?"

"Just about every middle-school kid you can imagine. You don't for a minute think it's real. Hello? Who are you and what did you do with my dad?"

He was usually about as cynical and scrutinizing as they came. He used to always quote Sherlock Holmes to her, telling her to never theorize without all the data. He'd go into his spiel any time she'd voice an opinion on something.

"Well, there really was a fire out there," he said. "It wiped out half the island."

"That could have been anything. A brush fire. A volcanic fissure. A gas leak even." She couldn't believe she was having this conversation with the man who had always drilled into her head to question everything and focus on provable facts.

He nodded. "That's what the Army said it was, a gas leak. They said the video was doctored."

"And you don't believe them?"

He pulled his tablet out of his briefcase and turned it toward her.

"Just watch this," he said. "This was the cell phone video sent to the media."

She watched as a young girl in the distance stood with her back to the camera, facing what looked like an enormous flying creature, spitting flames, burning everything—and everyone—in its path. The footage, shot from about thirty yards back, was too blurry for details, but the creature was flying low. A man rushed into frame from the left, trying to save the girl—or at least it looked that way. But then the beast hovered for some reason when it got to her. The flames stopped. It seemed to deliberately pause, as if they were having a staring contest.

Its massive wings whipped her long brunette hair into a frenzy. Then it turned and blasted flames at the camera, frying the videographer and probably the man.

Vikki blinked as the video ended. She wondered who could have sent the video—assuming it was real in the first place, which she doubted. In any case, an investigation would turn up the mundane truth. It always did. Meanwhile, as far as she understood it, nobody was allowed near the site.

"I've seen this video a dozen times," she said. "It's on YouTube. The likelihood of a species like this existing and being able to shoot flames is practically zero. And besides, why would someone even stick around to film it?"

"You're right," he said, taking the tablet back. "I agree with you. The odds are pretty slim. Don't you find that girl a little unusual?"

"You mean because she was just standing there? She was obviously traumatized. By something, anyway."

"And the dragon, or whatever it is, just stops when it gets to her? Changes its mind?"

"Coincidence," she said. "That's if it was real to begin with."

"Well, if it isn't real, the Army is spending quite a bit of time and money trying to keep it a secret."

"Maybe they created it."

"What, the dragon?" He shook his head. "I watched the video more times than you can count. This moves like an organic lifeform."

"CGI can work wonders these days. They can turn a plane into a dragon or a dog into a T-Rex. Or even create something out of nothing. Whatever it is, we know what it's not. A dragon. If you ask me? The whole thing sounds like a hoax. It's not like anyone's been to the island reporting on the damage."

"All good thoughts," he said. "But then why would the Army be sending out a search party for this girl . . . and the guy who was running to help her?"

"I heard nothing about that."

"You wouldn't. It's sensitive information—came to me through unofficial channels. Neither of their bodies were found. Why are they so important? My contact on the inside doesn't even know."

She had to admit, it was puzzling. "Maybe they have their reasons. Maybe they want to see if they're still alive."

"This isn't *Saving Private Ryan*. The Army doesn't send out search parties for someone unless they have some kind of special significance. And in this case, nobody knows who the girl is. And as for the guy, well that's another story."

"What about him?"

"Toro Cortez was one of the most decorated soldiers in history. Two Silver Stars, five Purple Hearts, and about a dozen more medals. They called him 'Toro' because he once charged straight through an ambush—like a bull—when everyone else dove for cover. He was a legend in Vietnam."

"I'm sure that's why they're looking then. He probably means a lot to the Army."

Her dad shook his head. "I don't think that's it."

"Dad, I don't get it. What happened to the guy who said don't come to any conclusions until you've verified the facts?"

"That's exactly what I did. Verified the facts. Sent one of my most trusted scientists to the island in the interest of Army research. And he saw some things that I think you need to see."

"Me!? What things?"

"I want you to come to your own conclusions. You're the only one I trust to get to the facts. This is your space. Besides, you specialize in pterosaurs. You're perfect for this."

She grabbed the little dinosaur-shaped stress ball on her desk. It was a gift from her mom when she'd first gotten the job. She looked at the faded writing on the side of it. "*From Mom. Happy Digging.*" Her hand was already trembling as she squeezed the purple toy. There was no way she was traveling anywhere—least of all to a place with cliffs and lizards.

"My space is the past, not the present. You need a biologist. Or a zoologist. Besides, you know I don't do fieldwork anymore." He had to understand. Between curating and cataloguing fossil collections, teaching, writing papers, doing lab work, and a million other tasks, she had plenty to keep her busy.

She could see the disappointment on his face as he sighed. "What happened to the girl who was always curious about everything? I remember you went nuts over a raccoon skull we found in the woods.

You couldn't wait to get it home and study it. You used to love going on adventures. Remember you used to dream about finding a new species?"

She glanced at the old family photo on the credenza by the window.

"That dream died with Mom."

She swallowed hard, her gaze lingering on the old photograph.

"That was a freak accident and you know it. It could've happened to anyone."

"But it didn't." If she had one wish, it was that her mom had been a little less adventurous.

He threw up his hands. "You can't live your life in fear, Vik. Listen, I'm sending a small team out there tomorrow to follow-up. I'd really like you to join them. If you're not impressed after that, I won't bother you again about it. This could be big for you."

She put the dino stress ball down and took a breath, glancing at the tall box marked *Fossils - Fragile* that had been placed in her office in the morning.

"Dad, I'm sorry to disappoint, but you'll have to find someone else. We just got a new shipment in and I'm way behind. The best I can do is a media interview to hopefully stop all the speculation. Other than that, if you don't mind, maybe we can change the subject."

"Okay, fair enough. By the way, have you heard from Matt recently?"

The blood began rushing to her face as her nails dug into the desk.

"Is that your way of getting back at me?"

"No, no, I just thought you never really gave him a fair chance. He's a scientist. A nice guy. You had a lot in common. Better than that cop guy. At least Matt was a decent fellow."

"Who cheated on me. You left that part out. Why are you bringing this up?"

"Because he's coming to your house tomorrow to take you to the helicopter."

"The *what*?"

Chapter Four

Matt

As soon as Jim Barnes stepped onto the patio at the 20th Street Café, he spotted Matt at the far table, waiting as planned.

"Did you order my drink?" said Barnes.

Matt put his beer down and shook his head. "I was afraid to."

Barnes hadn't been to Philly in ages. The Parkway area hadn't changed much, except for a few new cafés. Patterned after the Champs-Élysées in Paris, he'd hoped it would've been expanded by now to be lined with restaurants. Then again, there was something to be said for less hustle and bustle.

The waiter approached, smiling. "You're here. I was told you're particular about your drink."

"Yes, I'd like a Tanqueray martini, straight up with an olive, extra dry. In fact, just show it the Vermouth bottle. Got all that?"

The waiter repeated it back.

"If you don't want the Vermouth," said Matt, "why don't you just order gin?"

"Cause I like it in a martini glass. Got a problem with that?" He smirked.

"Nope. No problem. So, what'd she say?"

"What do you think she said?"

Matt frowned. "Can I just tell you what happened between us? It'll solve a lot of problems."

"No can do. I told you, it's gonna have to be up to you. I can't get in the middle. Because, if I know, then I'll have to keep a secret from my daughter, which I'm not gonna do. And if I tell her and take your side, then I become guilty by association. And I don't wanna do that either. So, man up, Matthew. You'll have to work it out between the two of you."

The waiter arrived with his drink. He took a sip. "Perfect," he said.

Matt leaned forward. "So do I still go tomorrow?"

"Of course. Vikki's a tough nut to crack. She's just like her mother was. If you're on the up and up, and I'm not saying you are—but I believe you're a good guy—she'll come around. Besides, I have my own reasons for wanting her to go."

"She really is the best person for this," said Matt.

"I don't doubt it. It's why I agreed to it. Now it's up to you to convince her. You have the evidence?"

Matt nodded.

"Good. I'm just glad it's you going, and not me. Vikki and her mom were the outdoorsmen, or women . . . whatever you call it. And go figure, now I'm seeing a woman who runs a horse ranch. She made the mistake of asking me to pick up the phone once. It was a buyer for one of her horses. They asked what color it was. I said brown with a white nose and blackish legs. Linda came up behind me and grabbed the phone, laughing. She said it was bay. The color was called bay. Who knew? Anyway, I don't know much about horses, and even less about dinosaurs."

"It's why we need Vikki."

He nodded. "Good luck convincing her. My advice?"

Matt raised an eyebrow.

"Don't even bring it up—the old stuff, I mean. This is business. Focus on the mission. Focus on the findings. Get her curious. Because I'm telling you, she'll fight like the dickens to avoid going out in the field. And if you start bringing up old memories, you'll only give her ammunition to back out."

"I'll try," said Matt, lifting his beer. "But what if *she* brings it up?"

"Then tell her the truth."

Matt leaned back and sighed. "I've been trying to do that for months. She doesn't answer the phone, doesn't reply to my emails. I even left a letter in her door. I didn't want to come across as a stalker, but . . ." his voice trailed off. "The truth, is, she means a lot to me, and I'd like to be able to prove it."

"Well then, tomorrow's your first step."

He liked Matt and believed he was sincere; it was easy to see he was trying. Still, Barnes was dying to know what had set Vikki off, but it was up to them to work it out. He'd learned long ago not to get in the middle of relationship drama.

He watched the hostess seat four middle-aged women at the table across from them. One asked for separate checks, and the hostess politely said she'd let the waiter know. Barnes admired the patience she showed—patience he knew he didn't possess—before turning back to Matt, who had a distant look on his face. He'd always known Matt to be pretty self-assured, at least at work. He wasn't the nervous type.

"Let's order some food," he said, trying to break the mood. "It's on the company. Fuel up for the big adventure."

Matt smiled. "I already had a big adventure."

"But we don't talk about that, right? Because this time, you have a plan."

Matt nodded. "Yes, sir." He lifted his glass to toast.

Their glasses clinked.

"Now, let's eat." Barnes signaled for the waiter.

Even though he was trying to lighten things up, as he watched Matt's nervous smile across the table, he couldn't shake the feeling that tomorrow's "brief investigation" might change everything—for all of them. He didn't want Vikki to be in any danger. He just wanted her to see the evidence and decide for herself. It would be good for her—and good for the truth. And if she reconciled with Matt, all the better. Still, his stomach was beginning to flutter. Was he doing the right thing?

Chapter Five

Unwelcome Guest

Vikki woke with a knot in her stomach and a resolve she'd never felt before: today, no one—not even Matt—would change her mind. She'd even rehearsed her "get lost" speech before bed, just in case he showed up early. With any luck, she'd slip out before he arrived. There was no way she was chasing after some fire-breathing monster— though a small part of her wondered what her father wanted her to see on that island.

Why did he decide to send Matt without asking her first anyway? Besides, with her first date with Kevin on the calendar, she had enough to worry about.

Thankfully, Kevin had been kind enough to agree to meet for brunch at Parc, rather than dinner, so she could avoid Matt. It was a perfect morning for a walk to Rittenhouse Square and eating on the patio. She loved their *Eggs Norwegian*—poached eggs, with smoked salmon and hollandaise. Now she just had to get out of the house on time. The idea of a real date made her stomach twist, with both nerves and hope. Finally, maybe, she'd found someone decent.

She rushed to get ready, rifling through her closet for the perfect outfit and shaving in record time. Then came the makeup. Her hair and finishing touches ate up another half hour.

She glanced at her watch. Crap.

Scrambling to put on her shoes—and nearly tripping—she checked her hair in the mirror one last time.

Satisfied she wasn't forgetting anything, she took a deep breath and steadied herself before heading to the door. As her hand reached for the doorknob, she thought she heard a faint knock.

She held her breath as she opened the door—and then sighed, throwing up her hands.

There waited Matt, hand raised in mid-knock.

"Well, that's a nice greeting," he said.

He stood there grinning in his khaki safari jacket, his *Grayson* name tag gleaming on his lapel. He was a scientist, for Chrissake, not a soldier, but she supposed it made him feel like some kind of adventurer.

Her jaw muscles tightened as memories of him came flooding back. She'd learned to distrust that grin a long time ago. It was the grin of a shady used car salesman. *We'll take care of the financing, no problem! You're in great hands!*

Dumbfounded, she realized it wasn't an exaggeration to say that her biggest problems these days started with him. After all, it was because of him that she didn't trust men, especially ones who seemed overconfident. And that jacket? It looked stupid.

"Going hunting?" she said.

"I had a bet with your dad you wouldn't answer," he said. "Guess I lost."

"Well, you both lose, because, as I told him, I have way too much to do. He just doesn't know how to take no for an answer."

"Can I—"

"I actually need to get going. I have a date." Her eyes flicked over his face, searching for any sign of disappointment. He looked briefly saddened but quickly forced a smile.

"A date. Nice. Well, when you see what's on that island—"

"Yes, I heard, Matt. You can send me pictures and I'll give you my assessment." She was trying to sound as business-like as possible.

His smile didn't waver. "I *have* pictures. I was there."

"Well, that's good, but I really have to go."

"Can I show them to you? Vik, please, just give me that. It'll just take a few seconds. If you're not interested after that, I can go and tell your dad you weren't here. Deal?"

She thought about it. It was like opening the door to an insurance salesman. She knew it was a mistake.

She nodded and invited him in. "Make it quick. I don't want to be too late." In reality, she'd left herself time to walk in the nice weather, so she had a few minutes to spare.

As soon as he entered the living room, Matt headed straight for the fireplace and clumsily removed the huge Panini canvas that hung above it. She'd spent a fortune on the antique frame, but the real value was sentimental—it belonged to her mom.

"What do you think you're doing?" she snapped.

"It's not heavy."

"That's not the point!"

He pulled a mobile phone-sized device from his jacket pocket and placed it on the coffee table. Instantly, a bright, blank projection filled most of the wall.

"Can you close the blinds?" he said.

Baffled, she complied. The sooner this was over, the better. She sat on the couch as he stood with a remote in his hand.

A crystal-clear aerial image appeared, revealing a mountainous forest with a small village nestled within it, and a rocky clearing that extended toward a cliff. Beyond the cliff was the brightest, turquoise blue sea she'd ever seen. As he zoomed in, she saw countless charred homes and dead trees.

"Okay, so it's a lot of damage," she said. "It's devastating, but there could be lots of explanations for that."

"Okay," he said, zooming in further. "Which of those explanations can cause *this*?"

At first, she thought she was looking at some kind of natural crater, but as he zoomed in further, her eyes widened.

It was a footprint. An enormous footprint. There was no way it could be anything else.

"There's another one about ten yards away," he said. "Then nothing else around it."

She stared at it for about thirty seconds before shaking her head in disbelief. She could hear the thumping of her own heartbeat. Could this really be a new species? A living one? Not a dragon, but something else perhaps? She realized she was speculating without the facts. Surely, the truth would be far less exciting than giant creatures that spit fire.

"This is impossible," she said. "There must be some—"

"I know." He raised his hands. "I didn't believe it either."

"So, this . . . alleged thing. It's bipedal?"

"Hard to tell if it walks on two legs or four," he said. "I didn't exactly have a clear view. But I didn't see any other prints on the island when I circled around. Whatever it was must've touched down for a second and flew off. If this thing is real, it's twice the size of a T-Rex."

"It can't be," she said. "Nothing like that exists. Are you sure this footage is real?"

"I took it myself, trust me."

She shot him a look.

"Okay, well trust me on *this*," he said.

She thought about it. Even Matt wouldn't have made this up. And he did seem dead serious.

She looked again. "Something's not right," she said. "It has a hallux like a raptor, but four forward-facing talons."

"Hallux?"

"The back talon. Raptors have them, but only three forward talons, not four. Also, this one's more on the side, so it doesn't use it for perching, which makes sense considering the size. Wait a minute. Is that webbing I see between the toe prints?"

He zoomed in further.

"Hard to tell," he said. "Could be."

"Weird. It's too big to be an Archeopteryx. And anyway, they don't have webbed feet."

"Arky-lop-a-what? Is that a kind of pterosaur?"

"Nope. Dinosaur. Actually, the first flying dinosaur. It evolved into birds."

"Wait, isn't a pterosaur a dinosaur, too?"

"You sound like my school kids. No, it's a flying reptile. And if what we're seeing is real, we're not dealing with a pterosaur either. Otherwise, I'd suspect a Quetzalcoatlus, which is in the pterosaur family, but even that's only about the size of a giraffe, and the footprint's all wrong."

"Could it be amphibious?"

She shook her head. "There aren't any flying amphibians except for those little flying frogs."

"I'll take your word for it," he said.

She stood up and paced around the room with her hand on her chin, trying to think of any possible explanation. Then she stopped and studied the image again.

"None of this makes sense."

She scanned the surrounding area. "Wait a minute," she said, moving closer. "Pan to the left a bit. Is that another footprint? Between those fallen trees?"

She watched as he panned the image to the left.

"Oh my God!" she called out, which made Matt jump. "That's definitely a footprint. Zoom in."

As he zoomed closer, she could make out the markings.

"Five talons and the side hallux," she said. "Different than the hind feet. Those had four talons. We're definitely looking at a quadruped here, which is literally impossible."

"Why?"

"Well, not only because there's never been a flying vertebrate with four legs in the history of the planet, but something that size taking to the air would defy the laws of physics. It would be like an elephant flying, only bigger."

"It worked in Dumbo. I'm just saying."

She started pacing again. "Even the largest pterosaurs took off and flapped with their huge front limbs. And their hind legs had to be small and light so they could fly. These legs are all proportionate."

"Don't forget the webbed feet," said Matt. "Even this new print looks like it has webbing."

"But why? What could it possibly need webbed feet for?"

"You're asking me? Maybe it's a sea creature."

"It can't live in the sea, or it wouldn't be able to fly. Not with that size. None of this is adding up."

She was baffled. Never mind the fact that this was the largest footprint she'd ever seen, but it was hard to tell where this even fit in the evolutionary tree, assuming it was even real. And if it wasn't real, it was an awfully good fake.

She walked closer to the image.

"The claws almost seem lizard-like," she said. "More reptile than bird."

"So, more alligator than albatross," said Matt.

"Exactly."

"How so? I mean, what makes reptile claws different?"

"Less curvature." She studied the image in more detail. "Interesting. Yes, this is definitely reptilian."

"Because of the claws?"

"The front footprint is pretty far off to the left. We can assume the right front foot smashed on those downed trees before it took off. But either way, dinosaur footprints are closer together—their legs are under their hips. Reptile footprints are off to the side, like this one. Please tell me you got samples."

"I'd love to tell you that, but I wasn't able to land. They had it blocked off. There may be more evidence there, too. That's why we need you."

"What makes you think I'll get any closer than you did?"

"We have that taken care of. Trust me." There was that word again.

She shook her head. As curious as she was, everything about this was setting off red flags: a secured military site, flying in some God-knows-what kind of contraption, the shady coverup going on.

She took a breath. "I'm not sure I'm the right person for this."

"Why not?"

She sighed. "Because, Matt, there are three things in this world I *don't* trust. Reptiles, helicopters, and, if I'm being honest, *you.*"

"Whaddya have against reptiles?"

She could feel her face grow red. "You have to ask?"

"That was a freak accident."

"You really have been talking to my dad."

"Vik, maybe what we really need to talk about is the elephant in the room."

"No elephants in here."

"I mean us. I can explain what happened. I mean it's so stupid, you'll actually laugh."

She took a moment to compose herself as she searched for the right response. As unpredictable as this whole trip sounded, could she really afford *not* to find out what was going on with those footprints? Maybe she could set her own requirements—make it a little safer.

"Okay, I'll make you a deal," she said. "I'll go on this little mission of yours, but I don't want to hear you utter another word about elephants or relationships or us. This is strictly business. And I want to get in and get out. Fast. And no helicopters. I want to go on a ferry or something."

"No problem," said Matt. She could tell by his smirk there was something he wasn't telling her.

"Oh no!" she said.

"What?" Matt looked concerned, probably thinking she was about to back out.

"I forgot to call Kevin to tell him I wasn't coming."

A look of relief washed over his face. "See?" he said, grinning. "Nobody's perfect."

She wanted to hit him with something, but for now, he was her only ticket into what would surely be pure hell.

Chapter Six

The Blue Meanie

After a three-and-a-half-hour flight to San Juan, Vikki had been relieved to get off the plane and into a taxi. She hated heights. Or maybe it was the feeling of not being in control. She and Matt hadn't spoken much in the plane or the taxi, and when they did, it was about their latest research. Fortunately, Kevin seemed understanding about the canceled date.

The ride took about an hour, mostly along the expressway, offering glimpses of the island's northeastern coastline before they reached Ceiba. As they approached their destination, the Hartford Research Institute's Puerto Rico facility came into view—a sleek white building with blue-tinted windows and a prominent HRI sign adorning its facade. She spotted a *Ceiba Ferry Terminal* sign just past the HRI building and felt reassured.

As they exited the taxi, she followed Matt into the building.

"So, you're working for my dad now," she said. "He never told me."

"Can you blame him?"

She couldn't help but smirk as she followed him into the elevator. "I suppose he knows better."

He pressed the *Roof* button. A flicker of panic surged through her.

"Wait," she said. "Why did you press Roof? I said no helicopters. I thought we were getting the ferry."

"We're meeting Reggie," he said. "Don't worry. He can be a little odd. A bit of a conspiracy theorist. But he's friendly."

"Who's Reggie?"

"Reggie Davis. He's gonna take us to Isla Lagarta on the Blue Meanie. It'll be fun."

"The Blue Meanie? Why's he on the roof?"

"That's where he said to meet. Relax. It's okay."

She clenched her fists, resisting the urge to snap.

"You know what makes me really un-relaxed?" she said. "When someone tells me to relax."

Matt smiled nervously, but it did nothing to calm the knot tightening in her stomach.

The elevator ride took forever, her palms growing sweatier with each chime of the floor indicator. Finally, they arrived at the roof and the doors opened. She followed Matt through a corridor and out into the balmy air. It was about 85 degrees, but it felt like a hundred. Good thing she'd stuffed her jacket into her carry bag.

A tall Black man in aviator sunglasses and a wide grin came forward to greet them.

"Dr. Matthew!" said the man. He had an American accent. He turned to Vikki and extended his hand. "And you must be Dr. Vikki. I'm Reggie and I'm pleased as papaya to be your pilot this pleasant afternoon. And I promise that's all the alliterations I'll bless you with today."

"*Pilot*?" said Vikki, shaking his hand. "There must be a mistake. I thought we're taking a ferry?"

Reggie burst out laughing and looked at Matt.

"Is that what you told her?"

As the fine hairs on her arms rose, her breathing turned shallow, and she felt herself teetering on the edge of passing out. "This is why I have trust issues," she said. "I don't do helicopters."

"Well, I didn't lie exactly," said Matt. "I was just . . . sloppy with the truth."

"Sloppy with the—"

"Oh, he's not totally wrong, Dr. Vikki," said Reggie. "This isn't exactly a helicopter. It's the Blue Meanie. Besides, the only ferry that could get us where we're going is one that flies. Now follow me, kind people."

Though her legs were practically numb, she followed Matt and Reggie around a white, stone wall, hoping it would at least be a small plane.

But as she turned the corner, there it was—in vivid blue reality. She should have known.

"That's . . . a helicopter!" she said, her knees going weak.

She felt her soul leaving her body. How could Matt not get that this was her worst nightmare? He, of all people, knew.

"Ah, but with modifications," said Reggie.

"Because you painted it blue?"

Her muscles turned rigid as she stared at the small helicopter. It looked like a royal blue oval with large windows and blue landing skids wrapped in padded cushions.

"What you're looking at," said Reggie, "is a modified Robinson R44 Clipper II. Those are inflatable floats attached to the landing gear, but I've added a lot more bells and whistles. So, it is kind of a ferry really."

Vikki rolled her eyes.

"But she can fly," Reggie continued. "And by fly, I mean she can go up to 200 miles per hour."

"That doesn't make me feel better." This was getting worse by the minute.

"Ah, I got you. I didn't say we're gonna *go* that fast. But she can if we need."

"That's good to know. Why don't I take the ferry, and I'll meet you both on the island?"

"Trust me, you can't." He grinned. "Hop in."

As Reggie opened the side door to the two rear seats, Vikki glanced inside the four-seater vehicle. It was about the size of a Toyota, with tan leather seats.

"Ladies first," said Matt. "I'll climb in the other side."

"I'm not gonna forgive you for this," she said, glaring at him. She meant it. She wanted to punch him right then and there.

He grinned. "You can add it to your list."

She reluctantly climbed into her seat as Reggie closed the door behind her. Before she knew it, the engine was running—much noisier than she expected.

The sharp smell of fuel hit her nose, and then, without any fanfare, the copter lifted off the roof. Between the pulsing rhythm of the blades and the rocking of the copter, she wished she was anywhere else. Anywhere but here.

Even in a car, she never liked being in the passenger seat because she felt out of control. This was out of control on steroids.

She held her hand against the inside of the door as the helicopter's sudden lift pressed her into her seat. "You need armrests on this thing."

"That's why the good Lord invented seat belts." Reggie flicked several switches, his easygoing expression growing more serious. That alone made her nervous. "It's about to get louder so put your headsets on. The jacks are above you."

"Louder? It's already loud."

She dared not look out the bubble-like front windows, but a quick glance out her side window nearly sent her into a panic. She felt like she was in a car dangling from a parachute.

The helicopter lunged forward, its rotors whirring loudly as it banked sharply down and to the right toward the shoreline. The abrupt movement sent a swooping feeling through her stomach, like a rollercoaster plunging down a hill.

She closed her eyes, praying the ride would soon be over.

Before long, they were over the open sea, and the helicopter leveled out. She was almost starting to get used to the feeling of being so high up, but not so much that her stomach wasn't doing somersaults.

"You know, I'll bet y'all anything the Army is behind this dragon thing," said Reggie, his voice coming in clear through the headset. "Just like they hid the aliens and the chupacabras. And all right here in sunny Puerto Rico."

Good heavens, this was going to be a long ride.

"Can't say I've heard anything about that," she said, as she looked down at the rippling sea. Now she knew what Matt was talking about when he said Reggie was odd. Is this what she was getting herself into? Next, it'll be unicorns and leprechauns.

"Look it up! 1975. All sorts of animal killings, all over the island. Bodies totally drained of blood through these little circular incisions. And then? Same thing happens twenty years later in '95. Sheep, cattle, you name it. Weird, huh?"

"Pretty strange," she said, humoring him. "Alien vampires I guess."

"Wait, then it starts happening in other places. Argentina, Bolivia, Brazil, Chile, Mexico. All Latin. And what was causing all this damage? A damn creature the size of a bear but with scales like a reptile. Yessiree, and spikes from head to tail, like Godzilla Junior. If that ain't alien, I don't know what is. A local called it a goat-sucker, or Chupacabra, and the name stuck."

"I thought they were supposed to look like dogs," said Vikki. She remembered seeing a TV show about it.

"That's in the states, but that was a whole different thing. That was some rabid coyote shit goin' on. Bunch of silly rumors."

"I heard about the Latin ones," said Matt. "But I heard the vets said the animals weren't really drained of blood. It was an urban legend."

"Okay, alright. I accept that. So maybe our boy got full and didn't finish drinking."

"And the point of all this?" said Vikki. "It's not like we're dealing with chupacabras or aliens or anything like that."

"Ah, the point, my good friend," said Reggie, "is that it's too many coincidences all in the same place. I'm just sayin' the government's been known to hide stuff. What about that secret military base?"

Vikki leaned forward. "What secret base?"

"In the El Yunque rainforest. They don't call it the Area 51 of the Caribbean for nothing. There's a secret American base there—or at least there was—blocked by a bunch of orange painted drums. Army guys threatened anyone who went near it. People would see trucks with cages goin' in there at night. I mean really big cages, like bigger than elephant size."

Matt shot Vikki a quick look. "When was this?" he said.

"I'd say maybe five or six years ago. The only thing we do know about the base is part of it was used for the HAARP program."

"Harp?" said Vikki.

"HAARP stands for High-frequency Active Auroral Research Program. Allegedly . . ." he made a quote sign with his left hand, "it's for studying the ionosphere through a big-ass, high-power, high-frequency transmitter. But they've been doin' all sorts of sound wave testing, including weapons. Don't know what it has to do with any of this weird stuff, or if it's just a coincidence. And don't get me started on the undersea structures spotted off the coast, causing all kinds of strange noises. At least, according to the reports. And get this . . ."

"What?" she said.

"A lot of folks started experiencing buzzing sensations."

"Seriously?" said Matt.

"It's all right there on the Internet. Told you, all the crazy stuff happens in Puerto Rico. Wouldn't be surprised if all this secret Army crap had something to do with this dragon of yours."

Vikki rolled her eyes. "Whatever it is, it's not a dragon."

Matt turned to her and shrugged, as if to apologize for Reggie's ranting. "How do you think it flies, anyway?" he said, trying to change the subject. "I mean it's too big to fly, right? That footprint was enormous."

Vikki shook her head. "I need to see what we're even dealing with. We may as well be chasing the Loch Ness monster."

"Hey, that's actually real," said Reggie. "Did I tell you about—"

"Reg, no offense," said Matt, "but I don't think Vikki cares about the Loch Ness monster at the moment."

"Well remind me, and I'll tell you sometime. It's an interesting story. That's a reptile too, just like your boy. Or girl as the case may be."

Vikki narrowed her eyes. "How did you know?"

"How did I know what?"

"How did you know we're looking at a possible reptile here? I don't recall sharing that with you."

"Well, who do you think flew the copter over with Dr. Matthew here? I saw the pictures. Dinos don't fly, and they sure don't swim, and this thing had webbed feet. Something that big that can fly didn't develop webbed feet just to walk better in the marsh. This baby swims. Ergo, a reptile. Easy peasy. But this ain't no pterosaur. Those prints are too big and too far apart for that."

Vikki looked at Matt wide-eyed, then at Reggie. "I'm impressed," she said. "Did you study paleontology?"

"I'm just a big nerd," said Reggie. "But I didn't answer Dr. Matthew's first question."

"What was that?" she said.

"How does it fly? My guess is . . . the only way it could. Some kind of methane sac. That would explain the fire, too."

Matt looked at Vikki and grinned. "We may not need you after all," he said.

"I'd be more than happy to go home."

As the helicopter navigated over the waters, Vikki suddenly spotted a tall, hilly island up ahead with a beautiful white sand beach. The crystal-clear waters near the shore revealed a vibrant array of colorful coral.

"Is that it?" she said.

"Yep, that's Isla Lagarta," said Reggie.

"So we *could've* taken a ferry. Those waters look as calm as could be."

"Yeah, but you see, that's not the way we're going," he said. "We have to circle around to the cliff and land in a small clearing in the rainforest."

"Why?"

"So the military doesn't spot us. Luckily, with my modifications we can avoid detection. Mostly."

"I don't get it," she said. "Aren't we sanctioned to be here?"

Reggie glanced back at Matt. "You didn't tell her?"

"Tell me what, exactly?" she said.

Matt had a sheepish look on his face. "Um . . . we were kind of unceremoniously chased away when we tried to land."

"Kind of!?"

"Yeah, this is a bit of a stealth operation," said Reggie, as the copter took a dip and veered suddenly to the left.

"A bit?" She gripped her seat and stared at Matt. She could feel her face grow red. "Really!?" she added. This changed everything.

He sighed. "Add it to your list."

Vikki gritted her teeth, clutching the armrest as the helicopter dipped lower. This was shaping up to be the worst field trip of her life.

Chapter Seven

Isla Lagarta

Vikki gripped her seat tightly as the helicopter banked sharply toward the rugged left flank of the mountainous island. A pristine ivory beach lay at the base of the towering, weathered cliff. For a minute, she thought they were going to crash into the rocky precipice, but then Reggie cut sharply to the left and hugged the cliff.

"See, you can't navigate like that with a normal copter," said Reggie, calm as could be. The copter pressed forward, remaining so close to the rocks she felt like she could open the window and touch them.

"Can't do this either," he added.

"Do what?"

Without warning, she was pushed down into her seat as the copter rapidly rose up the side of the cliff. She gasped, trying to catch her breath. In seconds, they cleared the top of the cliff and hovered above a dense rainforest she recognized from Matt's pictures. The photos didn't do it justice. They were also a lot less nauseating. She was almost afraid to look out the window, but when she did, she spotted some downed trees and a small clearing.

Unexpectedly, the copter dropped toward the clearing, plummeting like a free-falling elevator.

Her stomach was in her chest. She turned to Matt, trying to get the words out. "You could . . . have . . . told me it was gonna . . . be like this."

"Would you have come?" Even Matt looked like he was about to lose his lunch.

She shook her head and braced herself as the ground grew closer. The copter shifted in the wind until, by some miracle, it slowed and touched down softly.

The engine grew quiet, leaving nothing but eerie silence as they sat amidst the lush foliage. Vikki glanced out the window. They were deep in the jungle now, surrounded by trees and who knows what. She wondered if the military had spotted their dramatic arrival.

"So, just how unwelcome are we?" she said to Matt.

"Very. We need to get in, get some samples, and get out."

She wasn't counting on a covert operation. If she'd wanted that, she would've joined the Navy SEALs. She contemplated just staying in the copter.

"Okay, everybody," said Reggie, unlocking all the doors. "What do you say we get on our little adventure?"

"Should we be doing this?" she said.

"We're here," said Matt. "May as well make the best of it."

Famous last words. She'd put that on his tombstone.

She shook her head, then took off her headset and opened her door. Hesitantly, she exited the copter and stepped onto the dark soil. The air was so humid, you could practically drink it. Matt and Reggie joined her. Matt was holding a machete, which unnerved her a bit. Matt may have been cocky, but he wasn't the machete type. Or any tool for that matter, other than maybe a spectroscope or hydrometer.

"Do you even know how to use that thing?" she said.

"It's not that complicated."

"What are you expecting to see out here?"

"Branches. And maybe a dragon or two."

She rolled her eyes. She could just see Matt facing off against a dragon with his machete.

"This way," said Matt, pointing to a miniscule break in the trees to the right.

"There's no path there," she said.

"There's a path."

"You call that a path?" she said. It was maybe wide enough for a rabbit to get through.

"It's sort of a path."

"And you wonder why I left you." She walked behind him as he sliced the branches with his machete. "You just do whatever you want, don't you? Nothing phases you."

"You sound like my mom," he said. "*Matthew G. Grayson, you're incorrigible!*" He said it in a falsetto British voice, even though his mother wasn't British.

"What's the 'G' stand for? Gaslighter?"

"Funny. I'm pretty sure you know it's Gordon. And if you give me a chance to explain wha—"

"No need," she said.

"Right. No elephants."

"*Elephants*?" said Reggie, lagging behind. "There's no elephants here! This is Puerto Rico."

"We know," said Vikki and Matt in unison.

"You two have issues. I'm just sayin'."

They continued ahead as Matt cut through the underbrush.

A mosquito buzzed near Vikki's ear, and she slapped at it. She was already sweating. All she wanted to do was get back to the comfort and safety of the museum.

The loud blip of a radio ahead stopped her in her tracks.

"Quiet," whispered Matt, suddenly turning serious. He held up his hand and pointed ahead in the direction of the radio sound, then put his finger to his mouth. Vikki nodded and looked back at Reggie, who also had his finger to his mouth.

A burst of static blared from the radio, startling her. It sounded like it was a good distance ahead, but she couldn't tell how far. Her chest tightened. She didn't sign up for this. Amidst the insects and heat, she'd almost forgotten they were trespassing in Army territory. The reality that soldiers could begin shooting at any minute settled into her gut like a brick.

"This . . . is . . . Fort Majestic," said a crackling voice on the radio. It was faint, but she could hear most of it. "Gamma . . . secure. I repeat. Gamma is secure. Find them and clear the area. Over."

"Find who?" she whispered to Matt. "Us?"

He shrugged his shoulders.

A branch cracked behind them.

"What was that?" she said.

"Is that a person or an animal?" said Reggie without turning around.

Vikki turned and saw immediately what it was. She grabbed Matt's arm. Reggie must've seen her eyes bulge, because he quickly turned around.

The little girl from the video was peering at them through the foliage. Vikki felt a cold chill down her spine. She wasn't sure why. Even in horror movies, she'd always found kids terrifying.

She tried to wave to the girl to indicate they were friends, but the girl scooted off.

Vikki darted after the girl, with Matt and Reggie close behind. If this little girl was alone in the jungle being hunted, she was going to need help. Plus, the girl would be able to tell her firsthand what she saw, at least if she spoke English.

"We're making too much noise," said Matt, as they dashed through the underbrush.

"At least we're going the opposite way of those radios," said Vikki.

"And away from what we came here for," said Reggie.

The girl was ahead of them, frantically sprinting though the dense brush and jumping over thick, woody vines. Vikki followed as closely as she could, the other two catching up behind her.

"We're not here to hurt you," Vikki whisper-shouted ahead, trying not to be too loud.

"Quiet," said Matt. "You'll have the whole Army after us."

The girl kept running.

"She probably speaks Spanish," said Reggie.

"How do you say we're here to help you in Spanish?" she said.

He shrugged his shoulders, then his eyes lit up. "Amigos!" he called out in a loud whisper. "We're amigos!"

The girl kept running.

Vikki stumbled over a fallen vine, but Matt grabbed her arm.

"Those are Liana vines," said Reggie. "They—"

"Act first, explain later," said Matt. "Go!"

They continued pushing through as the rainforest grew denser and denser. The mosquitos were also getting worse. Vikki kept waving her hands in front of her face to keep them away.

"Look," said Reggie.

Between the trees, she could see light from a clearing up ahead. As she squinted her eyes, she could see the girl standing in the middle of the clearing and facing them, just staring at them silently.

"Well that's not creepy," said Vikki.

"Move slowly," said Matt. "We don't want to scare her."

They proceeded toward the clearing as calmly as they could.

"Just a walk in the park," said Reggie. "Like a leisurely stroll."

The girl was still standing there staring at them, though she seemed poised to run in any direction.

Vikki emerged from the brush into the open field, the others beside her. Together, they approached the girl slowly. She looked to be about eleven or twelve at most.

"Amigos," said Reggie, holding out his open hands.

"We'll see about that," said a gruff voice from the right. Vikki turned to see a local man in his seventies wearing a raggedy t-shirt and aiming an assault rifle at them.

Chapter Eight

Snakes and Copters

"Hands above your heads," yelled the disheveled man with the tattered clothes. His fierce eyes made it clear he wasn't messing around. Vikki noticed he had a series of tattoos on both his arms. He looked like a mercenary, or at least someone who used to be one.

She immediately held her hands high in the air and Matt and Reggie did the same.

"Drop the machete," said the man, aiming his weapon directly at Matt. The grizzled stranger squinted his eyes, and she could see the sweat beading on his forehead from the heat.

She glanced over at Matt, who still had the machete dangling from his hand. He casually let it drop to the ground, and it stuck in the dirt. He kicked it over for good measure.

"Listen, we don't have any money," said Reggie.

"Money? Give me a break. What unit?"

"Uh . . . you mean unit of currency?" said Reggie.

The man rolled his eyes. "What unit are you with!?"

Reggie hesitated.

"What unit?" the man repeated.

"We're not with any unit," said Matt. "We're here for research."

Vikki remembered something her father said. She knew exactly who this stranger was. And now she recognized him from the video.

"You're Toro," said Vikki. "I don't remember your last name, but I heard the Army's after you both."

"Oh you heard," said Toro, still staring daggers at them.

"We're not part of that," she said. "I swear."

"Then what exactly *are* you a part of?" he said, keeping his gun pointed in their direction. "Because I'll tell you now, nobody's gettin' anywhere near this girl."

Vikki admired the man. She admired anyone who stuck their neck out for a child, as this man has done more than once, including now.

"We only wanted to help. I'm a paleontologist. Someone sent a video to the news media. You were both on it. I was asked to gather samples and—"

"Asked by who?"

"My father. Dr. Jim Barnes. He's a science advisor with the Hartford Research Institute in Sante Fe. I'm just here to see what's really going on."

"And the Army just let you wander in here and investigate on your own."

"Not . . . exactly," said Reggie. "I think they're after us, too."

Toro seemed to be evaluating them as he kept his aim.

The young girl began moving toward them, but Toro didn't flinch.

"They're telling the truth," said the girl, in perfect English.

"Wait, you speak English?" said Reggie, as Toro slowly lowered his weapon.

"I should," said the girl. "I'm from New Jersey. And if you don't want to get captured, you better come with us."

The girl glanced back at Toro and he nodded.

"You're gonna wanna bring that machete," he said, motioning to Matt.

***

Vikki and the others followed Toro as he disappeared into a dense area of trees, which ultimately led into a narrow trail. Vibrant green leaves dripped with moisture as they trudged through the moss-covered ground, the earthy scent reaching her nose. She carefully picked her footing as twisting vines and tangled roots snaked across the path.

"What's your name?" said Vikki as she caught up to the girl. Up ahead, Toro cut through the branches with his hand knife as if he'd lived in the jungle all his life.

"Adelina."

"Adelina. I like that name. And Toro listens to you? Just like that?"

"Not always. But he trusts my judgment. And I trust his."

"If you don't mind me asking, how did you know we were telling the truth?" She tried not to bombard her with questions, though she was more than curious how a girl from New Jersey ended up on an obscure little island. It wasn't exactly a tourist destination.

"I just knew."

"So, you sense things," said Vikki. "Is that why the . . . flying creature turned when it saw you?"

She felt Matt's presence behind her. "You just can't bring yourself to say dragon, can you?" he said.

Vikki exhaled. "Because it's not."

"I think Adelina is done answering questions," said Toro, without turning around.

"No, it's okay," said Adelina. "I do sense things. Especially with animals."

"Like Doctor Doolittle?" said Reggie from behind.

"No, it's not like that at all," she said. "But I can tell what they're feeling. I see images. It's hard to explain."

"And what was the dragon feeling?" said Vikki. The sticky humidity clung to her skin, making her clothes damp.

"I thought you didn't believe it was a dragon," said Toro, slicing a large vine.

"I don't."

He stopped and turned around. "Well, you're wrong," he said.

"The dragon was angry," said Adelina. "But he was in pain, too. He wanted to be free."

"But he *was* free," said Vikki.

"No," said Adelina. "He wasn't."

"So you—"

"They're over there!" yelled a voice in the distance.

"Run," Toro hissed under his breath. "Follow me."

He sprinted ahead with the deftness of a jaguar.

Vikki and Adelina raced after him. Toro veered to the right, slashing through the jagged brush. Vines and branches snagged their clothes as they struggled to keep up. Vikki winced as the rough bark of criss-crossing trees scraped her arms.

She turned to make sure Matt and Reggie were following. They were.

Her breath came fast, her pulse thumping in her throat. She was sure anyone could've heard them pushing through the dense underbrush.

"Stay where you are!" yelled a voice from behind them. She couldn't tell how far it was, but she didn't see anyone when she looked back.

"Ignore them," said Adelina. "Keep moving."

Vikki paused.

"Trust me!" Adelina grabbed her hand and pulled her forward.

On instinct, Vikki reluctantly followed her. The path grew rockier and more awkward to traverse, her foot slipping on slick, moss-covered stones. A shiver ran up her spine as she struggled to keep her balance. What if she fell?

Up ahead, Toro stopped and waved for them to come quickly.

Adelina ran forward to join him, and then—three-quarters of the way there—the little girl's body suddenly slipped down and completely out of sight.

"Oh my God!" said Vikki.

"It's okay," called Toro from up ahead, still waving her on.

"But she—"

Toro took a leap and fell into the same hole Adelina did. As Vikki approached, it appeared to be some kind of camouflaged trap that was covered in leaves.

"Jump down," called Adelina from below the leaves, her voice echoing.

"What's happening?" said Matt, catching up. "Where's Toro and the girl?"

"Now!" yelled Adelina.

Vikki took a deep breath and jumped through the leaves. As gravity pulled her body down like a boulder, she slid about fifty feet down a dark, muddy hill until she fell backward and came to a painful halt. It was pitch dark and she couldn't see a thing. From the sound of it, Matt and Reggie arrived just behind her. Somebody's foot kicked her hard in the back.

"Sorry," said Matt.

"Get up and then push through," said Adelina, her voice just ahead.

Vikki paused. She felt a tightening in her chest. She realized she didn't really know Adelina or Toro. Maybe the military had good reason to be after them. Could she be jumping out of the frying pan and into the fire?

She took a deep breath and decided to trust her instincts. After all, there wasn't much she could do about it now.

"Hurry," said the young girl.

She did as Adelina said, rising to her feet and reaching out blindly. Her fingers brushed through a thick row of hanging vines as she pushed forward—hoping none of them hid any creepy-crawly things.

"There better not be snakes in here," she said. She felt something tug at her hair. She swung her hands wildly around her head in the darkness. Her fingers caught something hard—a twig or a branch. It was probably nothing. At least she hoped it was nothing.

Anxious to get out of there, she pushed through the dangling vines and soon spotted a dim, flickering light around the bend. Toro held a lantern, its warm glow casting a golden hue over the glistening cavern walls. Adelina stayed close by his side. A musky scent hung heavy in the air, and the damp chill was as eerie as it was refreshing.

"Won't they just follow us down here?" said Matt.

"They gotta find it first," said Toro. "Unlikely, through all that brush."

"Besides," said Adelina. "We rigged it to close again once we're down here. We just tug that vine over there." She pointed to a single hanging vine near the entrance where they'd dropped in so clumsily. "We make a good team," she said, smiling at Toro.

"So, is he your granddad or something?" said Reggie.

"No, we just met when he came to save me from Gamma. But I wasn't in danger. Not really."

"Turned out she saved *me* from that monster," said Toro.

"Gamma?" said Matt. "That was the name we heard on their radio."

"That's what they call him," said Adelina.

"It's a code name," said Toro. "Those guys are behind this thing, and I'm gonna find out exactly who they are."

"How do you know?" said Reggie. "Maybe they're just trying to stop it."

"Says Mister, the-Army-is-behind-it all," said Matt. Vikki was thinking the same thing.

"Follow me," said Toro. "All of you."

Vikki, Reggie, and Matt followed Toro and Adelina into a dark, underground tunnel that seemed to wind around endlessly.

"Dumb question," said Reggie, his voice echoing in the stone passageway. "How do we get back out?"

"There's an exit toward the cliff," said Toro. "It comes out by a waterfall."

"And you built all this?" said Vikki, ducking as the cavern grew shorter.

"Hell no. The Taíno tribes used this back in the 1500s. Tryin' to escape the Conquistadors, I suppose. Don't know if it was built for that or for the gold mining they were forced to do. Ponce de León was not a nice guy. Anyway, it served our needs."

"How do you know all this?" said Matt.

"You live here long enough, you learn things. Took me a while to find it, even *with* the map."

They emerged into a broad underground chamber, already illuminated by several lanterns like the one Toro was holding. The air was noticeably cooler, dropping at least a few degrees. Vikki shivered slightly as she scanned the area. She couldn't believe what she was seeing: stashes of weapons and gear, bags and cans of food, canteens of water. It looked like a military compound.

"How do you keep these lanterns burning?" said Reggie.

"Burning?" said Toro, looking at him like he had four heads. "They're LED. They last 30 days. With all the power outages on this island, everyone's got 'em."

Matt walked around, inspecting all the gear. "It must've been fun trying to get all this stuff down here," he said. He knelt and picked up a pinch of soil from between the stone cracks and sniffed it. Typical Matt.

"Oh, that was easy," said Adelina. "We made several trips over the last few days. We were on one when I saw you."

"Yeah, real easy," said Toro, rolling his eyes. "They got soldiers all over this area. I had an easier time in Nam."

Vikki looked again at the tattoos on Toro's arms. On his left arm was what looked like four helicopters, and on the other was a snake. "Is that where those copter tattoos are from?" she asked. "Vietnam?"

Toro nodded. "Slicks. That's what we called the transport Hueys. We had four of them. I was the first to make the jump, and the second I hit the jungle, Charlie shot down all four. I watched everyone I knew die in an instant." He rummaged in a box, his voice low. "Had to finish the mission on my own."

His stare grew distant. "I did it for *them*. Those were my brothers. My friends."

A heavy silence settled over the group. Vikki could see they were all intently listening, as was she. She shifted her weight, searching for words.

"That's awful," she said. "I'm sorry."

Toro pulled out a bottle of water from the box and offered it, but she politely declined, as did the others. He took one for himself and sat on a wooden box and drank it.

"We were supposed to be supported by two gunships," he continued, "but they were the first to fall. Charlie was tough, I'll give 'em that."

"So they shot down all six?"

"Don't be so surprised. We lost more than half the Hueys we sent in. When all was said and done, almost 12,000 copters were shot down. Eventually, I got picked up by a gunship under heavy enemy fire." He took a deep breath and exhaled. "Anyway, here I am to tell the tale. I'll tell you one thing. I'm not about to be done in by my own country after all that."

"And the snake?" asked Reggie, pointing to the snake tattoo. "What's that one mean?"

"Immortality, at least if you ask the Vietnamese. They say the snake can shed its skin and have a whole new life. It's what I did here. And that's what we're gonna do. You have a copter. We're gonna shed our skins and get off this damn island."

"I hope he means that metaphorically," said Reggie.

"You did camouflage the copter, right?" said Toro.

Reggie glanced at Matt, who avoided eye contact and pursed his lips.

"*Ay mamita*. Well, you better hope it's still there, for all our sakes."

Toro got up, went to a giant rectangular wooden case, and opened it. Inside were weapons of every kind: machine guns, knives, pistols, and some Vikki couldn't even identify.

"You're telling me you brought this whole case down here? Through the jungle?"

"Hell no," said Toro. "The box was already here. Minus the weapons. This box must be five hundred years old."

He picked up each weapon and studied it, the way one might pick the perfect melon at a supermarket. He put some aside and grabbed an old leather satchel, its surface scuffed and worn from years of use.

Vikki wondered if all this was necessary. Toro was a soldier; he saw battle everywhere. Her father used to say, *If all you have is a hammer, everything looks like a nail.* Had anyone considered the easy route?

"I'm a paleontologist," she said. "And Matt's a research scientist. Can't we just tell them our credentials? What's the worst they can do, kick us out?"

"I've seen the worst they can do," said Toro, loading his chosen weapons into the satchel. "They've been roundin' up witnesses. Those witnesses won't be talkin' to anyone ever again. You think they're gonna trust you to cover up their lie? You all had a look around up there. Didn't run into many villagers, did you?"

"Well, someone had to send the video," said Vikki.

"*I* sent it," said Toro. "With this." He pulled a charred cell phone out of his pocket and held it up. "Found it on a dead man. Well, his hand anyway. Good thing his fingerprint still worked."

He glanced at the group. "I've been listenin' to their radio transmissions. They're hiding something. Dunno what yet, but I'll look into it when we get to the mainland. Meanwhile, we need to get that copter before they send in more troops—if they didn't already scrap it for parts."

Chapter Nine

Soldier of Misfortune

Vikki followed Toro and the others through the underground corridor, its path twisting in different directions as it gradually ascended. The passageway was dark and dank, with only Toro's lantern casting dancing shadows on the walls. She took deep breaths, steadying herself as she navigated the incline. The air was heavy with the smell of damp earth and mold, and the constant drip of water echoed off the walls—blending with the sound of their labored breathing. The cool humidity clung to her skin as she walked. Still, it beat the hot, mosquito-infested jungle—and at least she wasn't sweating. She fixed her eyes on the lantern's light as it bobbed ahead, painting an eerie glow over the path in front of them.

The passageway grew narrower. Vikki gripped the slick walls on both sides as she climbed over uneven stones and dirt, testing each step carefully in the dark. She tried not to dwell on what might be waiting for them once they emerged from the cave and re-entered the rainforest. With any luck, the copter would still be there—if they made it that far without being seen. The thought was too unsettling to even entertain. Feeling suddenly frazzled, she caught up with Adelina and attempted to start a conversation, hoping to fill the heavy silence.

"Where are your parents?" she said. She was almost afraid to ask.

"They died five years ago when I was seven. I've been living here with my Uncle Tony."

"Did he . . ." Vikki wasn't quite sure how to put it.

"Uncle Tony didn't make it," she said, surprisingly matter-of-factly. "Nobody did back at the village. I only made it out alive because I was picking fruit. I dumped the whole basket when Gamma came."

She felt a pang in her heart at this emotionless recitation. *What else has this girl endured?*

"I'm sorry, Adelina. You know we won't let anything happen to you."

At first, Adelina didn't say anything. Either she was suppressing her emotions, or she was an incredibly strong child. Vikki scanned Adelina's face in the dim light and thought she spotted a tear on her cheek—though it could well have been the humidity.

"Are your parents still alive?" said Adelina.

"My dad is. I lost my mom, too. It was a weird thing, really. She was a paleontologist like me. She was in the Wasatch Mountains on a dig. Anyway, it's unbelievably high up there, and just when she was digging near the edge of a cliff, a snake jumped out of a tree and bit her. I mean, what's the likelihood of that, right? She was so startled that she jumped up and fell back. Unfortunately, she was . . ."

The grief surprised her, tightening in her throat like a familiar fist. All the old memories and emotions surged back all at once. She paused, taking a few deep breaths to steady herself before continuing.

"My mom was so close to the edge that she lost her footing and tripped over a rock. She went right over. I still can't bear to think of it." She sniffled. "So, anyway, it seems we both lost relatives to reptiles."

She put her arm around Adelina just as they rounded the corner. Blinding light flooded the cavern from ahead, and she could hear the intense rush of the waterfall. As they made their way into the light of day, the mist enveloped her face and arms, and the thrumming power of the falls pounded in her chest. It was time to re-enter the jungle.

***

"Grab onto the vines," Toro shouted over the roar of the falls. Adelina had already run up ahead to join him.

As Vikki stepped out of the cave onto the slick rocks—Matt and Reggie just behind—her left foot almost gave way, and her heart skipped a beat as she glanced down. They were higher up than she'd realized. She couldn't help but think of her mother falling helplessly. How terrifying that must have been.

"The vines!" yelled Toro.

Vikki took a breath and gripped the vines as he directed, tugging to make sure they were firm. Her eyes scanned the hanging foliage for any signs of snakes.

She moved slowly and deliberately along the narrow stone path, clenching each vine until her knuckles ached. The rough branches dug into her palms as she pulled herself forward. She closed her eyes for a moment and stood still. Her breathing grew shallow, and she could feel her heart thumping in her chest. Drawing on her meditation practice, she inhaled deeply, counted to four, and exhaled through pursed lips. *Keep it together, Vikki.*

Slowly she made her way along the jagged rocks, following Toro and Adelina as they moved farther ahead. She glanced back to make sure Matt and Reggie were still behind her.

"Don't worry," said Matt. "I'll grab you if you fall."

"Don't say *fall*," she said, clinging to the vines for dear life. A quick look down at the rushing waters was a mistake—her arms quivered, and for a moment, she feared she might pass out.

She reached for the next vine and hesitated.

"What's wrong?" said Matt.

"I'm checking for snakes." She hated how her voice shook.

"The only snakes on this island won't be on these vines," Toro called from up ahead. "They'll be in the grass looking for mice."

Trusting Toro, Vikki pressed on. The narrow path finally led to a plateau. Toro reached down and helped her up, and relief flooded through her as her feet touched solid ground. He helped Matt and Reggie up behind her, and for a moment, she savored the feeling of safety.

"Your copter should be just up ahead, fingers crossed," said Toro. "We went in a big circle underground. Follow me."

They moved into the familiar shade of the jungle. The air was cooler, or maybe she was just chilled from the cave. The call of an exotic bird—"keh-keh-keh"—echoed from the branches above, accelerating in speed and volume until it repeated. She spotted one on a branch up above: a small gray bird with a chestnut belly and a long tail.

"What kind of bird is that?" she said.

"Lizard cuckoo," said Toro. "We have them all over the island."

Toro stopped unexpectedly and held up his hand, signaling for silence. He turned, finger to his lips. Up ahead, a soldier stood guard, radio and rifle in hand. Toro motioned for quiet, then slipped away into the trees on the left.

"What's he doing?" said Matt.

She shook her head, her breath caught in her throat.

The soldier remained oblivious, scanning the jungle. Vikki held her breath, praying no one would make a sound. A noise rustled in the trees to the right; the soldier turned, distracted. Toro, however, burst from the left, catching the guard by surprise. In a flash, he wrestled the man to the ground. Moments later, Toro stood, weapon in hand,

and ordered the soldier up. He marched the captive back toward the group.

***

Toro shoved the captured soldier to the ground, zip-tying his hands and taping his legs with practiced efficiency. He leveled the rifle at the man's face.

The man couldn't have been more than twenty-five.

"What unit?" said Toro. Vikki recalled when he'd asked that of her and the others when she first saw him.

"Paramilitary," said the young soldier, lifting his chin in defiance. "You need to come with us, Sergeant."

Toro rolled his eyes. "Hired by who?"

"General Wilson Krupp. If you want to know anything, you'll have to ask him."

"What was that thing?"

"What thing?" The soldier's eyes narrowed, daring him.

Toro jammed the back of the rifle into his cheek. The man groaned but held his stare.

"Gamma! The thing that just about killed everyone on the island. The thing that looked like a dragon. What is it!?"

The soldier shrugged. "I don't know." Even Vikki could tell he was lying through his teeth.

"You don't know," repeated Toro. "Well, you *do* know who I am, and I'm gonna bet you know you know my service record."

The soldier smirked. "That's right, Sergeant."

"So, let's talk about what else you know. You know what I'm capable of, and you know I'm an American, just like you."

The man squinted his eyes and paused. "That's correct."

"Good. Now that we're clear, you're gonna tell me what that thing was, before I start treating you like the enemy. And you don't want me to treat you like the enemy."

The soldier took a breath. "I'm telling you the truth, Sergeant. I don't know. All I can tell you is, whatever it is, the Army was in control—until something went wrong."

Toro turned to Vikki and said, "How NOT to train your dragon!" He redirected his attention to the soldier.

"Did the Army create it?"

"Not that I'm aware of."

Toro scowled. "What *are* you aware of?"

"Only what I told you. I'm telling you I never saw it. I don't even know what it is, but the Army has it under control." The soldier eyed him. "You some kind of mercenary now?"

Toro sneered, though Vikki could see a glint in his eye. "Mercs take money. I do this for pleasure. Now you better start talkin'."

The soldier shifted uneasily, then puffed his chest out in defiance. "We need you and the girl to come with us."

"Why?" snapped Toro.

"You have to ask General Krupp."

"How do I reach him?"

"You can come with me, Sergeant. I'll take you right to him." He grinned.

"No thanks. Try again." Vikki was glad Toro was sticking to his guns, literally and figuratively.

"Hey," said Reggie. "Ask about Fort Majestic. We heard them talking about it on their radios. And then they said Gamma was secure."

Toro glanced at Reggie and then at the soldier.

"You heard him. What's Fort Majestic?"

"It's where you'll find Krupp," said the soldier.

"Where is it?"

The man smiled thinly. "I don't know."

Toro bashed him with the gun again. "You're lying. How were you gonna get us there if you don't know where it is?"

"I'm telling you, none of us know. It's top secret." The soldier shook his head, more serious now. "It's on a need-to-know basis only, and apparently, I don't need to know and neither do you. Besides, that's not where we're going. My job was just to—"

A radio blip interrupted them from the other side of the trees.

"Don't say a word," Toro warned, pressing the muzzle of the gun to the man's face. Vikki saw real concern in the soldier's eyes—whether for himself or his fellow troops, she couldn't tell. As his eyes darted back and forth, he appeared to be contemplating whether to shout a warning.

Toro ripped a strip of duct tape from his roll and slapped it over the soldier's mouth. The man started flailing, trying to break free.

Vikki exchanged a quick glance with Reggie, whose jaw tightened. Matt's eyes flicked toward the trees, alert for any sign of movement. Adelina scurried over and clung to her arm.

Toro turned to the group. "We have to get out of here. Now."

They hurried to where the soldier had been posted, then slipped past and continued along the jungle path. Picking up the pace, Toro said, "Can any of you use weapons?"

"I've fired weapons at a range," said Vikki.

"Since when did you fire weapons?" said Matt.

"I dated a cop for two years," she said, though she'd rather forget those days. Still, it was definitely coming in handy now. At the very least, it was satisfying to see the shock in Matt's eyes. She might as well have told him she was a CIA operative.

Toro handed her a Glock 22. She recognized it immediately as the same weapon she'd used at the range.

Matt still had his machete, but he looked at it disappointedly and tossed it on the ground.

"I was in Iraq," said Reggie, catching up to them.

"Desert Storm?" said Toro, handing him a high-powered rifle he pulled out of his bag.

"Iran-Iraq war. The Iraqis were the good guys then."

Toro's eyes lit up as he seemed to spot something up ahead. "Well, it's Christmastime in the jungle," he said. "And looky there, the biggest gift is just ahead."

Vikki looked past Toro and saw a sight for sore eyes in the clearing ahead. The Blue Meanie was in the middle of the field, parked just where they'd left it.

Gunshots rang out behind them. Then a voice on a loudspeaker said, "Stop where you are and await further instruction. Sergeant Toro Cortez. Stop where you are."

"Keep moving," said Toro.

The shots resumed and a barrage of bullets hit the trees around them.

"They're trying to kill us!" said Vikki.

"No, they're not," said Toro as they approached the helicopter. "It's just warning shots."

Reggie opened the rear door for Vikki. "Get in."

Vikki climbed up into the back seat and lifted Adelina onto her lap.

"Climb over to the middle," she said. "Away from the windows."

Matt entered from the other side and Toro rode shotgun beside Reggie.

A loud ping hit the side of the copter. Then another.

"They *are* shooting at us!" said Vikki.

"Now they are," Toro said from the front seat.

"Bulletproof windows," said Reggie as he started the engine. "One of my upgrades."

A stench of fuel filled the cabin as the engine thrummed to life. As the rhythmic thump of the rotor blades reached full force, the surrounding palm trees bent under the sudden torrent of wind, leaving the copter fully visible.

More bullets clanked against the copter's metal.

"Let's get out of here!" said Matt, putting on his headset. Reggie reached back with one hand and gave Adelina an extra headset from up front.

The helicopter lifted immediately and shifted abruptly to the left as it ascended. The whirring rotor sounds vibrated the back of Vikki's seat. As she put on her headset, she gazed out the window to see a group of soldiers looking up at them and talking into their radios. One soldier ran to an officer, probably to report. The officer turned and pointed to the sky behind him. Just then, she spotted two small planes in the distance, approaching from the island. Her heart quickened.

"I think we're gonna have company," she said, holding her pistol tightly in her lap.

Chapter Ten

Aerial Ballet

The distant roar of engines grew louder, slicing through the humid island air. Vikki's grip tightened on her pistol as the two small planes appeared on the horizon, closing fast. Her heart hammered in her chest—there was no time to rest.

"They're getting closer," she said.

Adelina rocked silently, clutching Vikki's sleeve like it was a lifeline. Vikki wasn't quite sure what to do, so she pulled her in closer. Brave as that little girl was, it was the first time Adelina actually seemed her age.

Vikki looked over at Matt, who was crouching down in his seat. "Maybe we shouldn't be running from the Army," she said.

He stared back at her, wide-eyed. "You wanna go back there and see if they fire more bullets at us?"

This whole day had been one disaster after another. She just wanted it to be over.

"We're lucky," said Toro. "Those are Piper Cherokees. We have them on the island for tours. Nothin' to worry about."

Vikki flinched as a loud rat-a-tat of bullets striking metal erupted from the back of the copter. Out the side window, she could see one of the planes flying dangerously close, just behind them on her side.

"Nothing to worry about, huh?" said Vikki.

"Are they firing at us?" said Matt.

Adelina covered her head with her hands and ducked down.

Reggie turned to Toro. "You have an annoying habit of jinxing us."

"Who knew?" said Toro, rooting through his satchel. He pulled out some kind of sniper rifle. "Hover, so I can get this door open," he said to Reggie.

"You crazy?" said Reggie. "There's a vent door just below the window. Use that!"

Another loud noise came, this time from Matt's side of the copter.

"The other one's shooting at us, too," said Matt.

"Gonna need your help," said Toro, as he attempted to fire his weapon through the vent. A barrage of bullets hit Toro's window. Despite the deafening sound, he didn't flinch.

"What do you need me to do?" said Matt.

"Not you. Her. She's the only damn one back there who can use a weapon."

"The little girl!?" said Matt.

"I'm twelve, not six!" said Adelina.

"He means me," said Vikki.

She unfastened her seatbelt and sprang into action without thinking.

"You got vents back there, too," said Reggie.

"Whatever you do, stay down," she said to Adelina. She climbed over to Matt's side and pushed her weapon through the small vent that looked like a cat door.

"Keep your body clear of the opening," said Toro.

"Ya think?" she said. Her heart raced as she tried to aim her pistol through the little vent door. As the other plane approached, she fired three times. It seemed to have no effect. The wind wasn't helping. She tried two more times but wasn't even hitting the plane. It was hard to aim through the vent.

A bullet cracked against the window, and she jumped back. Just then the copter rose and tilted to the left. Her stomach dropped as she grabbed the seat back to keep from falling toward the window.

"Just making it easier for you," said Reggie. "Aim a little ahead of the target. I'm climbing to 2,200 feet."

"Don't tell me that," said Vikki. She wiped her palm on her pants leg and realized her hand was shaking. She pressed her hand to her thigh to steady it.

As the copter rose above the plane and tilted to the left, Vikki could see she had a cleaner shot. As she balanced herself against the window, she feared she could fall through the glass at any minute. Matt put his arms around her waist to keep her steady. She watched carefully as the plane ascended to meet the copter. She prepared to fire at the cockpit window as soon as she had it within view. She did as Reggie said and kept her weapon aimed slightly ahead.

Just as she was about to take her shot, a series of loud pings hit the copter from Toro's side, startling her. Toro fired back and then yelled, "Got 'em!"

Vikki returned her attention to her target and fired five quick rounds, but by then, she missed her opportunity. The bullets soared harmlessly into the air. "Dammit," she said. The copter rose again and the plane ascended to keep pace.

"Going to 3,000 feet," said Reggie.

She barely paid attention to the climb. All she could feel was the cool of the glass on her forehead as her whole world centered on the single point of her target. Nothing else existed. She was weightless.

Vikki fired, then took three more shots. The plane was close enough now that she could see a couple of bullet holes in its side—proof she was at least hitting something.

"You got one shot left," said Toro. "You only got fifteen rounds in that Glock."

Vikki kept her eyes on the cockpit window, aiming just ahead of it. She could feel the sweat running down her forehead, threatening to sting her eyes. The thought of killing another human being, and all the implications that went with it, flooded her mind. It occurred to her that this one action could change the trajectory of her entire life. But so could inaction. After all, this was self-defense. It was kill or be killed. Her hand shook, but she wiped her brow, took a deep breath to calm her nerves, and then pulled the trigger.

She missed the cockpit window.

Part of her was relieved, though she wasn't sure which outcome would've been worse—hitting him or not. Then she noticed a burst of smoke coming from the front of the plane. She must have hit something. She held her breath, watching in horror as the plane glided toward the ocean.

"They lost power," said Reggie. "You got the engine. Good work."

Vikki's pulse quickened as she watched the plane descend rapidly toward the sea. For a moment, everything moved in slow motion as it settled onto the waves and drifted with the current. She exhaled, relieved she probably hadn't killed anyone, and climbed over Adelina back to her seat, her hands still shaking. She couldn't imagine enduring this kind of fear and uncertainty day after day, as soldiers did. The thought that she might have taken a life had haunted her since she pulled the trigger.

She glanced over at Matt, who was staring at her wide-eyed—she couldn't tell if it was surprise or respect.

"What?" she said.

He shook his head, a smile slowing forming. "Nothing. Remind me not to get on your bad side."

"You're already on my bad side."

He smirked. "Point taken."

Matt's gaze shifted to Toro. "So, how long before the Army sends some fighter planes? Real ones."

"Dunno," said Toro. "I'm not even sure these guys were Army, but I'm gonna find out."

"How?" said Reggie.

"I got a friend in San Juan."

"Are you guys going to leave me in San Juan?" said Adelina.

"Nobody's leaving you anywhere, *niña*," said Toro.

"This friend of yours," said Matt. "Can you trust him?"

"Emilio? We're like brothers. I served with him in Nam. He had some big secret job with Army intelligence. He's retired now, but if anyone can find out what's going on, he can."

"I bet you ten-to-one Fort Majestic's in San Juan, too," said Reggie.

"You're dreamin' if you think they're gonna hide a dragon in San Juan," said Toro.

"No, seriously." Reggie turned his head toward Vikki. "I told y'all about those crates being carried up to the secret base. Right there at the top of El Yunque. And those weird animal sounds. It all adds up."

"Dragons don't fit in boxes," said Toro. "At least not the one I saw."

"Maybe it grew before you saw it."

"It ain't a Chia pet. Trust me, you don't want to be anywhere near this thing."

Vikki was in Toro's camp. As curious as she was, she'd had enough misadventures for one day.

"I don't know, man," said Reggie. "It would be pretty damn cool to see a live dragon."

Toro huffed. "I can name a few hundred people who would disagree."

"From a distance, I mean. Think about it. Every culture has dragons in their history. They didn't just all decide to make it up independently. The Middle Ages in Europe, ancient China, the Mesoameri-cans, I could go on and on."

"And he will," said Matt.

"I'll do you one better," said Reggie. "Why did three civiliza-tions—the Egyptians, the Mayans, and Caral-Supe in Peru—thou-sands of miles apart with no knowledge of each other—come up with the identical idea to not only have pyramids, but to have them in the exact formation of Orion's Belt?"

Toro threw his hands up. "I give up. Why?"

"It wasn't a riddle," said Reggie.

"We learned about Orion's Belt in school," said Adelina.

Vikki was only half-listening to the conversation. She had taken out her cell phone and, seeing she still had signal bars, tried calling her father. Something about nearly dying made her realize she needed to hear his voice. There'd been too many things left unsaid since that fateful day her mom fell, and it couldn't have been easy on him either. Besides, they weren't out of the woods yet, and he needed to know the full extent of what was going on.

She waited—no dial tone, no ringing. Just silence and a blank screen. She tried his office number, then another. Nothing hap-pened.

"Guys?" she said. "I'm trying to call my father at the Hartford Institute. My phone's not working—any of yours?"

"What do you mean, not working?" said Matt.

"It won't connect. No ringing, no message—nothing. But I have bars."

"Maybe his line's down," said Reggie.

"That's the problem, I'm getting it no matter who I call."

Matt took out his phone and tried.

"Same here," he said. "Looks like they're jamming us."

Vikki felt like she was in some sort of odd purgatory—safe for the moment, yet not safe. Not even remotely safe. They had trespassed in Army territory in a top-secret zone, captured an American soldier—or paramilitary mercenary, or whatever he was—killed at least one pilot, left the other stranded in the ocean, and extracted Toro and Adelina, who, for some reason, were persons of interest. And now their phones were blocked. It was only a matter of time before the Army caught up to them, one way or another.

And the *pièce de resistance*: after all that, they barely knew anything more than when they started.

She shook her head as she gazed blankly out the window. No matter how it was sliced, this mission was a bust—though there was something to be said for helping Toro and Adelina escape the clutches of the Army. Still, she couldn't imagine life ever getting back to normal. And they weren't out of the woods yet. Not even close.

Chapter Eleven

General Krupp

Major General Wilson Krupp studied the enormous creature in chains as it bared its razor-sharp teeth like a rabid dog. Except this beast was nearly thirty feet tall and twice as long—its yellow eyes glowing in the dim light, along with the iridescent scales that lined both sides of its cold, reptilian face. Gamma clicked his talons in frustration and then suddenly lurched forward and scratched them against the thick glass, making a loud cracking sound.

Krupp didn't jump back. He didn't move at all. The creature was clearly furious, but Krupp figured he wouldn't dare release his fire in a sealed enclosure. He was too smart for that. Instead, the beast stared down at him in defiance, as if to say, "Just wait till I'm free again."

"Set it to 140," said Krupp. "Soften him up a little."

Gamma let out a bellowing roar that shook the lab. Krupp was never so grateful for three layers of acrylic glass.

"We should put him down," said Dr. Simmons. "This isn't right."

"Hell, no. He's too valuable."

"But we have the others."

"He'll learn. Do it."

Simmons nodded to the lab techs, and they began to increase the frequency as requested. Undetectable by humans, it was the perfect level to transmit a bit of pain to the massive animal through its neurochip. Almost immediately, Gamma lunged toward the glass, snarling, his huge talons smashing against the clear barrier.

Krupp once again stood firm. He'd seen this behavior before. As the frequency hit 140 kHz, the great beast moved back a few feet, knowing the sooner he complied, the sooner the unbearable sound would stop. These creatures were smart. Their spatial memory and ability to navigate complex terrain to achieve a goal made them uniquely suitable for the job. According to Simmons, they could distinguish colors, recognize and bond with certain individuals, and could even count livestock at feeding time. But most of all, they were sensitive to sound. *Sonic stimuli*, as Simmons put it.

"Cut the transmission," Simmons shouted. The lab tech obediently manipulated the controls on the monitor.

Gamma slowly relaxed his breathing and lowered his huge body onto the ground. The yellow eyes remained as angry as ever, if not angrier. The beast was just biding his time, but he acquiesced nonetheless. He didn't have a choice.

Krupp still had trouble fathoming how the sonic waves had such an impact on these behemoths while being undetectable by humans. He'd probably never understand it, but Simmons did and that was all that mattered. Dr. Simmons was a brilliant two-time PhD, rightfully in charge of studying Gamma. But sometimes the most brilliant people lacked the big-picture-thinking to fully grasp the priority of a mission. And this mission would save countless lives.

It had been a long time since Krupp's days as the Commanding General of INSCOM and chief of Army Intelligence. After the most devastating period of his life, he was all set to retire. But that's when the DIA contacted him and told him about the discovery in the British Indian Ocean, just off the coast of Diego Garcia Island. He saw the potential right away. This could change the world, and one setback wasn't about to set him off course. This was his life's purpose now.

He headed down the corridor to Sector 12, where Alpha was being held. After traversing the long corridor and crossing the glass bridge, he saluted the guards and approached the enormous window. He still marveled at the mysterious behemoth. It was hard to tell how old Alpha was. He was larger and slower than the others, and his jagged scales were riddled with scars. According to Simmons, he could be hundreds of years old, or more.

"What's your story?" he said to the beast, who was resting on the concrete. "Where do you come from?"

The large, yellow, apathetic eyes gazed blankly at him, the way his German Shepherd, Holly, used to do at home when she would rest on her dog bed.

He heard footsteps coming from behind.

"General, I have an update," said Colonel Adler. He had worked with Adler at INSCOM and insisted on him being part of his team at Fort Majestic.

"Curtis," said Krupp. "What's the good word?"

"No so good, General. Cortez and the girl got away. They're headed for San Juan. Two of our pilots went down. One survivor."

Krupp shook his head. "Toro Cortez, still making waves. Send a unit to San Juan and prepare our contacts there. We need to find them before they create a huge pile of crap we can't dig out of."

Adler nodded and started to leave.

"One more thing," said Krupp. Adler turned around. "I know I don't have to tell you how important this program is. Right now, we're pushing that video as a big ole hoax. I wanna know why Gamma changed his flight path when he saw that girl. I need them both here ASAP. We gotta keep this contained."

"Yeah, I hear you. Only one problem. They're not the only ones. They've got three others. We got a positive ID on one of them, Dr. Vikki Barnes, a paleontologist. And we traced the copter to the Hartford Research Institute in Santa Fe."

"I know it well. Get me on the line with Dr. Jim Barnes at HRI. He's Vikki's dad. He and I need to have a little conversation."

Chapter Twelve

Trouble in San Juan

"Home sweet home," said Reggie as the mainland came into view—though nothing about their return felt safe.

"Too many people," said Toro.

Vikki wasn't sure if he meant Ceiba in general or because they were trying to avoid being seen.

"What happens if we get caught?" said Adelina.

"It'll be okay," said Vikki. "We'll explain to them who we are." She knew it wouldn't be that simple—she wished it were. But there was no sense in alarming Adelina.

"We're not gonna get caught," said Toro, turning his head from the front passenger seat. "Because we're too fast for that, right?"

Adelina nodded. "Right."

Vikki craned her neck to gaze out the front window of the helicopter as they approached the HRI facility—she recognized the white building with its blue-tinted windows immediately. At this angle, the twilight sun glared in her eyes. She hoped Reggie's sunglasses worked well.

"We're landing on the roof?" she said, as the copter shifted in the breeze. Taking off from the roof was bad enough, but something about trying to land on a small roof in the wind sounded worse. She never could've been a MedEvac pilot.

Reggie chuckled. "Well, we're not landing in the street. Don't worry. Be happy."

She wished she had Reggie's attitude. The truth was they were all fugitives now.

She braced herself as the helicopter lowered onto the roof, pitching and rocking until it finally touched down.

She took a deep breath—not so much for relief, but to steel herself for whatever lay ahead. Adelina placed a hand over hers, trying to comfort her.

"This place have a stairwell?" said Matt.

"You suggesting we take it?" said Reggie.

"The less people see us, the better."

"You kidding me?" said Toro. "*Madre mía!* How long do you think we've got before the Army—with all their tactical gear and satellite tech—spots a damn giant blueberry with propellers on top of this building. They'll know we were here, trust me. Let's just move. Fast." He shook his head. "I'd slide down a freakin' sliding board if you had one."

Reggie clicked open the copter doors. "Don't have to tell me twice," he said.

"Wait, leave your phones," said Toro.

"Leave them?" Vikki said. She checked her phone. Even on the roof of the building, she was still getting no signal.

"If they can jam your phones, they can track your phones," he said. "Leave them. Now let's go."

Vikki tucked her phone under the seat and exited the copter, helping Adelina down.

Reggie led them all inside to the elevator, where they waited for it to reach the roof. As it opened, Reggie stepped in first to the left. Matt went straight to the back, and Vikki and Adelina stood beside Toro.

After Reggie pressed the *down* button, they waited as the doors closed and the elevator began its slow descent.

As excruciatingly slow as the elevator was, the stairs might have been faster.

The floor indicator chimed at the fifth floor and the elevator stopped. Vikki held her breath and glanced at the others as the doors slowly opened.

Two men in Army uniforms entered. This wasn't good. She glanced at Matt, who was standing wide-eyed against the back of the elevator like he was in a lion's cage trying to look invisible.

After the elevator doors closed and they began moving again, one of the men, a Latino, turned around and glanced at Reggie. The man squinted, suspiciously.

"Reggie?" he said. "Reggie Davis?"

Vikki's muscles tensed. They'd been recognized quicker than she thought. She prayed Reggie would give a fake name.

Reggie looked at the man, confused, but then his eyes lit up.

"Carlos!? You shaved the beard. I didn't recognize you, my friend. How's Maria?"

Vikki exhaled, her shoulders loosening just a bit.

"She's good," said Carlos, grinning. "You stayin' out of trouble?"

If he only knew the half of it.

Reggie chuckled. "You know me, ha ha."

After they exited the elevator, Reggie led them out of the facility to a taxi stand by the ferry station—the ferry she'd wished they would've taken to the island.

They stood outside, watching the street. The humid air clung to Vikki's skin. After a few minutes, a police car drove by slowly. Vikki swallowed, half expecting the cop to pull over and come out. She kept her eyes on the ground, trying to look casual.

A minute later, another police car approached in the middle lane. Did the other cop spot them and radio it in? Her heart thudded in her chest until the car passed without stopping.

Finally, after about ten minutes, a taxi arrived. Toro directed the driver to take them to an address on Calle San Francisco, where his friend Emilio apparently lived.

The ride took about an hour, and then they arrived in a residential area of Old San Juan, where rows of pastel houses glowed in the orange wash of the setting sun. Vikki followed Toro and the others out of the vehicle.

"Which house is it?" she said.

"It's around here somewhere," said Toro. "I'll know it when I see it."

They walked a few blocks through the warm Puerto Rican air. Vikki marveled at the rows of brightly colored shops—blue, yellow, peach, and white. The neighborhood felt far more upscale than the ramshackle homes with tin roofs and ancient, beat-up cars they'd passed earlier. After several stores and restaurants, the area became more residential, with white townhomes, ornate columns, and wrought-iron balconies. Then came a quieter stretch of modest single homes, mostly white stucco.

"Are we in the right place?" said Vikki. She was beginning to have her doubts.

"That's it," said Toro, pointing to a peach-colored house with a small front lawn.

"You sure you can trust this guy?" said Matt.

"Emilio and me, we go way back," Toro replied. "I told you, we're like brothers."

"It's a fair question," said Reggie. "I mean, you did say he's with Army intelligence."

"Retired."

Toro pounded on the door, loud enough to wake the dead.

Vikki wasn't quite sure what to expect as she waited for the door to open.

Toro banged again, even harder this time. She wouldn't have been surprised if half the neighborhood came out to see what was happening.

"Whatever happened to being discreet?" she said.

The door swung open. A portly man in his seventies appeared, wearing a white t-shirt. He looked surprised at first, as if he didn't know Toro at all. Then a big smile formed on his face as he held out his arms.

"Toro! *Mano*! It's good to see you!"

Toro embraced him. "It's good to see you too, my friend."

Emilio looked over Toro's shoulder at the group. "I take it you are not here for a pleasure visit."

"These are my friends," said Toro. Vikki blinked, surprised at the word—or to be included so readily. "We need your help," he added.

"Si, si, what can I do? You need *chavos*?"

"No, nothing like that. We're good with money. Can we come in?"

Emilio opened the door for them.

"Of course," he said, waving them inside. "You're all welcome. *Mi casa es su casa*."

Inside, Vikki marveled at the terracotta floor tiles, peach archways, and bamboo furniture with seafoam green cushions. Tall potted yucca plants gave the living area a garden-like feel, but as she glanced around, the house itself seemed barely lived in—no photos, no TV, no clutter.

Emilio led them to a long dining table draped in a white cloth. "Please," he said.

Vikki sat between Matt and Adelina. Reggie and Toro sat opposite, with Emilio at the head.

As Toro recounted their harrowing tale, Emilio remained wide-eyed, occasionally saying, *"Ay bendito!"* or *"Venga!"* Vikki couldn't tell if he was more shocked or amused.

"So, where do you think this Fort Majestic is?" said Emilio, after Toro finished his tale.

"You mean you don't know?" asked Reggie. "You know the rumors about the secret base in El Yunque, right? Maybe it's there."

"El Yunque? There hasn't been anything there since they were doing HAARP testing back in—"

"HAARP testing!" said Reggie. His eyes lit up as he looked at Vikki and Matt. "What did I tell you guys? I bet that has something to do with this!"

"What's all this harps crap?" said Toro. "You gonna play the dragon a lullaby?"

"The high frequency wave testing program," said Vikki.

"Exactly!" said Reggie. "High Frequency Active Aur—"

"It's doesn't matter," said Emilio. "That was maybe ten, fifteen years ago. It was just atmospheric testing."

"But it wasn't *just* that, was it?" said Reggie.

"My friend gets a little excited about conspiracy theories," said Matt. He glanced at Vikki with a knowing smile. Even Adelina smiled.

"Think about it," said Reggie. "Do you seriously think there's an advanced technology, a 300-million-dollar investment, that the military isn't gonna exploit for some advantage?"

Matt threw up his hands. "That's probably true, but it doesn't mean—"

"Okay, then what about the crates that people saw being taken up there from Ceiba—directly from the Roosevelt Roads naval facility?"

"Rosy Roads?" said Emilio. "It's an airport now. That hasn't been a naval base in ages. But yes, I heard the rumors about the crates, too. That was probably true."

"See! I told you guys. Y'all need to listen to me more."

"So, basically, you don't know anything," said Toro, looking at his old friend.

"I wouldn't quite say that," said Emilio. "Yes, there was a base at the top of El Yunque."

"I knew it!" said Reggie, slapping his hand on the table.

"Even I don't know all the details," said Emilio. "But I do know when the hurricane hit in 2017, they moved it to a tiny uninhabited island called Nibo."

"Nibo?" said Toro. "I never heard of it."

"You wouldn't. It's not on any civilian maps. It's off the coast of the Dominican Republic. We claimed it as part of a deal between the US and the DR. If your Fort Majestic is anywhere, I'd bet it's there."

"How do we get there?" said Toro.

"You don't. Like I said, it's not on any maps. Even military records list it as a classified exclusion zone, closed off and erased from tourist guides. It's dangerous to get to, and it's heavily guarded. My advice? Don't get involved in any of this. It's above you and it's above me."

Vikki had heard enough.

"What we need to do," she said, "is head back home and report what we found to my father. Let it go through official channels. We did what we could. Let's just get back and stay safe." She put her arm around Adelina, who huddled next to her. "I have spare rooms for you and Toro back in Philadelphia. We can figure things out once we're there."

"Listen to her," Emilio said. "It's the wisest decision."

Toro paused and then nodded. "Okay. Then can you help get us back? We got eyes on us everywhere."

Emilio smiled. "In the morning, I can see what I can do. You can all sleep here tonight. I have no extra bedrooms, but there's couches and I can bring blankets for the floor. I assume you don't want to be seen in a hotel."

"Gracias," said Toro. "You assumed right."

"You have blankets in Puerto Rico?" said Vikki.

Emilio grinned. "You'd be surprised. Now what do you say I cook you all dinner? You must be hungry."

Reggie patted Toro's shoulder. "You were right about this guy."

Emilio proceeded to take out pots and pans and all sorts of ingredients. Vikki offered to help, but he said he'd be delighted just to show her his recipe. She watched in awe as he cooked a delicious meal of rice and beans— *arroz con gandules*, he called it—along with shredded beef and fried plaintains.

After dinner, they all settled down into their spots around the living room. There were far worse places to spend the night than a lush indoor garden. As anxious as she was about the future, between the exhaustion from the day and the gentle whirring of the ceiling fan and the songs of the tree frogs outside, she dozed off in no time.

***

Vikki awoke to the glare of the morning sun filtering through bamboo slatted blinds, and the rich aroma of strong Puerto Rican coffee mingled with the scent of sweet pastries. She vaguely remembered hearing doors opening and closing in the back of the house much earlier—maybe in the middle of the night—but she'd been half asleep. Emilio must've been kind enough to run out and pick up breakfast.

She looked around and realized she was the last one still asleep. Everyone else was already at the dining table, enjoying the meal.

"You're alive," said Matt with a grin. "You have to try these malarkeys and—wait"— he turned to Emilio—"what are they called?"

"Mallorcas," Emilio said with a slight smile.

"It's a ham and cheese sandwich, but on a really special pastry," Matt explained. "And this coffee is to die for."

Vikki stretched and yawned as she joined them at the table. The sweet, fluffy roll filled with melted ham and cheese tasted like heaven. "Still warm from the bakery," she said.

"Bakery?" said Reggie. "He made these himself."

Vikki put her fork down and thought about it. If Emilio hadn't gone out, then what were those doors she'd heard in the night? A tinge of unease ran down her spine, but she tried to brush it off.

She glanced over at Emilio, who seemed unusually quiet—less jovial than the night before, more reserved.

"So, what's the plan?" said Toro. "You said you can help us?"

Emilio smiled, but it was a nervous smile, tinged with something like pity or hesitation. "Come with me," he said, rising suddenly. "I can arrange transportation. Maybe not in the way you'll find ideal. I'll show you what I mean."

As they followed him, Emilio kept glancing back at Adelina with a concerned look. Vikki wasn't sure why he was acting so suspiciously, and she could see Toro's confusion as well.

They followed Emilio up a single step and down a white, un-adorned hallway. At the far end of the hall, he opened a louvered wooden door and motioned for them to go through first. When they entered, the room seemed oddly bare, except for tall mahogany bookcases on either side, and a small portable table and set of four chairs in the middle.

Without warning, two soldiers emerged from behind each book-case, assault rifles aimed at them. Vikki froze as she heard the metallic click of the rifles—safeties off, ready to fire. Her heart hammered in her chest. She turned to see the door behind them had been closed and another soldier was standing with Emilio. Adelina grabbed her hand.

"I'm sorry, my friend," said Emilio, patting Toro's shoulder. "I had no choice. It's a matter of national security."

"*Maldito cabrón,*" Toro hissed, pushing his hand away. "Spineless."

Reggie turned to confront Emilio, but one of the guards grabbed him.

"Hey, if it's national security," said Reggie, "why'd you tell us the location?"

"He didn't," said Toro, gritting his teeth. "Nothing he said was true. He's a liar." He looked toward Emilio and spat. "*Mentiroso.*"

"Come on, amigo, it's not like that," said Emilio. The conflict in his eyes was evident.

Toro turned away from him. "I ain't your amigo."

"I didn't know yesterday," he pleaded.

"Where are we going?" said Vikki, as a soldier took her arm. "Where are they taking us?"

"These men will explain when you get there," said Emilio.

"Yeah, get where?" said Toro, his eyes narrowing.

"Where you wanted to go to begin with. Fort Majestic."

Chapter Thirteen

Rumble in the Jungle

Vikki had hoped never to ride in a helicopter again. Yet here she was in another one—this time an Army transport copter that had whisked them away from Emilio's home. She couldn't see a thing—they'd been blindfolded since takeoff—but presumably they were now flying over the ocean. They were all seated face-to-face along opposing side benches, like a battalion about to be dropped into enemy territory—Vikki, Adelina, and Matt on one side, Toro and Reggie on the other, with soldiers stationed at each end. The bone-rattling vibrations from the engine were jarring—far noisier than on the Blue Meanie.

She tried loosening the blindfold, as it was giving her a headache, but it was difficult with her hands zip-tied together.

"Are they gonna dump us in the ocean?" said Adelina.

"They wouldn't have bothered blindfolding us," said Vikki. "They're just taking us somewhere they don't want us to know about." She spoke carefully, conscious that at least a couple of soldiers were in the main cabin with them.

The uncomfortable zip ties were driving her crazy, so she kept maneuvering her wrists for a better position.

"You know, they blindfold you when they take you to Area 51, too," said Reggie from across the cabin, as if he was on a scenic tour.

"I don't know, I've never been to Area 51."

"If you had, you wouldn't be here talking to me. I'm just sayin'. They don't like when people know their secrets."

"Not helping, Reg," said Matt.

It was hard to tell how much time had gone by, but the silence that followed, combined with the constant thrumming of the Army chopper's engine, was causing her mind to wander. She figured once they'd been brought in front of military officials, she'd be able to provide her credentials. She could explain that she was there on behalf of the Hartford Research Institute on official business. She knew her father would back her up. But then again, if something was top-secret enough and some big military types thought they were a threat, who knew what they would do.

A hand pulled her blindfold off, jolting her from her thoughts. The young soldier glared down at her and then moved along and did the same to the others. He looked to be in his early twenties at most. Three other soldiers were seated in the cabin with them. One of them near the front, a tall, brawny guy with a shaved head, stood up.

"We're takin' off your blindfolds," he said, "because it's gonna be a rocky ride in and I don't feel like cleaning up puke today. If you start to feel sick, look out the window and focus on the horizon. It may help. Welcome to Nibo."

"So, Emilio wasn't lying about the name," said Reggie.

"Then again, maybe he was," said Toro. "Don't matter either way if it's not on a map."

The helicopter immediately shifted sharply to the left and dropped what felt like a few hundred feet before careening harshly to the right. Calling it a rocky ride was the understatement of the century. The tall, burly soldier barely managed to remain upright, gripping the rails along the wall, though he looked more annoyed than alarmed. It seemed like he'd done this drill a hundred times before.

Vikki was already feeling queasy. She glanced out the window as he'd instructed, hoping that might help. She could see Nibo, if that's what it was really called. Smaller in diameter than Isla Lagarta, yet towering even higher, the island appeared to be a lush, mountainous paradise, with steep cliffs and dense rainforests dominating the terrain. There was no beach to speak of, or anything that resembled a landing area, at least from this angle.

The helicopter banked in a wide arc, circling the island as if searching for a safe place to land.

"We're landing on that!?" she said. Adelina nuzzled into her while Reggie shook his head in disbelief.

"No way," said Matt.

"Yep," said the younger soldier who'd removed their blindfolds. She couldn't tell if he sounded overconfident or afraid.

The copter plunged like a roller coaster, then abruptly lifted before falling again. The cabin shifted from side to side as the chopper tossed in the wind, descending rapidly, and then swooping up to make another attempt at climbing. Vikki swallowed to try to calm her churning stomach. Was it her fate to die in a helicopter crash on a trip she didn't even want to be on? With Matt, no less? More than anything, she was worried for Adelina, who was clinging to her like glue. No child should have to endure this.

The helicopter rose higher as the engine strained, then it plummeted rapidly before steadying itself. Even if they did manage to land safely, what then?

"Is this normal?" said Matt, visibly sweating.

"They have to find an approach path," said Reggie. "With the updrafts and downdrafts, it's pretty normal to have to abort a landing and try all over again. Mountains are tricky."

Great. She wasn't sure if she could handle much more of this.

Vikki took a deep breath. She'd made up her mind. Whatever happened, she was going to focus on keeping Adelina safe.

The zip ties brought a sudden jolt of pain to her wrists. She realized she'd been clenching her palms into a fist—a combined result of determination and anxiety.

The copter turned sharply to the right, thrusting her sideways. She held on as best she could with her sore wrists as they rose steadily and headed toward the top of the island, flying above the lush forest. The strong winds rocked the cabin violently, and she thought the whole vehicle might blow apart. It was like trying to land on Isla Lagarta, but worse. Much worse.

Vikki couldn't help but notice Toro intensely focused on the zip ties around his hands. As everyone seemed more concerned about the descent, Toro kept shifting his hands, which were tied palm-to-palm, seemingly trying to wiggle loose. She looked at him and shook her head, hoping he'd get her message and stop causing trouble. He'd get them all killed.

The helicopter dropped another few hundred feet and corrected its trajectory just above the tops of the trees. She watched as the pilot deftly maneuvered the chopper into a small clearing.

She braced herself as they approached ground level.

Finally, they'd touched down, surrounded by dense foliage, just as on Isla Lagarta. She let out a sigh of relief.

The sudden silence without the engines caused her ears to ring for a few seconds.

A minute later, the cockpit door swung open. The pilot emerged and opened a side door in the cabin.

"Everyone up," he said. "Exit the door one at a time."

Reggie was the closest to the door and exited first. Then, Matt and Toro followed. Matt glanced back with an almost apologetic look as he stepped out. Meanwhile, Toro was holding his zip-tied hands at a funny angle. What was he planning?

As the pilot stood guard, she exited with Adelina, trying to keep her balance with her hands tied.

As soon as she stepped onto the ground to join the others, the humidity enveloped her like a warm, damp cloth clinging to her skin. Five soldiers immediately surrounded them, as if they'd try to escape on this remote island in the middle of nowhere. One spoke urgently into his radio, though she couldn't make out his words. Another soldier, an authoritative-looking blond man who hadn't been on the copter, approached briskly and said, "Let's go." He was probably their commanding officer.

Reggie and Matt moved first, following four soldiers—three familiar faces from their harrowing helicopter ride and the blond officer from the island. Vikki stayed close behind them with Adelina, whose eyes kept darting nervously between their captors. Toro brought up the rear, shadowed by two more soldiers. She glanced back at him, a knot of worry tightening in her chest as she hoped he wouldn't do anything reckless.

The winds were surprisingly calm at ground level, but soon after they began walking, the warm breeze picked up, blowing her hair into her eyes. Annoyed, she lifted her tied hands to brush it away—only for the hair to blow right back in her face. It was bad enough her fingers had gone numb from the plastic biting into her wrists. Now she had to keep raising her arms every few seconds. She wasn't sure what was worse, the anger she was feeling or the fear of what was coming next. She felt completely powerless. She needed some reassurance. Anything.

"Where are we going?" she said, hoping one of the soldiers would answer.

"Discharge training," said the burly soldier from up ahead, as straightforward and gruff as he was on the helicopter.

What on Earth was discharge training? She didn't like the sound of that.

"What's that?" said Reggie, reading her mind.

"The general will explain. Don't worry about it."

Easy for *him* to say.

As they forged ahead silently for the next several minutes, Vikki noticed Matt and Reggie pause to stare at something on the right.

"Keep walking up there," said a soldier from behind her.

Matt and Reggie heard him and continued ahead.

As she moved forward, she glanced to her right to see what they were looking at. She gasped when she spotted it.

An enormous footprint stretched across two fallen trees, its sheer size sending a shiver through her body. Concerned, she scanned the forest on both sides of the path, her gaze catching the scorched foliage that marred the greenery.

Whatever that so-called dragon was, it had been here. A chill ran down her spine despite the oppressive heat. It was at least ninety degrees, and the heat index had to be well over a hundred. Part of her longed to stop and investigate, but survival and protecting Adelina were far more pressing. Besides, the soldiers would've just nudged her forward anyway.

She continued walking, hoping they wouldn't come across whatever charred those trees. A mosquito landed on her neck. She tried to slap it with her tied hands, but with no luck. More of them were buzzing overhead. With everything else going on, this was all she needed. If she survived helicopters and Army interrogations only to fall ill from some awful mosquito-borne disease, that'd be the icing on the cake.

As her mind ran through the symptoms of dengue fever, a hand firmly grabbed her shoulder and she nearly jumped out of her skin. She turned to see Toro holding his finger to his mouth to quiet her.

"Keep walking," he whispered.

She looked back to see two bodies grotesquely sprawled out on the ground. They were most certainly dead, their necks clearly snapped. She held her breath. It was all she could do not to scream. Toro was gripping an assault rifle, with another hoisted over his shoulder—both likely taken from the dead soldiers. He had two military knives tucked into his belt.

"What did you do?" she said.

"What I had to."

Up ahead, one of the soldiers turned around.

"Get down!" Toro yelled at Matt and Reggie as he sprinted past her, his weapon raised.

Matt and Reggie dropped to the ground just as Toro opened fire, the rounds echoing through the air.

The soldiers barely had time to react before Toro's shots tore through them, dropping them like targets in a shooting gallery. The deafening roar of gunfire filled the jungle, mingled with the scent of gunpowder.

"Are you crazy!?" said Reggie.

"You could've hit us," said Matt.

Toro looked at them and shrugged, his weapon slung over his shoulder like he'd just come home from fishing. "That's why I yelled to get down."

Vikki couldn't even speak. She was too busy staring at the gruesome scene. She was still in shock from seeing men—seconds ago still alive—sprawled out on the ground like meat, their blood seeping through their uniforms, eyes wide open and faces frozen in surprise. The sight would be forever etched in her brain.

"What do we do now?" said Reggie. "They were just taking us to discharge training."

"You know what discharge training means?" said Toro. "It means brainwashing. Now, we got a choice to make. Fast. We get our heads wiped by the government or we find our way back to that chopper and get the hell outta here."

"And go where?" said Vikki, still shaken. "We were here on official business. Now we're murderers." Now she knew why the Army was so hell bent on finding Toro—he was a one-man wrecking crew. And now they'd *all* suffer for it.

Toro was silent. He appeared more angry than remorseful. He took his knife out and cut her zip ties. Then he did the same for the others.

"Man, you really didn't think this through," said Matt, wiggling his hands to get his circulation going again. "We'll have to make our getaway in a stolen Army copter, if we can even get to it. We just killed a whole squad of American soldiers, and by *we,* I mean you. Our chances of getting anywhere are zero!"

"I've managed so far," said Toro. "And thanks to me, we'll still have our brains, which is more than you'd have if they got ahold of you."

"I think you left yours somewhere," said Matt.

"He didn't have a choice!" yelled Adelina. Everyone turned to look at her. "Toro helped me. We were running from soldiers for days. They would do the same to us. Trust me. They tried already."

"*You* got me into this," said Vikki, pointing at Matt. "You're gonna have to find a way to get us out of it."

"Hey, your dad got us into this, so you can thank him," he said. "And I didn't know this was gonna happen."

"You just stumble your way through life, don't you?"

A rustling sound came from beyond the trees to Vikki's right.

"Quiet," she said.

"I heard it, too," said Matt.

More rustling of leaves followed, and then a long, deep rumble came from the distance.

"Was that thunder?" said Reggie.

Matt shook his head.

She waited to hear it again.

The rustling in the trees grew louder, and then another low rumble. It sounded more like a bellowing roar or grunt from a lion—an enormous one. A deep roar came from the left as well.

"Uh, that sounds like lions," said Matt.

"Lions in the Caribbean?" said Reggie. "Seriously?"

"I'm just saying what it sounds like."

"Plural?" she said. It was coming from multiple directions.

The winds picked up and the sky grew darker. A chill raced down Vikki's spine as she contemplated what it could be. She wasn't stupid. She saw the video and the footprints. She tried to remain rational and scientific, because the alternative possibilities were terrifying. Could there be two of them?

"It's thunder," she said. "A storm's coming." She wasn't sure if she was trying to convince them or herself.

"It's not thunder," said Toro. "Stay perfectly still."

The trees began swaying with the wind, and Vikki could hear the shuffling of leaves and crackling of branches in all directions.

"Where's it coming from?" said Reggie.

"Everywhere," whispered Adelina, in a way that made the hairs on Vikki's arms stand up.

Chapter Fourteen

A Circle of Seven

The rustling in the jungle grew closer until a loud crack of a branch came from up in the treetops to Vikki's left.

She shifted her gaze toward the sound but didn't see anything unusual in the foliage. As she strained to listen, a strange scent—somewhere between jasmine, urine, and decaying soil—wafted in on the soft breeze. Just as her eyes caught sight of a small tree frog clinging to a leaf, a dull rumble startled her. It wasn't thunder; it was closer, heavier. The forest floor quaked beneath her feet, each tremor sending twigs and scattered debris skittering and leaping into the air like startled insects. She blindly reached for Adelina's hand, but Adelina jumped in close instead, wrapping her arms tightly around Vikki's waist. The poor girl's breaths grew heavier, faster—on the verge of hyperventilating.

"Take slow, deep breaths," she whispered into Adelina's ear. "I'll tell you a little trick. Count to four while you breathe in through your nose. Then slowly count to five as you breathe out through your mouth." She tried doing it herself as the rumbling stopped.

The stillness was eerier than the noise, sending a shiver down her spine and a tingling sensation through her arms.

Matt and Reggie looked frightened, their eyes wide as they scanned the trees. Toro stalked around like a ninja, trying not to make a sound with his footsteps. Adelina backed up slowly, practicing her breathing.

More movement came from the trees on the right. Something was out there. Something big. And, since the rustling sounds seemed like they were all around them, likely more than one.

"It's working!" Adelina said loudly. "The breathing works."

Toro's harsh whisper cut through the air. "Shhh." He turned sharply toward her, his eyes betraying a flicker of fear beneath his tough exterior. Vikki tightened her sweaty palms. This man, who was never afraid of anything, was now visibly shaken.

The snap of a limb from the treetops on the right made her glance up instantly. She craned her neck to study the upper branches for any signs of movement.

As she scanned the trees like a cat pursuing a fly, she noticed a sudden silence. Even the birds stopped singing—birds she hadn't even noticed until they ceased their background chorus, as if they knew something was about to happen. All she could hear was the sound of her heart beating, the occasional crunch of a twig, and the whisper of a leaf. A flock of small parrots took off in the air, emitting their shrill warning calls to their brethren. Then another flock farther down. It seemed every bird in the forest took flight after that, as the air filled with the flutter of tiny wings.

The treetops above her parted with a sharp, cracking sound. An enormous, dinosaur-like head with bright yellow eyes broke through the trees and gazed down at her. A flash of razor-sharp teeth shone through the foliage, making the hairs on her arms stand up. Reggie and Matt saw it, too, from the shocked look on their faces. Matt's wide eyes locked onto hers in disbelief. Even Toro was frozen in place, his mouth hanging open as he stared up at the enormous head. She glanced back up just as the creature let out a guttural growl that made the ground tremble. She tried to move away, but tangled roots tripped her and she fell backward.

As she hesitatingly looked up at the terrifying creature, she lifted herself off the ground and tried to control her fear enough to tap into whatever remained of her scientific mind.

The eyes were reptilian. The face had greenish-brown scales but was otherwise shaped like a horse—or perhaps more like a sea-horse—with a long, tubular snout, certainly not like any fossil she'd seen. Spikes jutted out from the cheeks and forehead. This was most certainly biological, not mechanical, but was like no organic life form she'd come across in her research. No, this bizarre creature looked exactly like what people said it was. And now, as the behemoth peered down at her with soulless, glowing eyes, it appeared she was going to be its next meal. Her legs began shaking as she wiped the sweat from her brow, hoping the small movements wouldn't trigger the beast to attack.

"That's a . . . dragon," muttered Reggie. "That's a dragon." He kept repeating it, apparently in shock.

Vikki glanced over at Toro, who was as dumbfounded as she was. "Do we run?" she said.

He shook his head.

The gigantic beast emitted a low growl that shook the ground—a low, steady rumble, ten times louder than any jungle cat. Vikki held her ears. A new voice joined the bone-rattling choir from behind her. She turned around, almost afraid to look, and saw another beast, even larger, pushing through the trees directly behind their group.

"*Ay Dios!*" said Toro. "There are two of them."

"Three!" said Reggie.

Vikki turned just in time to see another dragon break through the trees on the right side of the path, farther ahead. Then another appeared on the left side.

"Four," she said.

"This isn't good," said Matt.

"Ya think?" said Vikki. She looked around for signs of any more of them.

"We coulda really used those soldiers about now," said Reggie, wiping his forehead.

"They're either trying to figure what to make of us or lining us up for lunch," said Toro, ignoring Reggie's dig.

She had barely noticed that the skies had grown dark when a loud, unexpected crash of thunder made her jump. Adelina ran into her arms just as a heavy, warm rain came pouring down with a vengeance, drenching their clothes. Vikki scanned the path behind them to scout out a place to run. Another crash of thunder brought a solid bolt of lightning in that very direction, causing an enormous tree limb to fall across the path.

As the heavy rain and thunder continued, the four dragons let out a deafening roar in unison, shaking the entire area. A fifth dragon joined the ones down the path, making it almost impossible to distinguish the storm from the beasts' thunderous cries.

"That's five," said Toro.

"Maybe we should run into the forest," yelled Reggie over the rain. He pointed back toward the fallen branch. "There's no dragons in that direction."

"The forest in a lightning storm?" said Matt.

"He's right," said Toro. "It's the safest place to be. Better than an open field or a single tree."

"We'll never make it," said Vikki. She gazed up at the sharp, intelligent eyes watching them.

"On the count of three," said Toro.

"We can't," said Vikki, holding Adelina close.

"We have to," he yelled.

The ground shook again, and she turned to see two new dragons tread out from the jungle near the fallen limb, blocking their only exit.

"That's seven of them," said Vikki. They were trapped.

The gargantuan creatures surrounding them emerged from the trees, rocking the ground with each slow step. They seemed to be forming a deliberate circle around their prey.

A crash of thunder nearly shook her out of her shoes as a jagged bolt of lightning struck the ground to the left.

Trying to ground herself, Vikki stared at the enormous talons—five on each of the front feet, plus the single hallux to the side. The feet were webbed, as she suspected. The hind legs were still hidden in the trees. She held Adelina tightly as she glanced over at Matt, Reggie, and Toro, all backing up.

Adelina broke away from her and stepped forward slowly, her feet sinking into the soggy ground as the downpour continued.

"No, don't!" Vikki shouted. She grabbed Adelina's arm to stop her, but the determined girl shook her off. She watched nervously as Adelina held out her arms and looked up at the beasts.

As the young girl stood frozen, two of the dragons jolted their heads in her direction, their eyes blazing with a fierce hunger. They seemed like a pack of giant Dobermans waiting for an order before attacking and devouring their meal. A couple of the other dragons grunted, their teeth bared in a menacing snarl. Vikki's heart pounded in her chest as she watched helplessly, her breath caught in her throat as she awaited their next move.

Adelina backed up slowly. Her face was pale.

"They're not like the one I saw," she said. "I don't sense any emotion at all. They're not afraid. They're not in pain. They're not even angry. It's like they're . . ." Her voice tailed off.

"Like they're what?" said Toro.

"Following orders."

Chapter Fifteen

Discharge Training

Vikki's fingers clenched the fabric of Adelina's dripping shirt as she gently tugged her backward. Any moment now, those furious beasts could lunge, their wrath reducing them all to nothing but blood and memories. She held her breath as Adelina shuffled back hesitantly, the crunch of dead leaves and snapping twigs in the sludge making each step feel like the match that could light the tinderbox.

"Slowly," said Vikki.

The two most aggressive dragons leaned forward, their snarls rumbling over the rolling thunder. Strings of saliva dangled from their gaping jaws, glistening as they dripped into the rain puddles on the forest floor. As their eyes darted toward Vikki, she gasped. She glanced through the rain at Matt, who was facing her from several yards away, standing perfectly still so as not to draw attention. He motioned with his head for her to slip into the jungle behind her, but, like him, she was afraid to make any sudden moves.

In an instant, the two colossal dragons lunged forward and let out a bloodcurdling roar in perfect unison, shaking her to her core. The sound reverberated deep within her chest, paralyzing her with terror, while the oppressive heat of their breath rolled over her skin like waves of fire. She was too horrified to even scream. She felt Adelina's hand clamp down on her arm and yank her backward, but it was no use—her legs refused to obey. She stood rooted to the spot, helpless, as one of the beasts lowered its massive neck toward her. As its cavernous mouth opened wide, revealing jagged teeth as large as her head, her legs trembled. Deep within its throat, a churning pool of molten lava began to glow brighter and brighter. The stench of sulfur invaded her nostrils, and the suffocating heat pressed against her chest like an iron weight. Unable to move, she braced herself for a horrible, fiery death. She wouldn't have been able to escape in time anyway.

An arm wrapped around her from behind. Matt had come out of nowhere and pulled her and Adelina backward.

"We gotta run," he said.

Just as Vikki turned, she noticed Toro raising both arms, as if to surrender to some invisible army. The rain had slowed to a light drizzle. His weapons lay scattered on the ground at his feet. Stepping out from the shadows behind him were four camouflaged soldiers holding him at gunpoint.

She glanced back at the two dragons that seconds ago were about to attack. As if by some silent cue, they began moving backward to join the other beasts, lumbering slowly back to their circle.

Another man emerged casually from the trees behind them—a highly decorated general with salt and pepper hair. He exuded an air of confidence, clearly in charge, and his smirk, along with his smug demeanor, indicated he wasn't concerned about the dragons in the slightest. As he stepped forward, another group of soldiers arrived behind him, their movements disciplined and synchronized.

A ray of sun shone through the trees into Vikki's eyes. The rain had stopped, and the skies had turned bright again. If she wasn't so petrified, she might have taken it as a supernatural sign of hope. But she wasn't feeling hopeful at all, not after everything that had just happened, especially knowing they'd left dead soldiers behind.

She glanced back at the general and noticed he had some kind of handheld device, like a small tablet. She grabbed Adelina's hand and turned to face the general, barely even noticing that her clothes were still soaked.

"Are you controlling them?" she blurted out.

"In case you hadn't noticed, *Vikki*," he said, emphasizing her name for effect, "I control the weather, too. I'm a regular damn Zeus. I even called off the lightning bolts for you. You can thank me later."

"The weather!?" said Matt.

"Nah, I'm kidding about that," said the general. "It was just a freak storm. We get 'em all the time on this island. But, yeah, to answer your question, Vikki, I *do* control *them*." He nodded toward the dragons.

"Why are you trying to kill us?" said Toro, as the soldiers kicked his weapons several feet away.

"Says the guy who killed a whole lotta my men. I liked you better when you were on our side. Speaking of which . . . whose side *are* you on, Cortez?"

Toro peered at him before finally answering. "The side that doesn't wipe out a whole island and try to cover it up. Now, you tell me . . . General Krupp. You wanna compare body counts? This girl lost the only family she had." He motioned toward Adelina, who was still holding Vikki's hand.

"Glad you mentioned her," said Krupp. He turned to face Adelina and stepped toward her, then bent down to her level. "What's your name?" he said. Adelina's nails dug into Vikki's palm.

"Adelina." Her voice was confident, but Vikki knew what she must've been feeling inside. The girl had an iron grip on her hand.

"Adelina," he repeated. "Nice name. I'm sorry about your family. I mean that. It was a terrible shame what happened. It really was." He seemed oddly sincere, considering his men tried to shoot down their helicopter.

"I'm sure you feel real bad," said Toro.

Krupp stood and faced the group, his jaw clenching as his expression hardened into a near-scowl. Everyone fell silent—all eyes were fixed on him.

"I want everyone here to know," he said, his face growing red, "that we have a situation with a certain dragon. We're getting a handle on it, but how this dragon came to be here—and what his friends are being trained for—is above top secret. And none of you, as far as I can see, is the goddamn president! Now, we can't undo what happened. But we can't have you sending videos to news anchors, or snooping in top-secret areas, or even worse, waging your own war against our own military. I mean, who the hell do you think you are? This is a serious national security matter. We will *not* be exposed. We will *not* be delayed. And we will . . . *not* . . . be . . . blackmailed!"

"Uh . . . we won't say anything," said Reggie. "We're all on the same side, here."

"Oh, I know you won't. We're gonna see to it. But first, there's the little matter of a young lady we have to find out about." He glanced back at Adelina and winked, and then returned his gaze to the group. "You see, I need to know if I have a dragon problem or if we have a really special girl on our hands with one helluva useful talent. Because my most ferocious and uncontrollable dragon stopped right in his tracks when he saw her and decided to call off his own made-up mission. Am I right?"

Nobody answered.

"That's not a rhetorical question."

Krupp looked directly at Toro.

"You were there," said Krupp. "You saw it. Is that what happened?"

"I was too busy trying not to get fried like an Arepa," said Toro.

Krupp turned sharply toward Adelina. "Then *you* tell me. Is . . . that . . . what . . . happened?"

Matt stepped in closer, about to intervene, but a soldier cocked a gun and aimed it at his head.

Adelina nodded.

"Okay, then. Let's find out if you can do an encore. Because I need to know if you have some kind of special ability that can derail my dragons."

Vikki wasn't sure what he was getting at, but it quickly became clear as Krupp nodded toward the two aggressive dragons and entered some instructions into his handheld device.

The two beasts stepped forward to face Adelina, growling, eyes locked onto her. Vikki lunged to shield the girl, but two soldiers yanked her back.

"No!" Vikki screamed, thrashing against their grip. "She's only twelve!"

"Stop this!" Toro shouted. "You can't do this!"

"Shut him up," said Krupp.

A rifle butt slammed into Toro's head, dropping him to his knees.

Vikki tried to break loose but the soldiers' grips on both her arms were too tight. She watched in horror as both dragons lunged toward Adelina.

Vikki fought to break free, but the soldiers' hands were iron. She watched in horror as both dragons lunged. Adelina covered her face, chest heaving with terrified breaths. Sulfur stung the air, and heat rolled over Vikki's skin. The dragons' throats glowed, ready to unleash hell.

"Stop them!" Vikki shrieked, struggling harder. Rage and terror blurred her vision.

"Adelina, run!"

At the last second, Krupp pressed his tablet and yelled, "Abort!" Both dragons froze, then slowly backed up to obediently resume their spots in the circle. He handed the device to one of his men and walked over to Adelina, who was slowly standing up.

"So, it seems like you're not so magical after all. At least not to Zeta and Kappa here, who would've barbecued you and then torn you apart and had fun doing it. But the fact remains, I need to see if there's some kind of special connection between you and Gamma."

"He wants . . . to be free," Adelina blurted out, still out of breath from the traumatic experience.

Krupp's eyes narrowed. "What exactly are you saying?"

"Adelina, don't," said Vikki.

"No, it's okay," said Adelina, calming down. "Gamma was in pain, and he was mad. He was just frustrated and wanted to be free."

"And you could tell that . . .how?" said Krupp.

"I could sense it."

Krupp looked at his men and grinned. "She could sense it," he said, mocking. He turned back to Adelina. "And what do you sense about my dragons here?"

She shook her head. "Nothing. They're like robots."

Krupp's expression grew more serious as he stared at her, then turned to the two men beside him.

"Take her back to base. We need to run some tests."

"No!" said Vikki.

Matt protested as well. "She's just a girl," he said.

The two men took hold of Adelina's arms, and she went with them quietly, her shoulders slumped

"You can't do that, man," said Reggie.

"I said no!" screamed Vikki, as they carted Adelina off into the trees. The unyielding grip on her arms kept her from taking any action.

"I'm afraid you're not the ranking officer here, Vikki," said Krupp. "But I do have someone who wants to say a few words you may wanna hear." He walked slowly toward her, took a radio from his holster, and handed it to her. After the soldier to her left released his grip, she took the radio and put it to her ear.

"Vikki?" said a familiar voice on the other line.

"Dad!?" She lowered the radio from her ear to look at it—to make sure it wasn't a trick. Hesitatingly, she returned the receiver to her ear.

"Vikki, listen to me. This is over our heads now. I've been advised by the general to back off."

It was his voice all right.

"You sent us here," she said. "Why did you s—"

"Listen, I'm sorry I got you into this. Just do whatever they say, and everything will be fine."

There it was. *Fine.* The operative word from her childhood. To Dad, it was always ignore or repress whatever emotion you were experiencing. Don't talk about what you might be feeling or how you might be hurting. Just fix everything by saying you'll be fine and then you'll actually believe it. Except it never worked.

"Fine?" she said. "You mean like Mom was fine?"

He remained silent. She regretted saying it as soon as the words left her lips.

"Vikki," he finally said, "I couldn't have stopped her if I tried. You know that. This is totally different. Now, they assured me if you cooperate, it'll be okay."

She thought about it. "It doesn't sound like I have a choice."

She could hear him sigh through the receiver. "You don't."

"Okay, I have one question then."

"Of course."

"What's discharge training?"

He hesitated for a few seconds, and then finally spoke. "They tell me it's safe. You'll . . . you'll be fine." That word again. But this time it was different. This wasn't the superficial *fine* of her childhood. From the way his voice cracked, she sensed he was either under duress or was instructed what to say.

"Dad?" she said, her voice quivering.

She looked at Krupp. "What did you do to him?"

Krupp grabbed the radio.

"Over and out, Dr. Barnes," he said. "You've done your civic duty."

"You're gonna brainwash us," said Reggie.

"You've all been reading too many spy novels." Krupp looked at his men. "I'm headed back to base. Round these guys up and bring them back. Anyone resists, you know what to do. Leave the dragons in the theater of operations. All of them."

"What do you mean all of them?" said Reggie. "Are there more?"

Krupp ignored him and headed back into the jungle in the same direction the soldiers took Adelina. It must've been a shortcut to a transport vehicle, because there didn't seem to be any buildings in the area. Meanwhile, Toro was back on his feet and was whispering something to Reggie.

Matt approached her. He appeared subdued, but confident. She couldn't tell if he was putting on a brave face or he was just in denial.

"Vik, we're gonna get out of this," he said. "We'll get Adelina and we'll go home." His eyes were steady and reassuring. For a moment, she felt like maybe she wasn't alone in this. But then reality set in. They were in over their heads. Whoever these soldiers were, they had Adelina, and now it seemed they had her father, too.

She looked at Matt and nodded, though she had a hard time believing it. She kept thinking about how her father sounded. Scared. He sounded scared. And he *never* got scared.

As the dragons all retreated into the jungle, their heavy footsteps growing more distant, the soldiers immediately got to work, corralling her and the others into a straight line. A tall soldier with red hair led the group up the same path they'd been on.

"This feels like déjà vu," said Reggie, who was just ahead of her with Matt.

After a few minutes, Toro came up from behind. "Listen to me," he said. "The military takes no chances. If you think you're gonna go through some training videos and they're gonna let us go, think again."

"What can we do?" whispered Vikki. "And don't say kill anyone. Besides, they have Adelina." She had visions of the dragons being sent back to get them.

"We can't help her from a cell," said Toro. "I can break in alone and get her."

"That's impossible."

"It's what I do."

Reggie turned his head. "That sounds like a bad plan," he said.

Just then, one of the soldiers behind them grabbed Toro's shoulder. "What's goin' on here?" he said.

"Now that you asked," said Toro, "*this*." He grabbed something from the soldier's belt, pulled something and tossed it. Immediately, there was a loud hiss, and the area was filled with smoke.

"Run!" yelled Toro. "Into the jungle. I'll catch up."

Through the thick haze, Vikki saw Toro twist one soldier's neck and then leap on another soldier's back. He was a one-man calamity squad. She didn't even see where Matt and Reggie ran to.

Frantic, she bolted into the jungle and ran as quickly as she could through the trees, the rough branches slapping against her face and neck. Her feet kept slipping in the rotten undergrowth, slowing her down. She could hear chaos behind her—yelling and gunshots—but kept running. She hoped she was heading in the same direction as Matt and Reggie, but she wasn't sure. All she knew was that she was in a remote jungle on an uncharted island with the US Army looking for her.

And now she was alone.

Damn that Toro. Either he was right and they would've been brainwashed, or he just doomed them all.

She pushed her way through the thick brush as the sounds of the jungle tormented her from all sides, from unknown screeching animals to strange insects buzzing in her ears. She kept feeling like something was dropping from the trees, but didn't dare take time to stop and check her clothes for creepy crawly things. She knew that somewhere amidst the fluttering of the birds and rhythmic chirping of the tree frogs, giant predators lurked that could devour her in an instant. That's if the soldiers didn't shoot her first.

As she swatted at the mosquito buzzing in her ear, a sudden wave of fear sent chills racing down her spine. What if she was stuck out here all night? The thought unsettled her more than anything else. But then her mind turned to Adelina—she had to find her, no matter what. She would've considered turning herself in, but now, thanks to Toro, the soldiers could just as easily open fire without asking questions.

She pressed on through the dense forest, her ears straining for any sound beyond the rustling leaves. She stopped suddenly when she heard a shuffling noise off to the right. It sounded like faint footsteps—it *was* footsteps. She froze, trying not to make a sound. Calling out was too risky, so she crept toward the noise, trying to make each step deliberate and silent. Though adrenaline was surging through her veins, a flicker of hope stirred in her chest—it had to be her group.

Making her way through the trees, she paused every few steps to listen. She could no longer hear the footsteps. Only birds cawing and fluttering to the background chorus of tree frogs.

As soon as she stepped onto the intersecting trail, two soldiers burst from the shadows, blocking her path. She gasped, instinctively spinning to flee, only to stop dead as another soldier emerged behind her. His weapon was leveled at her chest, his cold gaze locking onto her eyes.

One of the men spoke into his radio.

"Squad Two. We have Dr. Barnes. We set the dragons to code four. I repeat, code four. They'll get the rest. Heading back to base. Over and out."

Chapter Sixteen

Death and Immortality

Matt crashed through the tangled undergrowth before finally stopping to catch his breath. He looked over at Reggie in confusion.

"Where's Vikki?" he said, panting. The humidity was already getting to him.

Reggie bent down to take a breather and shook his head.

"I don't know, man. She's probably with Toro."

A gunshot rang out back where they came from.

The hair stood up on Matt's arms. "We need to go back."

"Are you crazy?" said Reggie. "Did you not just hear that gunshot?"

"I can't leave Vikki."

Reggie grabbed his arm. "Let's think about this for a second. I don't want to leave Vikki either. But we have a better chance of helping her if we can get the hell outta this place. They got tons of soldiers, and . . . oh yeah, dragons!"

As soon as Reggie mentioned the word, a terrifying screech came from above, echoing in all directions. Matt looked up to see an enormous dragon circling around, its wingspan so massive that it blocked out whatever daylight was trying to peek through the trees. As it circled and let out another ear-piercing shriek, a small ray of sunlight gave its wings a crimson glow. Razor-sharp talons jutted out from beneath its enormous silhouette.

Matt had a sinking feeling in the pit of his stomach. He and Reggie were being hunted, and the dragons' lookout had found them. Any minute now, the whole cadre of beasts would be upon them.

"Get down under the trees," said Reggie.

Matt swallowed. His throat was dry. "I think it's calling to the others."

The palms swayed with each flap of its gargantuan wings as it let out another ear-splitting shriek.

"Let's hope it doesn't do the ole flambé routine or we're toast," said Reggie. "Literally."

Matt heard movement in the trees behind them. It wasn't just the palm trees swaying from the dragon's wings. Something was back there.

"I think running was a bad idea," said Reggie.

A wave of dread washed over Matt as he realized they were trapped. "I think the other dragons found us," he whispered. "Quiet."

He crouched low, motioning for Reggie to do the same.

"He must be the scout," Reggie whispered, a little too loud.

The cracking of tree limbs grew louder, closer.

Matt held his breath. All he could hear was Reggie's breathing and the thud of his own heartbeat. He was prey. They both were.

The branches in front of them exploded outward, snapping like twigs.

It was Toro.

"Oh, you guys are alive," said Toro. "That's good."

Matt almost collapsed with relief, wiping the sweat from his brow.

"I'm glad you approve," said Reggie. He motioned toward the sky. "Meanwhile, we got a visitor up there."

"I know. I—"

"Did you see Vikki?" said Matt.

Toro looked surprised by the question. "No, I thought she was with you."

Matt's heart dropped. "We have to find her." He hoisted himself off the ground and helped Reggie up. "She could be out here on her own, or worse."

"We got a bigger problem," said Toro. "Those dragons are still out here. I gotta get to Fort Majestic. Adelina's there. With any luck, so is Vikki."

"Do we know that?" said Matt.

"I know we can't stay out here," said Toro. "So, either you come with me to look for the transport vehicles or take your chances out here with the dragons. But either way, I'm going in. Alone."

The dragon soaring above their heads let out another deafening call. Matt got a chill. Those other dragons were going to be coming any minute.

"I vote transport vehicles," said Reggie.

Matt paused for a moment, realizing there weren't many options. "I'll go with you two to find the vehicles," he said. "We'll see if we spot her on the way. But if not, I'm sticking around here to look for Vikki."

"Suit yourself, amigo," said Toro.

Keeping a close eye on the dragon circling above them, Matt followed Toro and Reggie through the thick brush of the rainforest. His heart pounded with each step, knowing an attack could come at any minute—either from above or from the sides. As he glanced up at the shadowy beast, he hoped the dense foliage would shield them from view, though he couldn't shake the thought of its piercing gaze scanning for movement. Birds of prey were known for their keen eyesight, able to spot prey from dizzying heights—but dragons were closer to reptiles, and he wasn't sure how their vision worked.

He wiped his forehead with his shirt. The trees provided some shade, but it was still hot and humid, and he needed water.

"The sweat's burning my eyes," he said.

"It's like walking through a bowl of soup," said Reggie.

"You guys know anything about these dragons, or whatever they are?" said Toro, swiping branches aside with a knife as he led the way like a seasoned jungle guide. He must've stolen the knife from one of the soldiers.

"I know they're reptiles," said Reggie.

"And what are their habits?"

"Dragons?" said Matt.

"*Ay, Dios*. Reptiles. Nobody knows dragon habits. Do they hunt in packs. Do they wait in silence?"

"I'm not sure," said Matt.

"It depends," said Reggie. "Some use a sit and wait approach, and others use active foraging."

Toro stopped walking. "You a scientist?"

"No, I'm a nerd. And a pilot. He's the scientist." He patted Matt on the shoulder.

Toro turned to Matt. "Okay, then what's active foraging?"

"Well . . . um," said Matt. In truth, he had no idea what active foraging was.

Reggie rolled his eyes. "Active foragers move through the habitat looking for their prey, unlike ambush foragers who sit there waiting for the prey to come nearby, and then bam!"

Matt felt his skin tingle just envisioning it.

Toro shook his head. "I don't wanna find out the hard way which these are, so we gotta assume it could be either." He patted Matt on the shoulder, either mimicking Reggie or as a gesture of reassurance—Matt wasn't sure which—then turned to resume walking. "Let's keep moving. We don't want to be sitting ducks."

As they pushed through the dense brush, Matt's eyes darted back and forth, searching for any sign of Vikki. His pulse raced with anticipation as he remained vigilant for the piercing gaze of giant reptilian eyes waiting to strike from the shadows. The trek seemed endless, with no trace of Vikki and no sign of civilization. He glanced up to check on the dragon, and gasped.

It was gone.

He wasn't sure if that was a good sign or a bad one, but he couldn't shake the feeling they were being watched. His nerves were already on edge and now he was on red alert.

"Where's the dragon?" he said, almost nonchalantly.

"What dragon?" said Reggie.

"What do you mean, what dragon?" He pointed to the sky. "That one. The one that isn't there."

Reggie and Toro looked up as they walked.

"Maybe it gave up," said Reggie.

Toro huffed. "Maybe it didn't. Nothing we can do about it. Stick to the plan."

"We have a plan?" said Matt.

They continued following Toro for what felt like an hour of nail-biting uncertainty but was probably half that time. He felt like he was going to drop at any minute, until finally, after trekking in the heat through the endless underbrush and relentless vines, they came to a massive clearing that led to a dirt road.

"Tire tracks," said Toro.

"Let's follow them," said Reggie.

"Not so fast," said Toro. "If we get out in the open, that makes us easy prey." He looked at Matt. "Okay, Mr. scientist, do these things hunt by sight or smell?"

"Well in Jurassic Park," said Matt, "the dinosaurs hunted by sight."

"But these aren't dinosaurs," said Reggie.

"Right," said Matt. "So, I'm not sure."

"Wait a minute," said Toro, turning to face Matt. "What the hell kind of scientist are you? You're giving me advice from Jurassic Park? I'd rather take advice from the pilot!"

"I happen to be a damn good scientist," said Matt.

Toro threw up his hands. "Studying what?"

"Soil."

"Soil! *Ay Dios*, I feel safer already. What, do you soil your pants when things get dicey?"

"Hey, I work with some very scary dirt," said Matt.

"Scary dirt," said Toro, shaking his head.

"So, you're a soil scientist," said Reggie. "No wonder she left you."

"Not funny, man," said Matt. "I happen to be a microbiologist specializing in metagenomic research."

"Meta-what?" said Reggie.

"I study enzymes from collections of soil. I look for contamination from explosives, unexploded ordnance, illegal testing . . . I also look for new chemical interactions, medicinal potential, all sorts of things. In this case, I was sent here to study the soil."

"What, like in case the dragon peed in the dirt?" said Reggie.

"That would be bizarrely lucky," said Matt. "But traces of residue in the footprints? Properties in the charred soil or foliage? That could tell us a few things about what we're looking at here."

"And what *are* we lookin' at?" said Toro.

"I don't know, I never made it back to the lab to analyze it."

"Uh, guys," said Reggie. "I think something's lookin' at *us*."

Before he even turned to look, Matt heard the familiar low growl in the trees to their right. A chill ran through his body. The deep rumble sounded like thunder rattling through his muscles and echoing down to his bones—a primordial roar that would have had to have come from its belly, not from its throat. He turned to see the terrifying yellow eyes staring from the foliage.

"Move," said Toro, heading into the clearing. Reggie joined him and Matt followed, nearly tripping over a rock.

The trees behind them shook violently as the beast tore through the vines and stomped into the clearing, rattling the ground beneath their feet. Four more dragons emerged from the trees on either side, flanking them.

"Damn things are herding us like sheep," said Toro. 'That's two on each side."

Another dragon burst through the trees on the left, joining the other two as it came to a halt. The dragon from behind lumbered forward to join those on the right.

"That's three on each side," said Reggie.

"They're . . . trapping us," Matt said as he staggered backward, his head reeling at their terrifying coordination. No wonder the Army wanted them so badly. His mind raced as he prayed Krupp would show up with his tablet, though deep down he knew it was hopeless. They were at the mercy of these beasts.

"There should be one more," said Reggie.

On cue, the seventh dragon—the one who'd been circling in the air—swooped down to join the three on the right. It landed with an eerie grace that belied its monstrous size, its massive wings folding with sinister precision.

"Do we run into the jungle?" said Reggie.

Matt's legs shook uncontrollably. He knew he couldn't outrun these things. But it was either that or give up and die.

"I think we need to split up," said Matt.

"Because that worked so well last time," said Reggie.

"Don't run," said Toro. "You two are gonna walk, very slowly into the jungle in different directions."

"What about you?" said Reggie.

"I told you. I'm heading to the fort alone. I'm gonna walk right past them. They sense fear. Adelina wasn't afraid, that's why she lived. And I was focused on her, so they ignored me."

"That's a crazy plan," said Reggie.

"It's my plan. It's how it's gonna be. Meanwhile, you two see if you can find a transport vehicle or a copter. Radio home or something."

Toro stood tall and stared at the three enormous reptiles on the left, who gazed right back at him with emotionless eyes.

"Now get out of here," he said without turning around. "Slowly. I got these big boys."

Matt glanced at Reggie, who shrugged. Matt nodded his head and began treading backward. Reggie moved slowly to the far side of the clearing, while Matt retreated to where they'd come from, his eyes darting back and forth between Reggie and the dragons.

One of the dragons on the right followed Matt with his eyes, and another on the left seemed to be tracking Reggie.

"I'm not sure about this," said Matt under his breath. His legs trembled as he stepped back inches at a time.

Toro paced slowly toward the imposing goliaths on the left, each of them towering silently like patient and calculating predators. It occurred to Matt that this was the single bravest thing he'd ever witnessed. Or the single stupidest. Time would tell.

"Toro, don't," Matt whispered, as loudly as he could without causing a disturbance.

"They won't do anything without their leader and his magic tablet," said Toro. "And he ain't here. Now back out of here while they're focused on me."

"You don't need to do this," said Matt.

Toro turned briefly to show him his right arm with the snake tattoo. "Remember," he said. "Immortality. We're gonna survive this."

Matt looked across at Reggie, who was shaking his head.

Toro stepped toward the dragons, undeterred. One of the creatures shifted a little and Toro stopped for a few seconds before continuing.

Matt kept watching as he crept back toward the trees. Still no action from the dragons. He was finding it difficult to breathe, and his heart was pounding through his chest. He tried to look away but couldn't. He wasn't sure what was making him more anxious, worrying about Toro's fate or his own.

Slowly, the center dragon on the left, the tallest one, extended its neck downward toward Toro. Toro stood bravely and looked up to meet the dragon's gaze. The creature took a deep breath and uttered a bone-chilling chittering sound. A faint yellow glow emanated from its mouth, and for the first time, Toro appeared to be trembling as he shielded his face. Matt watched helplessly as Toro yelled, "*Oh, mierda!*" and charged ahead in a desperate attempt to dive between the towering beasts.

The dragon slammed its enormous foot down on Toro with the agility of a cat. Its long, center talon punctured the man's torso with a wet pop that sent a horrified chill down Matt's spine. Screams filled his ears as blood spattered the jungle leaves with a pattering sound, like rain. He stared in disbelief as another dragon grabbed Toro's legs in its jaws and pulled, ripping him in half like a rag doll.

Matt hunched over, about to retch. He tried to hold it down and run. But his legs wouldn't listen.

Still in shock, he turned to flee into the jungle while the dragons seemed distracted. One darted toward him. He glanced back as he ran as fast as his legs would take him. The dragon changed direction toward Reggie, who'd already disappeared into the trees on the opposite side. Another dragon immediately joined in its pursuit.

As he frantically forged his way through the thick brush, Matt heard a sound he'd never heard before coming from the clearing behind him. It was almost like an air raid siren, but he knew it was coming from the dragons. The scent of sulfur filled the air, and as he turned to peer through the trees, two dragons were blasting flames in the direction where Reggie had run.

He could hear Reggie yelling and then all the dragons headed in that direction. Reggie didn't stand a chance. And it would only be a matter of time before they came for him, too.

Matt ran until he could barely breathe. The brush grew thicker and so did the air. Collapsing to the ground, he crawled to the narrow trunk of a tall tree and leaned back against it. As he finally reclined, he glanced up and spotted a small bunch of round, green apples—perhaps some kind of tropical apple—hanging high among the long, dark leaves. They were too small to be mangoes. Parched with thirst, he hoped a juicy, refreshing fruit might help him recover. He tried shaking the branch from below, but the stubborn green apples—or whatever they were—didn't budge. Clearly, they were unripe: their color and refusal to detach from the branch made that obvious. Eating them would probably do more harm than good. He was too weak to stand and try again, and certainly in no condition to climb.

He closed his eyes and started thinking about his chances. Here he was, alone on a remote island being hunted by at least seven dragons, who were apparently trained by the Army to be killing machines. He had no idea where Vikki was. All he knew was that if he had any chance of survival, he'd need to find water soon—perhaps a lake or a stream. He needed an energy boost to have a fighting chance of finding Vikki and maybe even getting to Fort Majestic. At this point, he'd sooner turn himself into the Army than be subject to the raw instincts of dragons—if indeed they were even operating on instinct, which he was beginning to doubt.

He thought of Reggie, whose humor and flying skills had made him feel better even in the worst of circumstances. And Toro, a warrior if he'd ever known one. That fierce snake tattoo represented immortality. That's how he'd remember Toro—not the screaming or the sudden terror that must've washed over him when he'd known there would be no escape, but the courage he'd shown at every turn, and the life of service that he gave in helping others. It was that service that made him immortal. He'd live on through the lives of those he'd helped.

Matt was now the only person left to save Vikki and Adelina. If he had even the slightest chance of success, he'd have to find a way to survive and get to a radio. Or at least get to Fort Majestic. Before this moment, he didn't believe in angels or the afterlife. He believed in cold, hard science. So, he completely surprised himself when he whispered, "Toro, buddy, you gotta help me here."

Chapter Seventeen

The Footprint of Freedom

Vikki was still reeling from the wild jeep ride as the soldiers led her to a shiny, oversized steel door built right into the mountain. It must have been at least fifty feet tall. The road to the facility had twisted and wound around the mountain so many times during the ascent that she'd gotten as dizzy in the vehicle as she did in the helicopter. She swallowed to unclog her ears. No wonder they called this place Fort Majestic. The massive door opened automatically with a whirring sound as soon as they approached. A guard was waiting on the other side, apparently to escort her somewhere.

Once inside, she followed the guard down a white, sterile corridor lined with thick glass windows that revealed enormous, empty rooms—some of which didn't even appear to have doors. One smaller room looked like a conference room. Just past it, the guard approached a steel door on the right, lifted a latch to unlock it, and swung the heavy door open. Vikki stepped inside. The first thing she noticed was the incredibly high ceiling. As she gazed upward, she heard the door close and lock behind her.

"Vikki!" yelled Adelina as she came running to greet her. Vikki turned and held out her arms to embrace Adelina, but then her eyes widened in amazement. On the opposite wall, where Adelina had come from, was an enormous floor-to-ceiling window, with a barrier rope a few feet in front of it. Beyond the window, resting on the floor of the adjacent room, was the largest dragon she'd seen yet—even more massive than the ones in the jungle. It looked ancient, with scars covering its body, and appeared either tired or drugged.

"He's sad," said Adelina. "I don't know his name, but he's much different than the others."

"How can you tell?"

"I just can. I can feel his pain. When I look in his eyes it's like he's trying to talk to me. He's not just sad—he feels . . . lost. Like he's been here a long time and doesn't think anyone can help him." Adelina moved back toward the window and stood against the rope to observe the captive creature. "I can almost feel his heart beating really slow," she added, "like he's tired of waiting."

The way the dragon seemed to be following Adelina's every move with curiosity, Vikki believed her. Then again, even the tigers at the zoo can look friendly until they start getting hungry. She wondered what a dragon eats, besides island villagers.

"Are the others here, too?" said Adelina.

"I don't think so. I think they're still out there."

"Why didn't they come with you?"

"It's . . . complicated. Toro did . . . well, what Toro does, so they managed to escape into the jungle. At least I hope they did."

Adelina seemed to be processing the news. For a moment, she appeared worried, but then she smiled slightly, if only to reassure herself.

"If Toro's with them," said the stoic young girl, "they'll be okay."

Adelina was an enigma. She'd been through such awful experiences, losing her parents at two, living with her uncle and then losing him in a terrifying dragon attack, and yet she still was able to empathize with these creatures. Somehow, despite increasingly dangerous encounters, she trusted them—at least the ones she could read.

Vikki wished she had the young girl's positive attitude, but she'd been burnt too many times to be so trustful. Then again, Adelina had been dealt an even harder hand, and she still managed to stay hopeful, whatever she might be feeling inside.

Vikki was trying to stay optimistic, too, but she felt like she was going to jump out of her skin. She was worried about the others. She may have been a little harsh on Matt, but she had good reason. Still, she didn't want anything to happen to him. Meanwhile, she wasn't even sure what was going to happen to Adelina and her. Was Toro right about brainwashing? Or could it be worse than that? Why were they locked in this barren room next to a dragon?

The door clicked behind them and slowly opened. She hoped maybe they caught the others safely and they'd all be together again. At least it would be the best of a whole list of bad options. Most importantly, it would mean they were still alive.

Instead, a silver-haired man in his seventies entered, wearing a lab coat and dragging a medical trolley behind him.

"I'm Dr. Simmons," he said. "Wesley Simmons. It's a pleasure to meet you, Dr. Barnes." After exchanging handshakes with Vikki, he turned to Adelina. "And you too, Adelina. I've heard a lot about you."

He seemed genial enough. He may as well have been a pediatrician, given his demeanor, but as her father once told her, even Hitler used to pet the dog. She glanced at the cart and spotted a glistening, stainless-steel tool peeking out from beneath a white cloth.

"I apologize for your situation here," he said, "but hopefully we can rectify that soon enough. I'm here to collect your vital signs."

"For what?" said Vikki.

"Oh, it's just standard practice."

"For prisoners?"

"Visitors, my dear. The creatures are quite sensitive, and we must keep a sterile environment. I hope you understand." He held out a pulse oximeter for her finger.

"What's that other tool for?" she said, motioning toward the cart.

He glanced back. "The forceps? Not to worry. It's not for you. For now, I just need your oxygen."

For now. What was he going to do to them later?

She hesitated, but then extended her hand. She couldn't help noticing that he shot a nervous glance toward the dragon.

"Oxygen's good," he said after checking the sensor.

He checked her temperature and blood pressure, then ran the same tests on Adelina.

"All good," he said. He looked at Vikki. "Pressure's up slightly for you, but that can be expected given the circumstances." He gave a slight smile that seemed uneasy. "Do you have any questions for me?"

"Do I h—" Vikki couldn't help but laugh at the absurdity of the question, but inside, her stomach was in knots.

"Let's start with what's going to happen to us," she said.

He crinkled his face as if the question pained him.

"I suppose General Krupp will want to talk with you both and will want some assurances as to your discretion. But you surprise me, Dr. Barnes. I've read your paper on basal tetrapods. Brilliant work. Surely, you must have questions about these wonderful creatures."

"The one that attacked the island wasn't so wonderful. What kind of assurances?"

"I beg your pardon?"

"You said Krupp would want assurances about our discretion."

"Ah, yes." Simmons glanced down briefly, then looked up. "I'm afraid that's between you and General Krupp. I'm a scientist, just like yourself."

He was clearly dodging the question. He knew something. He had to.

"Where do they come from?" said Adelina from across the room.

"Ah, that's the question I was waiting for," said Simmons, raising his index finger. He looked like her college professor when a student got an answer correct. "You've met Alpha." He motioned to the giant beast on the other side of the glass. "He's the oldest, and we came into possession of him back in 1995."

"Came into possession?" said Vikki. "You make it sound like you won it at an auction." She glanced over at the ragged creature, lying in its cell like a dying god.

"Not quite. The US Military was doing ultra-high frequency testing at Diego Garcia. Part of a program we call HAARP."

Vikki rolled her eyes and looked at Adelina. "Reggie was right after all."

"Where's Diego Garcia?" said Adelina. "Is it near here?"

"Heavens no. It's a long way from here. It's just south of the equator, in the center of the Indian Ocean." He looked at Vikki. "In military circles, we call it the Footprint of Freedom, because of its shape and strategic importance. Anyway, we were doing testing there and from what I understand, Alpha came soaring in at low altitude. He must've been attracted to the sonic waves. They have an acute sense of hearing and smell, you know. Beyond any species on Earth."

"What about their vision?"

"Poor, but adequate for their needs. Like whales, they rely more on echolocation. That, and their smell."

"So, he came from the sea," said Vikki. "That would explain the webbed feet."

"We don't know where he came from. Some of my colleagues think maybe somewhere near Papua New Guinea, since that was the direction he was coming from—or yes, even under the sea, possibly from a blue hole or surviving from a long-lost civilization. Frankly, we have no idea."

"Were you there when he first showed up?" said Vikki. Out of the corner of her eye, she saw Adelina wander closer to the window to watch Alpha.

"Oh, no, I was brought in by General Krupp much later." He looked at Adelina briefly and said, "I wouldn't get so close."

"So, Krupp was there."

Simmons shook his head. "The general was brought in to start the program months later. The DIA brought him in. That's the Defense Intelligence Agency."

"You said Alpha's the first one you found. How did you find the others?"

"We didn't find them," said Simmons, looking surprised by the question. "We made them."

***

"Clones?" said Vikki. "Do you guys not watch movies? So, Gamma . . . is a clone? And the others?"

"Gamma's the oldest living clone," said Simmons. "He has . . . issues we're trying to work out. Luckily, we've improved the process with the others since then. Beta was completely uncontrollable. Delta was an improvement, but didn't fare much better. Both had to be put down. I fear the same for Gamma."

"Wait, if Alpha is a male, how did you create the others without an egg?"

"We didn't need Alpha to produce eggs. We used his tissue and inserted the nuclei into lab-engineered egg cells. It's built on the same cloning techniques used since Dolly the sheep, but with next-gen bioengineering."

She'd read about bioengineered eggs being used for nuclear transfer. "How many are there now? Clones I mean."

"Eleven in all, with Omicron being the latest. Not counting Alpha of course, and—"

He paused mid-sentence and looked over at Alpha. Vikki turned to see Alpha and Adelina, both crouched down facing one another. Adelina had crawled under the rope and had her palm pressed to the window.

Vikki turned back toward Simmons, who was standing with his mouth open. "What's wrong?" she said.

"I don't believe it," he said, his eyes widening. He pointed to Alpha. "He . . . he moved to be closer to her."

"She has a way with animals. I don't get it either."

"I'm not so sure it's just that," he said.

"What do you mean?

"Lots of people who died on that island probably had a way with animals. Some of our own people had a way with animals. One was a renowned horse whisperer. All of them are dead. No, I think the bigger question here is, why do the dragons seem to have a way with *her*?"

Vikki looked more closely at Alpha. There seemed to be a certain intelligence in his eyes, no matter how poor his eyesight may be.

"We had Adelina in this room for a reason," said Simmons, "but I wouldn't have believed it."

"Is he usually this calm?"

Simmons shook his head, dumbfounded. "Not when people approach his window. He lunged at me just an hour ago. If it wasn't for that glass, I wouldn't be here talking to you."

Vikki thought about it. They say animals can sense emotions like fear or love. Dragons likely had the same ability, but perhaps exponentially greater. She looked again at the window. There were no openings that she could see.

"How do you feed him?"

"We lower his food in from the ceiling. Livestock, brought in from the Dominican Republic."

Vikki glanced up and saw the sliding hatch on the ceiling above Alpha's tank. She looked again at the ancient, withered skin on the creature. "How old do you think he is?" she said.

"We're not sure exactly. It's not like fossils where you can do radiometric dating on the surrounding rock. But from a bone extraction and a study of the growth lines on Beta and the others, we were able to get a sense of the relative growth rate. It's more challenging with Alpha, since the growth rate seems to slow down after 20 years. He's larger and much older than the others, so he could be hundreds of years old or more."

"Incredible." She glanced over at Alpha. "He has indicators of a plesiosaur and some pterosaur traits, but he's neither. He'd have to have come from a completely unknown branch of the evolutionary tree."

"Yes, but the bigger question is *where* he comes from, and all points would seem to lead to the sea, like you said yourself. But that poses an interesting dilemma, one that I'm sure is plaguing you at this very moment, and it's the same question that plagued me."

Vikki knew exactly what he was alluding to. "Everything evolves for a reason," she said. She recalled reading how snails evolved from having bright colors to dull patterns to be able to hide from predators, and how species in Japan adopted protective isotopic changes after Hiroshima. Even humans didn't evolve to have larger brains until they began making tools.

"So, if these dragons came from the sea," she said, "why do they fly? And *how* do they fly? The very weight they'd need to submerge would keep them from flying."

"Precisely," said Simmons, smiling. "The sea origin theory makes sense. Large sea creatures can hear much higher frequencies than people, dogs, or even bats, and these dragons hear in an even higher frequency."

"And that's how you control them."

His eyes darted around nervously. Then he leaned in.

"Yes, through a combination of targeted ultra-high frequency waves sent through an implanted chip. Through this, we can manipulate specific neurons. To put it another way, we're able to send brain signals. Outside the neocortex, of course. After all, they're not mammals."

She tried to process what he said. They can send brain signals via direct neuron manipulation. Then again, similar experiments have been done with rats, so why not dragons? She'd read the recent studies of birds and reptiles, including the new revelations on how the unique centers in their brain housing neurons were equivalent to the neocortex in mammals. No doubt, Simmons and company were at the forefront of science.

"And what about the flight?" she said. "How can they fly if they're heavy enough to submerge?"

"Methane-hydrogen sacs—buoyancy organs, completely independent of the pulmonary system."

"And both methane and hydrogen are lighter than air."

"Yes, and the very same flight bladder, if you will, allows them to fly and project their fire—it's sort of like a combustion engine: the gases ignite as they're expelled."

"And the catalyst?"

"Electrocytes. Electrified muscle cells. They can produce electric impulses at will."

"You mean like an electric eel?"

"Exactly."

She glanced at Alpha and marveled at the mind-boggling display of nature before her. But one thing still puzzled her.

"Why do they smell like sulfur? Methane's odorless. So is hydrogen."

"Their bacteria contains a complex mix of sulfurous compounds. We're still analyzing it—but I can tell you it's like nothing we've ever seen. There's much more to it, but *why* they have all this flight and fire capability, or as you put it, why they *evolved* to have it, we don't know. To answer that, we'd need to know where Alpha came from. But that, my friend, is a program for another day."

"And what's the program for this day?"

His face grew serious. "I better let General Krupp tell you that." His eyes flicked nervously toward the door. "I can tell you it's gone far beyond what I'm comfortable with. Keep that between us, scientist to scientist."

"Then . . . scientist to scientist . . . I can tell you I don't trust Krupp. I'm pretty sure he plans to brainwash us, and I don't like the sound of that. What do you know about it?"

Simmons shook his head. He began to fidget nervously with his cart. "I wouldn't know anything about that. I'm . . . I'm sorry."

Vikki liked Simmons, but she wondered if he was telling the truth. "Okay, then I do have one last question," she said, glancing over at Adelina.

"I'll try my best to answer."

"How much are you going to stay silent for?"

"I don't understand."

"You said the program has gone beyond what you're comfortable with. Are you comfortable with a fellow scientist and a child having their brains practically lobotomized? Is that on your acceptability list?"

Simmons leaned in, sweat forming on his forehead. "I truly don't know anything about that," he said.

Vikki gritted her teeth. "Can . . . you . . . help us escape?"

Simmons closed his eyes and took a deep breath, then opened them. He seemed about to speak when the door burst open. Two guards stormed in. Simmons jumped, knocking a small tool off the cart. It clattered to the floor. Alpha, perhaps agitated by all the noise, let out a low rumbling growl that shook the floor. Adelina jumped to her feet.

"We're here to take the participants," said the taller guard with a stern face.

"Participants?" said Vikki.

"Come with me, ma'am," he said. Then he motioned to the other guard. "You take the girl to Sector 9. I'll bring this one to the general."

"Vikki!" yelled Adelina. Her eyes were wide with panic.

Vikki looked at the two guards. "What's Sector 9?"

Neither answered. She looked at Simmons. "What's Sector 9?"

He shrugged. "Just cooperate," he said. "It'll be okay." He stepped back from her as if she were contagious. But he couldn't hide the horror on his face as he passively watched the determined guard escort her into the hallway.

As the guard led her away, she turned to see the other one leading Adelina in the opposite direction. "Where are you taking her!?" she yelled.

Chapter Eighteen

Stayin' Alive

Matt's arms ached as he tried to cut his way through the foliage without the use of his machete—or any tool for that matter. He wasn't even sure where he was headed. He had no cell phone, so calling for help wasn't an option. Somehow, he had to survive in this hellish jungle while avoiding the alarmingly intelligent dragons and who knows what else was out there. The annoying mosquitoes were the least of his worries.

The thick, humid air made it hard to breathe. Every step felt like he was trudging through invisible sludge. He prayed for any signs of water or food, but so far it was just thick underbrush, dangling vines, and an overwhelming sense of darkness caused by the canopy of leaves and branches overhead. The chorus of insects and tropical birds serenaded him from all sides as his tired feet crunched through broken twigs and dirt. He was running out of energy fast. His hands trembled as he wiped the sweat from his forehead. At this point, he didn't know if he was heading toward water or not.

He thought again of Toro's unending determination. He couldn't get his mind around how a man so full of strength and vigor—and who had survived so many harrowing ordeals in his life—could be cut down so quickly. Would the same thing happen to him, after all this effort? Either way, Toro had never stopped fighting, and he would need that same resolve to get to Vikki. He owed it to Toro to keep going, so the man wouldn't have died in vain.

As he trudged along through the brush, he thought about his options. He didn't know how to fly a copter, but if he could find one, he could try to radio for help as Toro suggested. That would be easier than trying to access the undoubtedly well-guarded fortress where Vikki was being held.

He paused and bent to pick up a handful of the clay-like soil, clearing away the decomposing leaves. With the humidity it was hard to tell if he was getting any closer to a water source. He crumpled a corner of his shirt and used it to wipe the sweat from his eyes. With any luck it would rain and he'd get a few sips of rainwater from his cupped hands, though that wouldn't help much. In the meantime, even a piece of fruit would hold him over if he could find ones that were low enough to reach.

He stood and continued his journey ahead, stopping occasionally to scan the trees for anything edible.

Exhausted and on the verge of passing out, he caught sight of something bright green ahead in the trees—brighter than any leaf around. Moving closer, the round shape became clearer. Was it a mirage? Were his eyes playing tricks? As he drew near, he knew. He swallowed hard in anticipation. Suspended before him was a fruit the size of a watermelon. And there were more.

Thankfully, a few of the melons hung low enough for him to reach. Mustering his remaining energy, he pulled one down, cradling it as if it were a precious child. It was heavier than he expected. Then he realized—this was no watermelon, nor any kind of melon for that matter. He recognized it instantly from his pomology course at Cornell: a calabash. Not the bottle gourd kind, but a true, round calabash from the calabash tree. His heart sank. Not only would it be difficult to cut, but it wasn't really edible. The one saving grace was that calabashes made excellent bowls—practically indestructible. If anything was going to kill him aside from the dragons, it would be dehydration. At least now, if he found water or if it rained, he'd have a container. But first, he had to figure out how to get it open.

He tried biting into the rind and nearly broke his teeth. Desperate, he lifted it as high as he could—straining the sore muscles in his arms—and smashed it against the ground. It rolled a few feet, uninjured. He didn't have the strength to try again. He was going to need something to cut it with, but he didn't have anything on him he could improvise with. Maybe a sharp rock would do the trick if he could find one.

A volcanic rock like basalt would be ideal, if only he could spot any, but it was unlikely in this part of the island. He scoured the ground for anything that might work. His best bet would be jagged pieces of sedimentary rock beneath the clay soil. He knelt and began digging with his hands, but the hard soil and the numbness in his wrists and fingers forced him to take frequent breaks. Again and again, he hit solid clay. He shook out his hands and tried again. Muscle cramps he could survive; dying of thirst was another matter. Ignoring his painfully broken nails, he went back in, trying to dig around the hard segments instead.

He felt something.

It may as well have been gold. No—right now, it was better than gold. Shale. Shale made a perfect tool; in fact, it had been used for sharpening knives since the Stone Age. Best of all, it broke into sharp shards, and this piece already had. He summoned the last of his strength and let out a slow exhale, shutting his eyes as he concentrated. Carefully, he pried the dirt away from the sediment with what remained of his fingernails. His fingers ached, but he kept scraping.

Got it. Carefully, he pulled out the flat, gray shard—about the size of a cell phone. He settled onto the ground and tried cutting into the fruit.

It didn't budge. All he was doing was scratching the skin. He knew he could cut it—he'd done it in class—but with only a piece of shale, it would take some work.

He stabbed at the skin multiple times until he finally penetrated the hard shell. Then it was a matter of working his way around the perimeter. By the time he'd made enough of a gash to pry the two halves open, his arm felt ready to fall off. The flesh inside was disgusting—a kind of decaying, gray pulp. At least, that's what it looked like. A strong chemical smell immediately assaulted his nostrils. He remembered that smell. He'd hated it in class, and he hated it even more now. Reluctantly, he dug his hands into the putrid guts and scooped them out of the gourd, trying not to gag. He used the shale to scrape the insides, making the bowl as clean as possible.

He remembered hearing that in small quantities, the flesh could have some health benefits but was otherwise toxic. Those benefits had never been proven. Still, despite every rational instinct in his brain, he was starving and thirsty—he needed something for sustenance. Holding his nose, he put a small handful of the pulp in his mouth. It was chewy, like eating raw oysters, except it smelled like a biochemical facility. After a few bites—as disgusting as it was—he wanted more. He *needed* more. But he forced himself to stop and think. He couldn't afford to get sick.

A tremendous rumble reverberated through the trees, sending shivers down his spine. Quickly, he grabbed the bowl he'd made and got to his feet. He shot forward, driven by instinct, pushing through vines and branches. He couldn't tell where the noise was coming from—he just hoped he wasn't running toward it. Another booming roar echoed, sounding like it was coming from all around.

He was practically delirious, his vision blurring—he wasn't sure if it was from the calabash or dehydration. *Immortal, Matt. Remember what Toro said.*

A ringing started in his ears—one of the first signs of dehydration. He forced his way through the brush, but didn't know how much farther he could go without collapsing. *Stay alive, Matt. Stay alive.* That was the name of the game now: survival. He started singing to himself to keep sane. That old Bee Gees song, "Stayin' Alive."

Another violent rumble shook the ground. The sound was getting closer. Black spots drifted into his vision. He pushed his weakening legs faster until he had to stop, his heart pounding with fear and exhaustion. The leaves, branches, and trees began spinning, clouding his mind. He stumbled, reaching out to grab anything he could. In his stupor, he noticed a clearing just ahead—a patch of light that caught his eye. He was so close.

With a meager burst of energy, he pushed forward. *Get to it, Matt. Don't give up now.* He stumbled ahead, nearly falling, until he approached the gap in the foliage. He shoved his way through until he emerged into an open path. He staggered and glanced around, but didn't see anything. Then he looked down.

Vikki's footprints were right below him—there was no doubt they were hers. A larger set of footprints accompanied hers, side by side. He traced the prints with his eyes until they led to a set of tire tracks further ahead.

A loud boom shook him to the core. The skies darkened, and a heavy downpour began, drenching his clothes. Though the sudden torrent instantly washed away the footprints, he laughed with pure joy—relieved it wasn't the dragons causing the noise. Holding out his bowl, he let it fill, then tilted his head back to gulp the refreshing rainwater. He gazed up at the dark clouds, letting the rain wash the dirt and sweat from his face.

"Thank you, amigo," he whispered.

Just as he took a deep breath, another deafening burst of sound made him jump out of his skin. It came from just ahead.

And this time, it wasn't thunder.

Chapter Nineteen

Secret Meeting

"Dr. Jim Barnes?" said the receptionist, squinting as she scanned her computer monitor. "Are you sure?"

"Yes, I know who I am," said Barnes. "I'm not on the schedule but Dr. Ford's expecting me." He glanced at his watch. He didn't have time for this.

"I don't see your name, but I'll let him know you're here."

"He's expecting me."

"You said that, sir."

He took a deep breath to try to calm down. "You're right, I'm sorry."

If anyone knew what was going on, Marcus Ford would. Ford was a Senior Intelligence Officer in the Science and Technology wing of the DIA, and prided himself on being the first African American to reach that position. He had worked with Krupp back in his Army Intelligence days and knew the general personally.

The receptionist made a brief phone call, which he assumed was to Ford, and spoke into the receiver quietly. She put the phone down and said, "He'll be right out." He was surprised Ford wasn't retired by now. He had to be in his late seventies at least.

Barnes was exhausted. The trip from Santa Fe to Washington, DC, had taken six hours, including a stop in Denver—plus a forty-five-minute drive to the Defense Intelligence Agency head-quarters. He had no choice, though; he couldn't risk having this conversation on the phone, even on a secure line.

After a few minutes, Ford entered the waiting room. He looked as dapper as ever, though a little older. His customary smile was missing—he must have picked up on the urgency of Barnes's request to meet. Ford reached out to shake his hand.

"Jim, is everything alright? What's it been? Five years? Six?"

"Hell, at least ten." He'd forgotten how firm Ford's handshake was. "Can we talk inside?"

"Of course. Good to see you, man. Come on back."

He followed Ford down a labyrinth of corridors to an unmarked walnut door. Ford opened a small, silver lock box outside the door.

"Phones go in the box," said Ford. "You know the drill."

He took out his cell phone and dropped it in the box. After Ford closed and locked it, he pressed his thumb against a scanner beside the door and waved Barnes inside.

Barnes had specifically requested a SCIF. Though he'd never used one before, he knew from his past government dealings that a *Sensitive Compartmented Information Facility* was basically a private, soundproof room with acoustic paneling and no windows. It was for when conversations needed to be had that couldn't risk prying ears. And this was one of those conversations.

He took a seat at the small conference table opposite Ford. Ford's brow was furrowed with concern as he leaned forward.

Barnes rested his elbows on the table, trying to appear comfortable and composed. He was anything but. "Thanks for keeping this off the books, Marcus."

"Of course. Now what's this all about?" Ford took out a small notebook and a pen from his jacket pocket and placed them on the table.

"I'm sure you saw the video about the so-called dragon."

"Jim, if you're gonna ask me about that dragon—"

"No, no, it's about Vikki."

Ford's eyes narrowed.

He decided to just get to the point. "I sent Vikki to investigate the island, and now Krupp has her."

"Wilson Krupp?" Ford looked completely confused. "I thought he was retired."

Barnes hesitated, then lowered his voice. "What do you know about Fort Majestic?"

"Nothing." Ford shrugged. "I mean, it sounds impressive, but I can't say I ever heard of it. What's this have to do with Krupp?"

He leaned forward. "Krupp's running a Special Access Program at a secret facility called Fort Majestic. It's so secret that my sources at the Pentagon don't know anything about it. Whatever he's doing is completely off the books. I've even tried my contacts at AARO and NBIC. Nothing."

"AARO? Since when is Krupp into UFOs . . . oh, sorry, UAPs? I still can't get used to the damn alphabet soup changes."

"Whatever this so-called dragon was, I figured it might classify as"— he made air quote signs with his fingers—"*anomalous phenomena*." He shook his head. "No such luck. And NBIC's biosurveillance folks handle biological events, like avian flu, so I thought maybe . . . I mean, both were longshots, but—"

"Did you try the Military Intelligence Corps?" said Ford, tapping his pen on the table.

"The MIC didn't know anything either."

Ford paused and put his fist to his chin, appearing truly stumped. "If it's a Black Budget program," he said, "it would be off the books for sure, and most of those are outsourced to the private sector."

"I know," said Barnes. "We handled plenty of them at HRI during the post-9/11 surge."

"How do you know Krupp's involved in this?"

Barnes folded his arms across his chest. "Because I talked to him. That's how I found out about Fort Majestic. He wouldn't tell me where it was though. He has Vikki and a couple of my employees in custody. He wanted me to get them to cooperate."

Ford's eyes sharpened as he leaned forward. "Cooperate how?"

"Basically, get them to acknowledge a gag order, which means putting them through something called discharge training. Any idea what that is?"

Ford shook his head. "Sounds like classic contractor speak. Anyway, there is no such thing, and I've been at this a long time. But I can guess, and it isn't good."

Barnes felt his palms begin to sweat. "No, it's not good. It's why I'm here." He leaned in further. "I'm off the record now, Marcus. I'm asking as an old friend. Do you know anything at all about this program? Anything that could get me in touch with someone."

"I really don't." He looked sincere.

Barnes's heart sank. "Can you at least find out where Vikki's being held? I'll go there myself if I have to."

"Did you try reaching back out to Krupp?"

"No can do. He contacted me through a protected number. You knew him better than I did. I thought maybe you could find a way to reach him. Maybe contact his relatives?"

Ford paused for a moment and contemplated. He would've been good at poker.

"I'll see what I can do," he said. "One thing's puzzling me though. Why'd you send her in the first place? You know how these things work."

Barnes grimaced. "Don't you think I haven't asked myself that every day? Especially after what happened to Laura?" His muscles tensed as he recalled his last visit to Vikki's office. He still couldn't believe he put her in this situation.

He looked Ford in the eyes and sighed, as if to expel every molecule of guilt he'd been wearing like a lead harness. "Vikki lost her passion. Ever since Laura died, I could see she was afraid to do anything. She'd take the easy route."

"I pushed her," he said, pounding his fist on the table. "I tried to get her to move forward, to take risks. So even if there was a small possibility there was some new species involved here—and let's face it, it sure seems like it—I thought maybe it could help light a little fire in her. Just a spark. To bring back that old curiosity she always had. Plus, I thought it could be an opportunity to get her back in touch with Matt."

Ford raised an eyebrow and put his pen down. "I thought they broke up. At the party, she almost spit out her martini when I mentioned his name."

"Don't ask. The thing is, I need them back. I need *her* back. She's my only daughter for Chrissakes. If I thought for one second anything might happen to her because of my stupid mistake, I . . ." He shook his head in frustration. This was his worst fear in life. All he wanted was for Vikki to be safe and happy. It's all he's ever wanted. It's all Laura wanted, too. He thought back to Laura's laugh, which used to fill the lab. These days he could only hear it on old voice mails. He couldn't lose Vikki, too.

Ford stood up and walked over to him, putting a hand on his shoulder. "I don't know a lot, my friend, but I know blame never solves a problem. You did what you thought was right. Now, I don't know if Krupp went rogue or if he's working on some off budget program for the DoD." Ford hesitated for a moment and sighed, tightening his grip on his shoulder. "He was always a . . . straight guy, so I assume this is all legit. I did hear the DIA brought him in for some consulting, but I thought he retired after that. I'll see what I can find out, or at least if I can get you a way to reach him. It won't be easy. I mean, we're talking Area 51 level secrecy here, above my pay grade. But I'll try. For now, let's hope she cooperates."

Barnes nodded. He never felt so helpless in his life.

Chapter Twenty

Trouble in Paradise

Vikki clenched her fists as she continued up the pristine white corridors, flanked by an armed soldier on either side. She wasn't sure if she was more angry or afraid. She just knew she didn't like being treated like an enemy by her own country—especially after everything she'd already survived. And all this for what was supposed to be a simple scientific expedition.

The soldiers led her through a set of double doors and across a glass bridge that led to another hallway. The passage was much wider, with ceilings so high they could only be meant for dragons.

Their collective footsteps echoed in the vast halls as they passed the empty rooms and enormous glass tanks. The whole environment felt like a long-abandoned research facility—except everything was perfectly clean and white. With everything so spotless, she was surprised they didn't have her wear a mask and gloves.

The soldiers didn't utter a word as they led her around a corner. On the right was a set of open double doors. Krupp was standing inside with his back to her. He was gazing out the window at a spectacular vista of rainforest treetops that led to a cliff on the distant horizon. Beyond it, the sparkling, turquoise waters of the Caribbean Sea shimmered in the sunlight. The term *trouble in paradise* had never rung truer.

She quickly glanced around the room at Krupp's sparingly appointed office. Behind his mahogany executive desk was a matching credenza with an empty vase. A silver-framed photo showed a woman and two teenage boys—his family, she assumed—but it was impossible to tell how old the picture was. There were no other pictures or pieces of furniture in the room aside from a couple of simple black chairs for visitors.

He turned to face her, a slight smirk on his lips and a cup of coffee in his hand. Her stomach churned at the sight of him. He nodded to the guards and they left silently, closing the door behind her.

His smug demeanor made her jaw clench. She dug her nails into her palms, fighting the urge to say something she'd regret later. She decided to get straight to the point.

"What are you going to do to Adelina? Or any of us. Are you going to kill us? Turn our brains to mush? Is that what the military does these days? I mean, a little—"

"Vikki, let me stop you there," he said, the smirk fading. His expression turned serious. "Is that what you think? You think I want to kill Americans? Or"—he made the air quote sign with his free hand—"turn their brains to mush?" He set his coffee down on the desk and stepped toward her. She stiffened up as he invaded her space—much too close for comfort.

"I don't want to kill Americans. I want to save them. Whether you care or not, this little project here just may be the most vital national security initiative this country's ever seen. No, not *may* be. It *is*."

There it was. Virtue signaling in the interest of national security at the expense of everything and everyone else.

"And what is this project, exactly?" she said.

"Let me ask you this. What do you know about Afghanistan? I mean the war, not the country."

"What do you know about my dad? I mean his current situation, not his career." She'd dealt with men like him before, always trying to *educate* her.

He remained stone-faced. "Your dad's fine. We don't have him if that's what you're thinking. Whether anything does happen depends on you. Now answer the question."

She wasn't sure what angle he was working. She figured she'd just be honest.

"Not much. I know we sent troops there after 9/11. It didn't go well." She couldn't imagine what Afghanistan had to do with any of this.

"It went *very* well, at least in the beginning. Like gangbusters in fact. We made damn quick work of al Qaeda and the Taliban. Did you know we wiped out all the terrorist training camps in the first hundred days?"

"Can't say I did." *Was he just trying to show how strong his army was—how he had the advantage here?*

"All of them. Gone. Regime ended." He began to pace as he spoke. "But then we tried to create a centralized government. Democratic. Hell, their tribal groups didn't want that. If anyone had even touched a history book, they'd know Napoleon made the same mistake in Spain, thinking they'd bow down and sing Kumbaya. So, with no clear exit strategy, we were stuck there in a counterinsurgency campaign we didn't plan on. For twenty years! Fighting a guerilla war, with al Qaeda and Taliban rebels stickin' it to us from the mountains. And who ended up in charge after all that?"

He stared at her. She didn't answer.

"The Taliban." He sighed. "By the time all was said and done, we'd lost around 2,500 service members."

She shook her head, still unsure where he was headed with this. "I agree, it's horrible," she said. "But what does this have to do with me?"

He stopped pacing and pointed to the photo behind his desk. "Michael and Brandon were two of those soldiers." He gritted his teeth. "My sons. Killed in action. They had their whole lives ahead of them."

An empty silence filled the room.

He stared at her, waiting for a response. Words failed her. A tight knot formed in her chest—nobody should lose a child, let alone two. Still, despite her sympathy, she couldn't shake the thought that such a devastating loss might have made him more compassionate toward Adelina—was an abuser any less abusive because he suffered trauma? All she could manage was a quiet, "I'm sorry."

"The point I'm making here is I don't want any more American families losing their sons or daughters in wars. Not in just wars. Not in unjust wars. And not in political wars. And I've got news for you. All wars are political."

"And you think these dragons can help." *Now his motive was starting to make sense.*

He leaned back against his desk. "These dragons," he said, "are like B2 Spirit bombers, but with two exceptions. One, they have mind-boggling sonar detection, which means they can dodge any kind of missile or tracer fire. And two, thanks to what I'm told is their unique membrane hydration, they can't be detected by any radar. So, we get in, we get out. And—"

Vikki folded her arms. "And you have a perfect killing machine, but sooner or later things go wrong, and these creatures may not want to sing your song. Gamma didn't."

His eyes narrowed. She must've hit a sore spot. Meanwhile, all those people on the island are dead—thanks to Gamma's aptitude at killing.

"Let me finish," he said. "It gets better. These dragons aren't dependent on satellite positioning. So, if any enemy knocks out our comms—which I can tell you isn't a matter of *if*, but *when*—it's no problem. We're still in the game. Plus, they're ferocious in hard-to-get places, they can submerge, and they can fly. These goddamn dragons are the most perfect weapons we've ever had. They're the anti-war machine. The ultimate deterrent. Sure, some things went wrong, but we fixed it. Nothing's without risk. It's the price of safety. Still think we shouldn't use them?"

She sighed. "Listen, if you want me to say I won't tell anyone, I'm not going to say anything. I get it. It's a military secret. It's a game changer. I don't know how you found Alpha and I'm not even going to ask."

"Ask away, Vikki." He smiled. "I mean, you're not gonna remember the answer anyway."

"So you *are* going to brainwash us." Her palms began to sweat and the air felt suddenly oppressive and heavy. She frantically scanned his office for any needles or something he might grab for.

"What, do you think I'm Dr. Evil? Brainwashing is so 1960s."

"You just said—"

"Discharge training, if that's what you're worried about, is a relatively harmless treatment that'll give you a little short-term memory loss. It could be a lot worse."

As he rose from the edge of the desk, she began to back up toward the door, her nerves tingling. "What do you mean *treatment*?"

He stepped toward her. "Vikki, it's the only way I can let you out of here. It's a sort of hypnosis, but with a bit of direct brain stimulation. It's perfectly safe."

"No. No way." She wasn't about to be the recipient of any direct brain stimulation, especially one that involved memory loss. She'd done deep brain stimulation on animals in school for behavioral control, but this sounded far worse.

Krupp pulled a shiny, rectangular, black device out of his pocket and her nerves prickled with alarm. He put it to his mouth and spoke into what was apparently a receiver. "It's time."

Before she could figure out what that meant, the doors burst open and the two soldiers rushed in and grabbed her. She tried pulling free, but they had an iron grip on her arms, her skin burning where they held her.

"You can't do this," she yelled. "I don't volunteer for this. I do *not* volunteer for this!"

As the soldiers dragged her out of the room, Krupp followed, his footsteps echoing behind her. "Hope you don't mind if I join you part of the way. I want to show you something." She didn't like the sound of that. The last time he tried to show her something, the dragons had almost torn her and Adelina apart.

The corridor was colder than Krupp's office, unless it was her anxiety giving her the chills. They led her to the right, the opposite direction from where she'd come. She was acutely aware of Krupp marching along just behind them. She stopped struggling; it was no use at the moment. But her stomach was in knots thinking about what awaited her. As she walked, she thought of possible ways to escape.

Before long, they escorted her into a cavernous, circular lab area with a series of colossal steel rollup doors positioned around the room like giant sentries. At the far end of the facility, lab technicians in white coats worked at a large control panel.

Krupp stopped at one of the steel doors on the left.

"Do it," he said.

One of the soldiers clicked a button on a small handheld device. The steel barrier lifted into the ceiling with a quiet whir, revealing an enormous glass window behind it—like the tank Alpha was in. But what was behind the window made her skin crawl.

A familiar, loud rumbling—a dragon's growl—rattled her bones as huge, scaly legs came into view. Razor-sharp talons gleamed like obsidian, and massive green-gray scales dripped with moisture. She craned her neck as more of the beast was revealed. The legs seemed to go on forever until its spiky chest appeared, rising and falling with each noisy breath. This beast sounded angry, its bellowing snarls sending deep vibrations through the floor.

The steel barrier rose fully. Instantly, the dragon lunged at the glass, its giant teeth crashing against it with a thunderous bang. The noise shook her to her core. She jumped back, her heart hammering, and looked up into its yellow, soulless eyes. The beast lowered its massive head and stared directly at her. With another roar, it smashed its snout into the glass, nearly shattering it. She froze, every instinct screaming at her to run. Its eyes fixed on her, unblinking, as if she were the only thing in the room.

"He's gonna break that glass!" she said.

"He's not gonna break anything," said Krupp, calm as could be.

"Why isn't he outside with the others?" Her legs shook as she watched the dragon pound on the window with every part of its body. A deep, thunderous boom reverberated through the lab with every strike, rattling her teeth and echoing in her chest. There was no way this glass would hold. The pane was already creaking and flexing under the dragon's assault. "It's because you can't control it like the others, isn't it?"

"He's not like the others," said Krupp. "That's Gamma."

She should've known. This was the beast from the video—the one Adelina had faced and, somehow, survived.

"Impressed? Scared?" Krupp's lips curled in a faint smile. "You shouldn't get too concerned. Adelina was in that tank not more than a half hour ago. Hell, maybe he misses her."

Vikki looked at him, horrified. The blood rushed to her face and her breathing grew fast and heavy. "What did you do to her!? She's a child!"

Furious, she struggled to break free from the two soldiers, but they only tightened their grip. She couldn't breathe—she was starting to hyperventilate. She'd never hated anyone like she hated these men.

"Relax, she's fine. It was a controlled experiment."

The dragon kept chomping at the glass in a rage. "Controlled how?"

She tried inhaling through her nose, like she told Adelina to do when she was panicking. She steadied herself with each breath—at least as much as she could with a vicious dragon about to crash through the glass.

"How . . . do you control . . . that?" She pointed at the rabid monster.

"Don't worry," said Krupp. "He was calm as a baby with her."

"Him!?"

Krupp turned to the lab technicians. "Put it on 150."

"What is that?" Vikki asked. "Temperature?"

"Frequency. Watch."

She did as he said and stared at Gamma, who was still trying to break through the glass. Within seconds, the dragon backed up and lowered himself to the floor. She couldn't believe it.

"He won't take instructions," said Krupp. "But he damn sure doesn't like pain."

"And you're saying he was calm when Adelina was in there," she said. "Before you did . . . *that*."

"Bingo, Dr. Barnes. You win the prize. And now you see why we have to study her."

"What exactly do you mean *study her*?"

"I'll show you."

Chapter Twenty-One

Crisis Point

Vikki's legs still trembled as the soldiers marched her from the lab, away from Gamma, Krupp's shadow looming just ahead. The click-clack of their boots matched the beating of her heart as they led her down another massive corridor, one of many leading from the circular lab. She still couldn't shake the shock of seeing Gamma attacking that glass; how it didn't break was a miracle. Her head buzzed, and she felt a ringing in her ears. She shook out her cold, clammy hands. She needed to focus and get a sense of where she was—think about the direction she'd come from, and where they were headed.

She realized the facility was shaped like a star, with the lab in the center and the oversized corridors branching out like spokes. It reminded her of the Eastern State Penitentiary back in Philly, where the hub-and-spoke design was meant to confuse prisoners and foil escape attempts. She wasn't sure if that was the intention here, but it had the same effect.

They came to a window on the left where several doctors and nurses were operating on a patient, who was in a reclining position. The patient's body was covered, and the doctor's white-coated figure blocked the view of the face. As they proceeded to the end of the window, Vikki could see the back of the patient's head, with electrode wires and leads connected to a measuring device. The patient sharply turned to her with a shocked expression.

It was Adelina. Vikki jolted back in horror. A tremor shot up her spine, tightening her throat. She could barely get the words out. "You can't do this!" she yelled. "Get her out of there now!"

She turned to push one of the guards, but then a firm hand gripped her arm and pulled her back. "Get her out of there!" she repeated.

"Quiet!" said the guard.

She tried pulling loose, but his grip was too tight.

"Vikki!" Adelina's terrified voice came faintly through the glass.

Vikki broke free and banged on the window, but both soldiers grabbed her arms and yanked her back. "Stop!" she cried. "What are you doing to her!?"

"It's not invasive," said Krupp. "Now, wave, so she doesn't panic."

She struggled, then gave up, realizing it was no use. The soldiers released their grip.

"Jesus," said Krupp, "they're just electrodes."

Vikki felt the blood rush to her face.

Krupp nudged her. "I said *wave*."

Vikki waved and forced a smile. Adelina waved back, calming a little.

"You can't do this to a child," she said through gritted teeth. "You're putting a minor through stress against her will. I'm going to—"

A shrill alarm blared, echoing through the halls. Blue and red lights flashed down the corridor. The doctors and nurses looked at Krupp through the window and shrugged, as if they were confused about what to do.

"Third time this month," said Krupp.

The lights suddenly grew dimmer.

"What's happening?" said Vikki.

"Power outage." He looked at the soldiers behind her. "Take her to Room 201, I'll go see what's up."

As Krupp left, the soldiers led her down the hall.

"What happens if the power's out?" said Vikki.

Silence. All she could hear was the hum of the emergency lights and the echoes of their footsteps in the dimly lit hall. She prayed Gamma wouldn't escape.

"If my life is at stake, don't you think I deserve to know?"

They just nudged her along and didn't say a word.

"Some of the systems don't work," said the soldier to her right, finally. "Generator keeps up the main building."

"What doesn't work?" she said.

"It's classified."

The dragons! What if they got loose? She felt a chill down her spine.

"Are the dragons in the field still controlled?" The blaring alarm was stressing her out even more.

"That's not your concern."

She stopped in her tracks. "My friends are out there, so I think it is."

"Walk."

They both pushed her forward, nearly knocking her over.

"What's in Room 201?"

The alarm still rang in her ears as she walked as slowly as she could, trying to delay the inevitable.

"Somebody's there to see you," said the soldier on her left, finally answering her.

"Who?"

"Keep walking."

As she picked up her pace, the alarm continued its repetitive, loud beeps. She wondered if it could be Matt and the others waiting for her—maybe they'd been captured and brought here. She needed to know they were okay. Could there even be a way off this island? She didn't believe Krupp's claim that they'd all leave unscathed in the end, despite her father's reassurances. Still, there was something about strength in numbers. She dared to feel a glimmer of hope.

As they nudged her along, her father popped into her mind. He'd sounded desperate. Where was he? Was he safe? Was he being held somewhere—or out there, looking for her? Could he be the visitor?

The alarm stopped and everything went dark for a second. She heard a click, and then the lights came back on. She glanced around, trying to get her bearings.

"We're back on regular power," said the soldier to her left.

"Thank God," said the other. He spoke into his radio. "General, is everyone safe? Over."

If Gamma had gotten loose, it would've been her worst nightmare.

Static crackled from the radio, followed by Krupp's voice. "Mostly. Red on Blue. Single unit down. Over."

She tried to make sense of the code words, but they meant nothing to her. At any rate, he didn't sound happy.

"Copy that," said the soldier. "Over and out."

They entered another hall and approached the first door on the right, marked 201. Her first instinct was to dig in her heels—she wasn't ready to find out what was in there. Her nerves tingled as one of the soldiers turned the knob and opened the door. Was it friend or foe on the other side? He pushed her inside.

She froze, her breath catching in her throat at what she saw.

On the other side of the unassuming door was a vast operating room, larger than the one Adelina was in. In the center of the room was an oversized exam chair that looked like a dentist chair. Next to it stood Dr. Simmons with a slight smile. Behind him was a mobile control unit with all sorts of buttons and wires hanging from it, and an IV trolley. A nurse with a surgical mask was standing at the far end of the room.

"There's no way," said Vikki.

Before she could turn to run, the soldiers grabbed her and forced her into the chair. The harsh lights burned her eyes as she struggled, her heart racing. The faint smell of antiseptic sent her into a panic.

"Someone help!" she yelled, hoping she'd cause enough commotion to alert anyone in the area. Blood rushed to her face. She kicked her feet wildly, thrashing her body in every direction trying to get free. The soldiers ignored her as they secured the tight, surgical restraints on her arms and legs. Her breath came in sharp bursts as she scanned the room for anything—anyone—that could help. She had to get out of here. Her left arm had some wiggle room. She tried jerking it loose.

"Stop squirming," said one of the soldiers as he fastened the last restraint on that arm.

Simmons pressed a button on the side of the chair that set it into a reclining position. He nodded to the nurse, and she wheeled over the IV trolley.

"What are you doing!?" said Vikki, as the nurse tightened a tourniquet around her right arm. "What is that?" She had never felt so helpless. What were they going to do to her?

Nobody answered.

The nurse searched for a vein, then cleansed her skin with a pad and inserted the IV. "This is just for anesthesia," she said. She taped the IV to her arm and then left the room. The two soldiers remained.

She looked up at Simmons, who was picking something off the cart. She could barely breathe, and she was getting dizzy. "What's happening? What are you doing?"

Simmons kept moving slowly and deliberately, examining the cart as if he had all the time in the world.

"Talk to me! I need to know what you're doing."

Still no response.

"Please answer me!" she yelled. "You owe me that."

She was at the mercy of a sadistic doctor in the service of a fanatical, delusional general. What kind of surgery was this going to be? Would they drill into her brain?

"I don't want surgery," she said. "You can't do this against my will. I don't consent to this. *I don't consent!*"

"The procedure won't hurt a bit," he said, walking behind her with whatever he'd picked up. The strong scent of rubbing alcohol filled her nose as he wiped the back of her neck, then her forehead, with a sterile pad. She saw sharp-looking tools on his cart, and none looked painless.

Several tears rolled down her cheek, but her hands weren't free to wipe them away. She twisted her neck, trying to see behind her, but the doctor held her forehead down.

"What kind of procedure?" she asked, her voice trembling. "Where are the medical techs?"

"Not at all necessary," he replied from behind. "This is highly specialized." He draped a cold medical sheet over her shoulders.

Vikki's breathing grew rapid. It was bad enough getting surgery, but a thousand times worse when you had no idea what was waiting on the other side.

The two soldiers stood silently by the door. Simmons walked to the back of the room and returned with a gyroscope-looking frame, which he placed over her head. She braced for pain.

"What are you doing with that?"

"Only what is necessary," he said. "On the good side, we won't need to shave your head." He seemed all business, unlike the first time she'd met him

"Don't touch my head." Her legs shook. "Get that away from me." She didn't want to become a vegetable because of some experimental surgery, and Simmons was being intentionally vague.

"Stop! Is this brain surgery!? Are you digging into my brain?"

"There's no need to worry. I'm performing an augmented transcranial magnetic stimulation. It's been modified from standard TMS. And, oh yes, there's no cutting involved."

"What is that? Modified how?" She knew about transcranial magnetic stimulation—it was used to study brain function and treat depression, not for whatever this was. "You have to tell me—what are you doing to my brain?"

"The net effect is that you'll have some short-term memory loss. Leave the *how* up to me."

"TMS doesn't produce memory loss," she said.

"As I said, it's been modified."

She strained against the restraints. "How many times have you done this?"

He glanced at the soldiers briefly, then looked down. "I'm afraid that's classified."

A cold wave of fear swept through her. He wouldn't even meet her eyes.

"How many times?"

He didn't answer.

"Dr. Simmons." She spoke in a hushed tone to avoid the soldiers hearing her. "If you can get me out of here, my friends are still on the island. One of them is a pilot. I can take Adelina and find them. If I get caught, I'll just say I escaped."

He ignored her and continued prepping his tools. Then he moved behind her to tighten the pins on the head frame.

"No, don't do that," she pleaded. "Just send out the guards. Please. Just send them out so we can talk."

"You know I can't do that." He moved back to his cart, not looking at her.

"I won't say a word. I'll say I cut one of the restraints. You can slip me your knife when they leave."

No response. This wasn't working. She was running out of time.

"If you just give me a chance, I'll take all the blame. You won't get in trouble."

Finally, he looked at her. "You are getting preferential treatment because of who you are," he said matter-of-factly. Then he turned back to his work.

"This is preferential treatment?" Her voice shook with disbelief.

He continued prepping his tools in silence, then pressed some keys on his tablet. She shivered, wondering what he was doing.

It seemed he was really going ahead with this. She had to try another angle. "You said yourself they've gone beyond what you were comfortable with." She lifted her neck. "Are you comfortable with this?"

"We're almost ready to begin," he said, as if he hadn't heard her. "I'm setting the parameters."

"Tell me, doctor," she said quietly. "Do you know for a fact he'll let us go?"

He continued ignoring her, typing away on his tablet. Judging by his pursed lips, he was getting annoyed with her questioning.

"Are you absolutely sure this procedure will work? Without fail?"

No response.

"Do you have any children, doctor?"

His hands were shaking slightly.

"Are you sure this'll work? Can you promise me?"

A bead of sweat formed on his brow. She could see it in his eyes—he wasn't sure at all.

"You've never done this before, have you?"

He reached for a needle on the cart and prepped it, his hands shaking more strongly.

"Forget the Army for now," she said. "It's just you and me. You have to decide now. Who do you want to be? Are you Oskar Schindler or Josef Mengele? Are you the guy who risked his life to save people or the guy who did unspeakable things to people because he was under orders?"

He turned to adjust something on the IV line above her head. She wasn't getting through to him at all. Spineless idiot.

"You can't be both, doctor, and there's no in between. Which are you?"

He paused. For a moment, she thought he might actually answer.

He shot a nervous glance to the soldiers and then approached her with the needle. Her legs tensed and she tried shaking her arm to make it hard for him, but the strap dug into her skin. It was no use.

"No, please don't do this. *Stop!*" Her heart was pounding.

He opened the IV port and dispensed the needle's contents into the IV line.

"My dad's company won't let this rest if I'm not home safely."

Her arm began to tingle. The anesthesia was running through her veins.

"Even if something happens to him, he'll make sure of it. We won't let this rest, we won't . . . let . . ."

The icy-cold prickles ran up her arm. It was too late to do anything now. She'd lost.

"I . . . won't . . ."

She was losing consciousness.

A distant, muddled voice said, "The general will see her in the recovery room after the procedure."

The sound of a door opening . . . hazy . . . a white ceiling . . .

Lift your head, Vikki. Fight it.

Blurry figures . . . leaving the room.

Blackness.

Chapter Twenty-Two

Voices

Matt ran through the thick brush, gripping the calabash bowl, not having a clue where he was going. He only knew he needed to get as far away from the sound of those dragons as possible. The deep rumbles echoed behind him, and it was hard to tell how close they were.

Too exhausted to go any further, he stopped, set the bowl down, and rested his hands on his knees to catch his breath. A sharp, stabbing pain tore through the right side of his abdomen—a side stitch from running, a harsh reminder that he was still dehydrated and needed to eat something. He leaned against a tree, trying to plan his next move. Ultimately, he needed to find a copter with a radio, but if he couldn't, getting captured would be the next best option. At least then he'd be in the same facility as Vikki. The trick was to end up in the hands of the guards and not the teeth of the dragons. Or the flames. He wasn't sure which was worse.

If the dragons or soldiers didn't kill him, starvation might. He contemplated the increasing likelihood that he might die out here. His biggest regret would be Vikki never knowing how much he really cared for her. As far as he was concerned, she was the one. She'd always been the one, despite the stupid misunderstanding that had kept them apart and his own inability to explain it.

He thought of the many laughs they'd shared back in the good days—the time at the Moshulu restaurant when his chair rolled backward on the tilted ship and she laughed hysterically, or when the llama at the zoo started chewing on her hair and wouldn't let go.

He smiled at the memory of happier days—three years of travels and dinners and movies—and then he remembered the darker times after her mom died. He tried to be there for her, listening and letting her grieve, taking quiet walks in Fairmount Park. It was around then that the *event* happened that she never forgave him for. And it happened at the worst possible time.

No, he wasn't going to let that be her lasting memory of him. He wasn't going to give up on her like that. Not after all they'd been through. He was going to get up and survive this somehow. Rather than just thinking about what he was running from, he had to remember what he was running *for*.

As he held his stomach and straightened up, Matt realized he'd been leaning against a palm tree. Not just any palm, but one thin enough to climb halfway and bend. More importantly, he recognized the slender, single trunk and the telltale scars at the base of its leaves—it was a juçara palm. He'd seen photos of juçara palms in his study guides, but they were native to South America. What was one doing here?

If he could reach its heart, he'd at least have some nutrition—at last.

Slowly, he wedged his right foot into the shallow grooves of the trunk's rings and hugged the tree, lifting his left foot to the other side. The trunk was smoother than he expected, making it hard to get a grip—not to mention there were no branches. As he hoisted himself up, the searing pain in his side flared. He tried to keep climbing, but his strength gave out and he slid back to the ground, the jagged bark scraping his skin.

Another roar echoed in the distance.

Determined, Matt started climbing again, gripping the trunk even tighter. He pushed through the pain, alternating his legs as he worked his way upward.

"Just like climbing ropes in gym class," he muttered. Except he wasn't a kid anymore, and this was a thousand times harder. Another sharp pain shot through his abdomen, but he gritted his teeth—just a little farther, and the tree would start to bend. He took a deep breath and forced himself up.

At last, the trunk began to give way. Hope surged through him. He climbed higher, feeling the tree arch down to the left. Now he just had to hold on and pray the tree didn't whip back upright. More likely, it would break; after all, the juçara usually had to be cut down to reach the heart.

As the tree bent and lowered to the ground, Matt's body flipped so he landed gently on his back. Still gripping the trunk, he pulled himself toward the top of the tree, inching his way to the swollen base where the palm stalk met the trunk. That was where he needed to cut.

Clinging tightly to the palm, he reached into his pocket for the piece of shale—and froze. It wasn't there.

His muscles aching, he craned his neck, scanning the ground below. The shard must have fallen out when he hit the ground.

Finally, he spotted the shard a few feet away. He reached back with his right arm, careful not to lose his grip on the tree. Stretching as far as he could, his fingers just brushed the rock—still out of reach. Thinking quickly, he tore a strip of bark from the trunk and used it to fish the shard closer. Once it was within reach, he grabbed it and began cutting.

To get to the heart of the palm—the only edible part—he had to slice through the tough outer bark just below where the leaves extended. It wouldn't be easy, especially with nothing but a piece of shale, but it was his only option for food. If he managed to get to it, at least it would be high in fiber to help keep him full.

He cut away the outer layers and peeled them off. The harder part was slicing into the center, which he did one layer at a time until his muscles burned with fatigue. When he finally reached the core, he broke off a long piece and let go of the tree. Instead of springing back upright, the tree stayed down. Palm trees bend, but only so much. It seemed like a fitting metaphor for his life at the moment.

Bit by bit, he scraped away until he reached the part he could chew. Unlike the marinated hearts of palm from a can, this was solid and crunchy, like raw asparagus, with a slightly earthy taste. It wasn't filet mignon, but he devoured it as if it were his last meal. And for all he knew, it was.

He froze when he heard a voice coming from his left. Finally, another human. Even if he were taken captive, he'd at least have a chance at survival—and a chance to get to Vikki. Slowly, he rose, careful not to make any sudden noises.

"I'm turning myself in," he called out. "Don't shoot."

The voice kept talking, then he heard a burst of static. Was someone speaking into a radio? Maybe they hadn't heard him.

"I'm turning myself in," he repeated, louder. "I'm not armed."

He started moving toward the sound, pushing through the thick brush. It was still a good distance away.

"Please," he called. "Take me with you."

As he got closer, he could make out certain words. He paused to be able to hear better.

The voice, broken up with static, said, " . . . Trying to reach you . . . General . . . Pick up." The voice was coming through a radio, but who was holding the radio?

"General Krupp . . . please answer," said the voice. Odd, the voice sounded familiar. Though coming through a tinny speaker, it sounded like Jim Barnes.

" . . . Broadcasting . . . all channels," said the broken voice. " . . . need . . . update . . . daughter." It *was* Jim Barnes.

Matt's heart was racing. He rushed ahead. Tree branches scratched his arms and face, but he didn't care. He was either about to get captured, or he might finally be able to respond to Vikki's dad. Either way, it was better than getting eaten by dragons.

"I'm coming to you," he called. "Please don't shoot." He still heard nothing but the voice on the radio—no activity in the area of any kind.

" . . . This is . . . Dr. Jim Barnes," said the voice. "Come in . . . repeat . . .come in."

He was almost there. The radio was just ahead.

Matt pushed the branches aside and emerged from the trees. His mouth dropped.

A soldier lay on the ground up ahead, the radio by his side. He appeared to be dead.

Matt approached carefully, stepping quietly over twigs and debris scattered around. An empty juice box lay near the man's head, next to a smashed computer tablet. Some kind of confrontation had happened here, and it couldn't have been Toro.

As he got closer, he began to gag.

The bottom half of the man was gone—missing completely, not just separated. Blood and guts spilled onto the soil. Matt scanned the area but couldn't see any sign of the missing limbs. Dragons must've gotten to him.

He rushed to pick up the radio and pressed the talk button, scurrying away from the body.

"Dr. Barnes," he said. "This is Matt Grayson. Come in."

All he heard was static on the other line.

"Krupp has Vikki," he continued. "I'm out here in the jungle. Island called Nibo. It may be off the Dominican Republic, but I don't know for sure. I don't have coordinates. We're at Fort Majestic. I repeat. Fort Majestic. Situation dire. Send help."

"General Krupp," said Barnes. "Can you hear me?"

"Dr. Barnes," said Matt. "It's not Krupp. It's Matt Grayson. Come in."

"Please respond," said Barnes, clearly not hearing anything he was saying.

Static hissed in his ear. He slammed the radio against his palm before tossing it to the ground. No one was coming.

As he started to walk away, the radio blared again.

"Matt Grayson," said the voice. It was a man, but it wasn't Barnes.

More static. "I'm afraid Dr. Barnes can't come to the phone right now. Please leave a message at the tone."

Now he recognized the voice.

It was Krupp.

He lunged for the radio, grabbed it, and pressed the button.

"General, is Dr. Barnes safe?"

He listened to the static, waiting for a response.

"Which one?"

What a joker.

"Both of them."

"That's an affirmative," said Krupp. "Though the elder one is not in my purview at the moment, so if an anvil should happen to fall on his head, don't blame me."

Matt shook his head, his fists tightening. He wanted to reach through the radio and strangle him, but he knew he had to play it cool.

"So, Vikki is okay?" said Matt.

"It's a relative term. She'll be better if you turn yourself in."

If he harmed her or Adelina in any way… He took a breath to calm down.

"Can you guarantee my safety?"

More static.

"Unless you get eaten first."

"General, then you can come and get me," he said, though it wasn't the words he wanted to say. "I'm unarmed."

He glanced down and noticed a weapon on the ground next to the guard. He knelt and picked it up.

"Oh, don't worry," said Krupp. "We will. You just stay put. We have your location."

Were they watching him all along, or did they track him through the radio? He wanted to ask a million questions, but he thought the better of it, forcing himself to stay quiet.

"You can count on my cooperation, General."

"That's good. Oh, and you can forget about using that gun. It's out of bullets. Over and out."

Matt scanned the trees nearby looking for some kind of camera, but didn't see anything. How on Earth did Krupp know about the gun? Satellites? Clearly, these people were full of surprises—even without the dragons.

Feeling utterly defeated, he stared at the useless gun in his hand as the static faded to silence.

Chapter Twenty-Three

Interrogation

Vikki's vision was still blurry, and her mouth was dry. Barely awake, she groped for the cup of water on the table beside her bed. She vaguely remembered gobbling down some Saltine crackers as if they were a surf and turf dinner. When was that? Where was she? Why was she even here?

She glanced around, trying to make sense of where she was. It appeared to be a hospital room, though larger than any she'd seen. Her narrow bed—a twin, it seemed—ran along the wall to her left. On the other side of the room was a recliner and a long metal cabinet stamped with a serial number—though she couldn't make out the number. The faint scent of disinfectant lingered in the air, and all she could hear was a low hum coming from a mini fridge tucked in the corner. Was this a medical center, or some kind of office?

The door creaked open, and footsteps approached. A doctor in a lab coat stepped into view. This *was* a hospital of some sort.

"Dr. Barnes," he said.

She blinked, struggling to focus. Was he talking to her? Or was that his name, too?

"Dr. Barnes, do you know who I am?"

She gazed up at him, still groggy. She knew him. Where from?

"I . . . know you," she mumbled. She started to giggle, though she wasn't sure why.

"Dr. Barnes, think!" he said. "You're just coming out of the anesthesia. Do you know who I am?"

She just wanted to go back to sleep. Her legs were shaking, which annoyed her to no end. She was still fully dressed, with a light bedsheet draped over her.

"Stop shaking," she muttered to her legs.

He grabbed both her arms.

"Come, sit up," he said. "Drink this."

She sat up with his assistance and took the Styrofoam cup of water he offered her. Slowly, she sipped from the straw.

"Do you have any more crackers, Doc . . . Doctor . . ."

"That's it," he encouraged. "What's my name?"

Dr. Simmons. Yes, that's who it was. She didn't dare say it. He must've done his procedure.

Her heart fluttered as the terrifying ordeal in the operating room came flooding back to her. The helplessness as the guards had strapped her down. The metal contraption that Simmons had attached to her head. The needle. She looked at the underside of her right arm and noticed the bandage where the IV had been. She tried not to let on how shocked she was.

She began to panic. Would she always be this confused? What had he done to her?

She frantically tried to remember whatever she could, but everything was jumbled. She shook her head from side to side as if to shake the cobwebs loose from her brain. A tear rolled down her cheek and she casually wiped it away. The dragon. She remembered the dragon. What was his name? Oh yes, Gamma. Damn anesthesia.

She gasped. The girl! She had to get to the little girl, Abel . . .Abigad . . . Adelina.

She looked directly at Simmons, trying to mask the sudden terror she was feeling.

"I don't know your name," she said, lying through her teeth. "What is it?"

"Do you know why you're here?"

She shook her head and crinkled her eyebrows, trying to feign innocent confusion. "No. Why am I here?"

"Dr. Barnes, I know you're not telling the truth."

"What do you mean?" she said. *How could he tell?* "What happened to me?"

"What is the last thing you remember?"

Inside, she was frantically searching her memories. They seemed to be intact, but how would she even know if he'd erased something?

"I don't remember anything. I remember my name."

"You're lying, Dr. Barnes. And you're not even being believable."

"I'm telling the truth." Her legs trembled again, though it was just happening intermittently now. Was that giving her away—did he think it was nerves? What if he decided to redo the procedure?

He leaned in.

"The reason I know you're lying," he whispered, "is that I didn't do the procedure. I only gave you anesthesia. Same as you'd get if you had your wisdom teeth out."

She began breathing rapidly. Every emotion she'd been feeling rose into her throat. He faked it? Why? Was he trying to help her, or was this another trick? She wanted to break down in tears, but she held it in with all her strength, clutching the edge of the bedsheet. She took a few deep breaths, forcing herself to calm down—the antiseptic tinge in the air coming more into focus.

He glanced nervously back at the door and then froze. Footsteps echoed in the hall. A door slammed shut. He turned back to face her, his intense stare full of urgency.

"We have to be quick," he whispered. "You were right. That's not who I am. But I had to put on the act in front of the guards. They've gone too far. All of them."

A lump formed in her throat. An hour ago—or was it a day?—she'd hated this man as much as Krupp, if not more. Now she was grateful for his humanity. But was he telling the truth, or was this a test to trick her into confessing? She scanned her memories. Everything seemed intact, aside from the anesthesia fog. Wasn't that proof enough?

She decided to give him the benefit of the doubt. "Thank you, Dr. Simmons," she said quietly, barely able to get the words out. She was torn between laughing and crying.

He breathed a genuine sigh of relief.

She giddily reached up to hug him, but he held a hand up and put a finger over his mouth.

"Not here," he whispered. "They may be watching."

She let her arms drop and lay her head back on the pillow, scanning the corners of the room for cameras or blinking lights.

"Listen," he said, glancing at the door, "the general will be in soon to evaluate you. You'll need to be more convincing."

"How?"

"If he asks what the last thing you remember is, think of something recent—nothing about dragons or your trip here. You know who you are, you remember your life before the last couple days, but you don't know how or why you're here. That confusion should really distress you. He'll expect it."

She nodded, though her stomach twisted at the thought of facing Krupp again. Acting wasn't her strength, but she'd have to try. "If this works," she whispered, "can you help me get Adelina so we can get out of here?"

He let out a heavy sigh. "I really don't know how you would escape. Your best choice is to be sent home. After that? Well, that's up to you, but at least you'd have options."

"What if you could get me to the power grid? They seemed worried about that. I could cause a distraction and—"

"The power grid!? But that could . . ."

His voice trailed off as he stared at the floor, lost in thought.

"I suppose it could be possible, but it's a terrible idea. I—"

He turned sharply. Another noise echoed in the hall—footsteps. They were closer this time.

"We'll talk more later," he said, his voice low. "For now, rest and wait for the general to come in. Convincing him is the first hurdle. And it's a very high one."

"I will," she said, her fingers tightening around the bedsheet as she listened to the footsteps fade.

***

Vikki opened her eyes and squinted until the face glaring down at her came into focus. She must've fallen asleep. It was Krupp. Just the sight of him made her ill. She discreetly clutched the fitted sheet, forcing herself not to react.

"Do you know who I am?" he said.

"Sure." She took a steadying breath. She could do this. She wiped her eyes and said evenly, "You're General Wilson R. Krupp."

He appeared taken aback by her response. His eyes narrowed.

"It says so on your uniform," she added, unable to suppress an uncontrolled giggle—whatever drugs they'd given her were still in her system.

He smiled slightly. "Who did you come here with?"

"I don't even know where *here* is. Is this a hospital? Was I in an accident? Nobody will tell me anything." She ran her hands over her arms as she lay on the bed, feigning panic and disorientation. It was only half an act. "I don't feel any pain."

She looked around at the empty room and tried shaking the dust from her head.

"Do you have a child?" he said.

The blood rushed to her face as she thought of Adelina in peril. *Keep calm, Vikki.* She took a breath before answering him. "No."

"You don't seem so sure."

"No, I don't have any children. It's a sore spot with me."

"What's your name?"

"Vikki Barnes. Dr. Vikki Barnes." The words tumbled out before she could stop herself. Was she supposed to know her name? Was that too quick? Too confident? She'd read somewhere real amnesia patients sometimes forgot their own names. The fluorescent lights above seemed to blur as the room began spinning. She tried to remain focused.

He peered at her.

"A doctor," he said, smirking. "What kind of doctor are you? Do you make house calls?"

She wanted to reach out and punch him. She'd been dealing with arrogant, smirking men like him for years. That *little-lady* attitude. But she needed to answer him—Simmons had said she should remember her past.

"I'm a paleontologist at the Academy of Natural Sciences. Did anyone notify them where I am? What day is this?"

"What's the last thing you remember?" There it was. The question she was waiting for.

"I was speaking to a group of school kids. A class . . . at the museum. I can't seem to remember anything after that. Did I black out?"

"Do you know a Matthew Grayson?"

The question threw her off. Did he notice the surprise on her face? She crinkled her nose in disgust, masking her nerves.

"Matt Grayson? I wish I didn't. He was an old boyfriend. What's he have to do with any of this?"

"An old boyfriend," he repeated, eyes narrowing. He seemed caught off guard by her answer.

"Why would you ask me about him? Is he why I'm here?"

"When did you last see Adelina?" he said, ignoring her question.

She blinked, feigning confusion. "I've never been to Adelina. I don't even know where it is." It did sound like a town in Italy or Spain.

"Adelina's a person. Think." His face flushed with impatience.

She shook her head. "I've never known anyone by that name. What's with all these questions? How did I get here?"

"Don't worry about—"

"What would an Army general want with me? Either someone explain or I'm just gonna get up and leave. Now, where am I!?" She pounded her fists on the bed. She hoped she wasn't overdoing it. "You can't hold me here . . . wherever *here* is."

He gazed at her, as if he was studying her every move . . . her every emotion. Her head was still spinning. She pressed her palms to her temples, wishing all this would just end.

"I have one last question," he said. "And then you'll get all the answers you want. Later. What do you know about dragons?"

"Dragons?" she said, crinkling her face. "Is this a joke? Is someone playing a joke on me? I mean, you're kidding, right?"

"It just so happens I'm not," he replied, wearing that stupid grin.

She pretended she was searching her memory. "There was that video on the news, but that wasn't a real dragon. Jesus." She laughed—much too loudly and too long, the sound echoing strangely in the sterile room. She subdued herself, suddenly aware of how forced it sounded.

He grinned. "I'm glad you find it funny."

"You sound like my middle school students, asking me about dragons. Is this a test? Did my dad put you up to this?"

He shook his head slowly, just staring at her, as if waiting for her to crack.

"Wait, did someone put a roofie in my drink?"

The door opened.

"Ah, Dr. Simmons," said Krupp, turning around. He glanced back at Vikki. "You're going to have to thank this guy. The ole doctor worked some voodoo magic. He'll have you ready to go in no time."

He looked over at Simmons. "I have to say you outdid yourself. Even you said it was a longshot, but wow. I'm impressed. Have her ready for transport in an hour. She'll have some questions for you."

"Will do, General," said Simmons.

"I have some questions for you, too, so see me before you release her."

Simmons nodded. "Of course." That didn't sound good.

The general left the room and closed the door behind him. The silence that followed felt heavier than before—for multiple reasons.

***

As soon as the general left, Simmons approached her.

"Excellent work," he said. "Whatever you told him, I think he believed it."

"A longshot!?" she said, sitting up and spreading the bedsheet over her lap. "You mean you could've fried my brain if you did the procedure?"

"What does it matter? I didn't do it. Now let's focus."

Her head throbbed from trying to invent answers while still under the drug's haze. Did Krupp really believe her? He'd looked suspicious more than once. She rubbed her eyes, fighting to stay alert. "I'm still in la la land from whatever you gave me."

"I told you, it was just a twilight drug, like for wisdom teeth. It'll wear off soon."

"I've never had my wisdom teeth out."

"You're lucky. My strong suggestion? Keep up the act and get transported home. Then you can do whatever you want to try to get Adelina back."

"I'm not leaving here without her." She yanked the sheet off her lap and tossed it aside.

He shook his head. "If this goes wrong, you may both be stuck here, or worse."

"What does he want to talk to you about?"

"I don't know."

"Do you think he's on to us?"

"I hope not." He didn't sound too confident.

"Tell me the plan."

He turned to make sure the door was closed.

She scanned the walls and ceiling again for any sign of a hidden bug, but saw nothing.

He leaned in. "I have no plan."

No plan? Was he serious?

"You said you could help me. That we'd talk later. This is later."

"You said you wanted to shut down the power, right?"

She nodded. "Unless you—"

"To do that, you need to get to level one. The elevator's just opposite the transport room I'll be taking you to. You want to find room A."

"Room A," she repeated. "Easy enough. That's where the power grid is?"

"Yes, it's the unit to the far right. But I wouldn't say it's easy. Also, it's not an actual power grid—just a microgrid patched together from diesel generators, solar arrays, and a transformer that brings in backup power for the base."

"That means nothing to me," she said.

He gave her a series of instructions—pulling levers, flipping transfer switches, shutting circuit breakers. And all that time, the alarm would be blaring. Her head spun, especially with the lingering drug haze. She tried to memorize each step.

"Now, here's the important part," he said, "and it's what makes this tricky."

"I'm listening." This was already getting confusing.

"You have to wait at least two minutes before turning off the main power switch on the generator. You'll just about have time before you have company down there."

"Why two minutes?" Two minutes would be like a lifetime with the alarm blaring.

"Because then it could fry the generator and there's no bringing it back up. We only want it down temporarily. You don't want dragons getting loose or we'll have bigger problems to worry about."

"So how do I bring it back up?"

"You don't need to. There's a backup generator—the black start generator. It kicks in automatically. But all the lights and power will still go off for about thirty seconds. Just enough to scatter everyone."

She reviewed the plan in her head, digging her nails into her palms. Her pulse quickened as she pictured all the things that could go wrong. "This sounds really risky."

He grabbed her arm. "Of course it's risky. Worse than risky. It's foolish. But if you insist on leaving here with Adelina, it's the only way I know."

"Then I guess it's the only way." She wasn't about to leave Adelina to be experimented on. Who knew what could happen to her in the time it took to return and hopefully get help. No, she wasn't leaving her here.

"Just make sure you get out of there, fast. Get up to Adelina. Everyone will be distracted. Get her and then get to your friends. The exit is back where you came in." He paused, glancing at the door. "One other thing."

"There's another thing?" As if she needed more.

He reached into the pocket of his lab coat and pulled out a small flashlight. "You'll need this."

She took it, feeling the cold metal in her palm, and hid it under the sheet next to her with a sigh. "I guess I'm ready, then."

"I hope you're ready because I have to wheel you to transport. I'm afraid you'll be on your own. I can't communicate with you, so I hope you got everything."

"I got it." She tried to remember all the steps. "Level one. Room A. Red Lever. Set the switch to Utility. Turn off the circuit breaker. Then shut down the generator."

"You left out the most important part."

She rolled her eyes. "Wait two minutes before turning off the generator."

"Yes, good. I'll wait a few minutes to notify the general. That should at least give you a head start."

She lay back on the bed and looked up at him, grateful to have him as an ally.

"Whatever happens," she said, "you made the right choice."

He nodded and smiled, though it was a sad smile. He looked as nervous as she felt. She doubted the plan would work—he did too. But she had to try.

Gripping the flashlight under the sheet, her hands trembling, she braced herself for what came next—knowing the consequences could be dire.

Chapter Twenty-Four

Remember Your Why

Krupp stared out the open window of his office at the picture-perfect canopy of rainforest treetops and the turquoise sea beyond. He could feel the warm breeze against his face, carrying a faint smell of cedar and gardenias, even at this height. For most, it would be a paradise. But for him, the real paradise was what this site represented—the future. A future without American soldiers having to die in battle to suit the whims of grandiose men with grandiose schemes. Of course, those same men would one day want to control this program, too. But that was a battle for another day.

He gazed out at the dense jungle. The dragons were out there somewhere. Ordinarily, nothing would keep them from flying into the great beyond, except for the controlled response—once they reached a certain altitude or distance, they expected the sonic pain stimulus. Whether the stimulus was active or not, the dragons believed it was—none of them dared test it. At least, not until Gamma—which was why he could never again be with the others. Dr. Simmons had done quite a job up to this point, even if reluctantly.

The staff sergeant tapped on the open door, interrupting his thoughts. Krupp closed the window and turned around. Back to reality.

"Colonel Adler is here as requested, sir."

"Thanks, Sergeant."

Adler entered, stone-faced as always.

"Curtis," said Krupp. "Have a seat."

Krupp sat behind his desk while Adler settled into the chair across from him. Adler squinted—about as much emotion as he ever showed. He usually did that when he suspected something was up, and this time, he was right.

"Something bothering you?" Adler asked. Adler knew him better than anyone.

Krupp sighed, glancing at the file on his desk. "What's our transmission level of the institutional knowledge we have on these dragons?"

Adler folded his arms. "I don't follow."

"If something were to happen to Simmons—just as a hypothetical example—are we covered?"

Adler's eyes narrowed further. "What tells me this isn't just hypothetical? Something going on with Simmons I should know about?"

Krupp shook his head. "Not yet."

"Is this about the procedure he did on the Barnes patient?"

"Maybe."

"How'd she do on the post-op?"

He thought back to his interview with her. All the I's were dotted and the T's crossed. All her actions seemed in line with expected protocol. All but one.

"Hard to say," he said. "It's easy to fake. But one thing jumped out at me."

Adler leaned forward. "What?"

"When Simmons came in the room after, she seemed a bit too happy to see him, like she knew him."

"Did he see her before you? I mean after she was awake."

Krupp nodded, frowning. "Maybe I'm being paranoid, but I can usually read the room, and those two had, let's say, a camaraderie. Hard to establish that in a two-minute briefing, which is all they would've had. Plus, I've been sensing some things about him anyway."

"What things?"

"Little things. Microexpressions."

"You're really putting that Ekman training to use," said Adler. The two of them had taken Paul Ekman's workshop on reading facial expressions as part of a Defense Intelligence program way back.

"The bigger question now is what our options are, hence my question."

Adler leaned back and sighed. "Well, the lab techs pretty much have the drill down by now, and Dr. Collins is coming up to speed. But what are you thinking?"

"I'm not thinking anything yet. Just want to know my options. Remember what I told you back at INSCOM? The Napoleon quote? Never interrupt—"

"Never interrupt your enemy when he's making a mistake. Is Simmons your enemy?"

He tried to recall his observations of Vikki's reaction to Simmons. They were both scientists. It wouldn't have been a stretch for him to feel a kinship with her. But to what extent?

"Maybe," he replied. Maybe not. But I'm gonna find out."

"Hell, either way it sounds like good advice. So, you're saying sit back and watch the show for now."

Krupp nodded. "For now."

Adler rubbed his chin. "You know, I remember something else you told me though. When you pulled me into this program."

"What's that?"

"In Nam, none of us poor bastards knew why we were there, other than some BS about stopping a domino effect. After that, you said you'd never back any mission that didn't have a good *why*. Now, I know your *why* on this program, and you know mine. If it turns out you do have to make a tough choice, my only advice is what you told me: Remember your why. Nothing can stop this mission—if you're getting what I'm saying. Nothing."

He knew exactly what Adler was saying, and he agreed wholeheartedly. "Can Barnes give us any trouble? The dad, not Vikki. I mean in case we have to contain her. You know, mitigate the threat."

Adler threw up his hands. "Accidents happen."

Krupp nodded, already weighing the cost.

Chapter Twenty-Five

Into the Darkness

The guard's grip on Vikki's bedrail was firm as he and Simmons wheeled her toward the transport room. When they stopped outside a set of double doors marked *Transport*, he brushed his hand on her cheek, and she suspected it wasn't for good luck. She forced herself not to flinch. One wrong move, and she'd never see Adelina again.

All she had to do was keep up the act—until she could make her move. Freedom was just a jeep ride and a helicopter flight away. That's if they didn't shoot her and toss her in the ocean en route. But freedom would mean leaving a twelve-year-old girl who'd lost everyone she'd ever known, to be poked and prodded and who knows what.

No, she reminded herself, she wasn't leaving Adelina behind. Not to these people. Not ever.

Simmons opened the double doors and they wheeled her in. The room—if she could even call it that—was not at all what she was expecting. She'd assumed it would be for medical transport, with a few beds on wheels, similar to hers. But this wasn't a hospital; it was a military compound. Instead, the room was a transportation hub and resembled a giant warehouse, with parked vehicles, docks for loading and unloading supplies, and conveyor belts.

They wheeled her off to the side and left her next to a muddy jeep that looked like it had been through hell and back. Two soldiers were outside near the dock, but they were too busy carrying equipment to worry about her—or so she hoped.

Simmons and the guard left and swung the door closed. She waited until she heard the doors click shut and their footsteps fade away.

It was now or never.

Hopefully, the others were still out in the field alive. If they weren't, all bets were off. She didn't even want to think about that possibility, not only for her and Adelina's sake, but for the others as well, especially Matt. Not when it seemed for the first time in a while like there was a caring human being inside his impenetrable shell of laissez-faire smugness. Still, none of it would matter if she couldn't get out of here with Adelina.

She took a deep breath, quietly climbed off the medical bed, and threw off the sheet, glancing back to make sure the soldiers outside weren't looking. She heard them talking but couldn't see them. Good. That meant they couldn't see her either. She'd have to act fast.

Grabbing her flashlight, she crept to the door and pressed her ear against it. Nothing—just the faint hum of fluorescent lights.

She eased the door open and peered up and down the hall. A soldier was down the hall to the right, his back turned, walking away. As he disappeared into a room, she took one last glance back, then darted across the hallway to the elevator and pressed the down button.

A door opened down the hall to her left. Before she could see who it was, she ducked back into the transport room and closed the door. Footsteps grew closer, stopping just outside the room. She held her hand over her mouth, barely breathing.

The person continued walking.

She jumped when one of the soldiers outside came in from behind her. She froze, hoping he wouldn't notice her. He turned, picked up a heavy crate, and cursed under his breath as he hauled it outside.

The elevator beeped outside her room. She listened. Nothing. She'd have to take a chance. Slowly, she opened the door. Her adrenaline surging, she bolted across the hall into the open elevator, not daring to look back.

She was breathing so heavily she thought she'd hyperventilate. If nobody saw her, they'd surely hear her panting. Frantically, she pressed the Level 1 button.

The clack-clack of footsteps startled her. Whoever had passed her room was coming back. The elevator doors were still open.

Come on, close, dammit. She jabbed the Level 1 button again, then spotted the Door Close button and slammed it. This had to be the slowest elevator in the world.

The footsteps approached as the elevator doors finally began to slide shut.

Just as they were nearly closed, a hand darted inside, stopping them. Slowly, the doors began to open again. Her mind raced for something to say. *Think, Vikki.* But panic left her blank. She could think of nothing.

The intruder peeked in. It was Simmons.

She let out a shaky breath. "You scared the hell out of me."

"I wanted to make sure you got out okay. Now hurry."

She rolled her eyes. "I'm trying."

As he left, the doors finally closed and the elevator began its slow descent. Though only one floor down, the creaky elevator's ride felt endless.

When the doors slid open, she peeked out cautiously. The hallway was empty. So far, so good.

To the left, a sign pointed to the stairwell, but she headed right. Her footsteps echoed off the cold concrete walls. This level, apparently for utilities, was a far cry from the sterile environment upstairs—dank, poorly lit, and heavy with the scent of damp metal.

She stopped before a set of double doors marked with a large "A," each with a small window. This was it.

She peeked in the window on the left door and immediately spotted two maintenance men in orange vests—a portly bald guy and a lanky, blond man who looked to be around sixty. She gasped. Simmons didn't mention there'd be people down here. Now what?

Before she could think, the two men turned and started toward her. One lifted his hand, maybe to wave. A jolt of panic shot through her. She could run, but they'd reach the elevator first. The stairwell was too far. She continued past the room and quickened her pace, scanning for a closet to duck into.

The doors behind her creaked open.

"Hey," called one of the men.

She kept walking, pretending not to hear. Thank God, she was fully dressed and not in one of those flimsy hospital gowns with the open backs.

"Are you gonna stop?" said the other.

She had no choice. Her legs shook as she turned. "Me?"

"Yeah," said the blond guy. "We're all done in there. Power should stay up now."

"Oh," she said, trying to hide her nerves. "Thanks. I came to check on that."

"It's all yours," he said. The two men turned and headed toward the elevator, one mumbling something she couldn't catch.

She exhaled, heart pounding, and slipped through the doors. Inside, she paused to catch her breath, then moved forward. On the left stood a row of what looked like heating and air conditioning units.

Black pipes crisscrossed above. Another set of white pipes ran parallel with yellow levers marked Water. Simmons said the power grid was on the far right.

She spotted a tall set of gray metal units ahead. That had to be it.

She studied the panels, searching for the right controls. She spotted a red lever on the end unit. That had to be the power grid. Flipping it would set off the alarm. She hesitated, reviewing Simmons's instructions: shut down the power grid, switch the generator to Utility, turn off the circuit breakers, then the main switch on the generator.

Her hand shook as she gripped the red lever. The maintenance men were probably gone by now. She hoped.

She pulled the lever down.

Instantly, a deafening alarm blared, echoing off the concrete. It was ten times louder down here.

A whir came from the unit on the right—almost lost in the noise. The generator. She flipped the transfer switch to Utility, then shut off all the circuit breakers.

The lights snapped off, plunging her into darkness. Only a small red light glowed on the generator. Between the blackness and the noise, she could barely think.

She fumbled for her flashlight and turned it on. She wanted to run, but something nagged at her.

The main power switch. Damn it. She'd forgotten to find it while the lights were on. The generator was probably still running upstairs. She had to act fast. Krupp—or someone—would be here any second.

She aimed the flashlight at the generator's control panel, looking for a power switch. She swept the light over the generator, searching.

There—a small red switch on the upper right, just above the control panel, with a sticker that read: *Caution*. That had to be it.

She reached for the switch, then stopped. Simmons said to wait two minutes before shutting down the generator.

The alarm's shriek made it almost impossible to think. She shone the flashlight on her watch, breath quickening as she watched the second hand crawl.

Ten seconds . . . twenty . . .

She aimed her light at the door, looking for any sign of Krupp or someone else—not that she could see much in the dark.

Thirty . . . forty . . .

This was taking forever. She swept the light around the room, searching for a place to hide if she had to.

Fifty seconds . . . a minute . . .

The elevators were probably dead. Anyone coming would have to take the stairs. She strained to hear footsteps between the alarm blasts.

A minute ten . . . A minute twenty . . .

Was that footsteps in the hall?

She couldn't wait any longer. All the fumbling must've taken at least twenty seconds. She hoped Simmons's "two minutes" was more a guideline than a rule. Holding her breath, she flipped the power switch.

The little red light went out. The alarm kept blaring.

A tiny blue indicator light glowed on the unit beside the generator. The black start generator. A chill ran down her spine. In thirty seconds, it would kick in—and with the power back on, she'd lose any advantage upstairs. This plan sounded better in theory.

She aimed her flashlight at the black start generator. If this was going to work, she needed darkness and chaos on her side. She made a snap decision: she had to shut it down.

Frantically, she flipped every switch she could find, yanking out wires until the blue indicator turned off.

A noise nearly shook her out of her shoes. She spun, flashlight trembling in her hand, just as the double doors burst open.

Two soldiers came running in.

Chapter Twenty-Six

Fire and Death

Vikki froze as the two soldiers rushed toward her, their lights blaring in her eyes. She could barely see, but neither could they, with her flashlight aimed right at their faces.

She did the only thing she could think of.

"Fire!" she yelled, keeping her light steady. "There's a fire in here!"

The men were at her feet in seconds. One shouted, "Where?"

She pointed to the far end of the room. "Back there. I think it's almost out."

As they rushed past, she called, "I'll go tell the others!" and bolted for the doors.

"Wait!" one of the soldiers called.

She paused, her heart racing.

"Tell those maintenance guys to come back."

"I will," she said.

As she slipped into the hall, she heard, "What the hell is this?" behind her—they must've discovered all the pulled wires. She darted down the dark corridor toward the stairwell, her flashlight flickering in her hand. The batteries were nearly dead.

She heard the doors swing open behind her and ducked into the stairwell, sprinting upward. Her flashlight, dim and weakening, barely illuminated the steps as she scrambled in near darkness.

A deafening rumble from above shook the stairwell, sending chills down her spine. It sounded like a freight train or a bomb, but she knew exactly what it was—her worst nightmare. The roar that followed vibrated the walls.

Gamma was loose. Adelina!

The doors above burst open. Soldiers barreled down the steps, yelling. She switched off her flashlight and pressed herself against the rail, hoping they'd rush past in the chaos. Flashlights bobbed above, casting haphazard beams down the stairs.

A loud click startled her—then the stairwell lights snapped on.

She gasped. Blood was everywhere. One soldier, missing an arm, screamed as he stumbled past. Others, their faces pale and terrified, nearly trampled her in their haste.

Another roar rattled the walls.

She swallowed hard, fighting the urge to vomit. Her whole body trembled, but she forced herself to keep moving. Whatever terror waited above, she couldn't leave Adelina in this chaos for another minute.

Just as she approached the exit door to Level 1, it swung open and then slammed shut. A bloodcurdling scream from the other side sent shivers down her spine. She clamped her hands over her ears and pressed back against the wall. This was a suicide mission. And it was her fault. She'd dug herself a hole, and now Adelina was at risk, too.

The screaming stopped. Another life snuffed out. A living, breathing human—gone. What had she done?

She listened, trying to catch her breath, as the booming footsteps faded away.

Her hands trembling, she eased the door open. The door creaked, and she froze, listening. What if she brought the dragon back and cost even more lives? What if she made things worse for Adelina?

When all she heard was the distant thunder of dragon footsteps, she took a shaky breath and slipped through the doorway.

Oh my God.

Blood and body parts littered the floor—shreds of Army-green fabric, bits of charred skin—it was a massacre. She spotted a doctor in a white lab coat, lying facedown in a grotesque pose. The stench of death made her gag; she pressed her palm to her face, breathing through her mouth, bile rising in her throat. Overhead lights glistened in the blood-soaked floor as she stepped around the bodies.

She had to get to Adelina. Now. If anything happened to that little girl, she'd never forgive herself.

Once she found a clear space, she ran to the left toward the operating room. That was the last place she'd seen Adelina. The hallway looked like a war zone. Giant holes in the walls on both sides made it look like a bomb had hit. Smatterings of blood dotted the floors and walls along the corridor. There were no bodies around, so either the people in this area had evacuated or they were eaten. She hoped with all her heart that Adelina had been moved to safety or was hiding.

She approached a T-section at the end of the hall. From what she recalled, she had to go right to get to Adelina. She didn't have a moment to waste, so she zipped around the corner to her right, skidding on the slick floor.

A soft object about the size of a large fish flew right in front of her face, nearly knocking her over. She caught her balance and turned to see what it was—and almost threw up. *It was a severed arm.* But what threw it?

She looked to her right and froze in her tracks.

Gamma stood silently about twenty feet away, staring directly at her.

She wanted to run but couldn't. It would be no use anyway. Gamma was too close. She gazed up, horrified, at the humongous teeth—strings of flesh and blood dangling from its jaws. And this time there was no glass between them.

Please don't see me. Please don't see me.

The creature glared at her and let out a low growl. It saw her, all right. Instantly, it lunged like an enormous lion. She shrieked and scrambled back, falling to the ground, curling into a ball. She was about to be ripped apart, and there was nothing she could do.

She closed her eyes and screamed until her voice gave out. Its hot breath blasted her hair and face, reeking of sulfur. Warm droplets of blood spattered her forehead—was it hers? She braced for the bite, for the agony.

But nothing happened. Only a strange, paralyzing numbness—she couldn't tell if it was physical or mental.

The heat faded. She was still alive. Or was she? Was this shock, or had she somehow survived? She opened her eyes, afraid to look.

All her limbs seemed intact. Gamma was backing away, each step shaking the floor—and her heart. *Why did he stop?*

A shadow moved behind her. She heard soft footsteps.

She turned and nearly collapsed.

"Oh my God, Adelina! You're safe!"

Adelina didn't answer. She walked slowly toward Gamma, her eyes focused, her voice gentle.

"It's okay," said Adelina to the giant beast. "You know me. I'm your friend."

Gamma stared at her, as if weighing her words.

"You can calm down now." Adelina moved closer. "We're not going to hurt you."

"Adelina, careful," Vikki whispered, not wanting to disrupt the fragile connection. She stood up slowly, watching Gamma's face.

The dragon seemed to be listening, recognizing the girl and sensing her intent. For the first time, Vikki saw him not as a monster, but as a broken, tragic soul—a misunderstood, fearful being, comforted by Adelina's presence.

She recalled studies showing reptiles can feel fear, trust, even pleasure, and sometimes form bonds with familiar humans or other reptiles. Gamma's emotions might be basic, but they were real—and far more complex than Krupp and his team ever understood.

Gamma's breathing slowed. Adelina had calmed the beast.

But not for long.

Gamma's face twisted in anger. His eyes grew fierce. He let out a growl that rattled Vikki's bones. Even Adelina stepped back, alarmed.

"Adelina, back up," Vikki said.

"Gamma, what's wrong?" said Adelina.

"Adelina, back up!"

Gamma rose tall, chest puffed, ready to attack. Vikki recognized the look.

"Adelina, get back! Now."

"She's right," came a voice from behind. It was Krupp. "Both of you, get out of the way."

He was holding some kind of giant sonic weapon—much larger than an assault rifle—with large spirals extending toward the tip.

"Get back!" he yelled.

"*No!*" shouted Adelina, rushing toward Krupp. Vikki grabbed her, pulling her aside as they both crashed against the wall. Adelina screamed as Krupp fired the weapon at Gamma.

A shrill screech pierced Vikki's ears, stabbing into her brain. She pressed her hands over her ears; Adelina did the same.

Gamma roared and unleashed a massive blast of fire at the arched ceiling. The corridor became a blazing sauna; Vikki could barely breathe as sulfur scorched her nostrils.

Krupp fired again and again. It took all Vikki's strength to keep Adelina from running to Gamma, but there was nothing they could do.

Gamma howled, vomiting flames at the ceiling. Chunks of burning plaster crashed at Vikki's feet, the dark smoke billowing around her. She looked up—sections of the roof were gone. She shielded Adelina, bracing for it to collapse.

Gamma staggered, delirious, his yellow eyes dull. Krupp kept firing relentlessly.

"Stop!" yelled Adelina. "You're killing him." She grabbed a broken piece of wood and jumped up, but Vikki grabbed her.

"We can't. There's nothing we can do." She couldn't risk any more danger to Adelina.

Krupp's weapon seemed to be running out of power as the blasts grew weaker and weaker. But the damage was clearly done, as the enormous, majestic dragon staggered and fell forward in slow motion. Vikki pulled Adelina close as Gamma's huge body hit the ground, shaking the whole corridor. More charred segments fell from the ceiling, adding to the piles of ash and debris smoldering on the floor.

The dragon lay motionless, its massive form stretched along the broad corridor. His tail twitched one last time—and then, nothing. The sudden quiet was both eerie and somber. She stared into Gamma's lifeless eyes and knew he was gone.

Adelina sobbed as Vikki held her tight. How much more could this poor girl lose? Gamma wasn't the monster. Krupp was the monster.

Krupp threw down the expired weapon. He picked up a radio and spoke into it. "This is General Krupp." His voice echoed throughout the halls. "Project Gamma terminated. Tango one and tango two in the bag."

He looked down at her and Adelina, his face an angry grimace. "You two," he shouted. "You did this. Not me. Now get up!"

Footsteps came from behind Krupp. It was Dr. Simmons.

"General," said Simmons. Krupp turned around. "Please don't blame Dr. Barnes. I gave her a strong sedative. She may have had an adverse reaction to the treatment. I'm sure she was delirious. Give me a chance to work with her."

"Time's up, Doc," said Krupp. In an instant, he pulled a pistol out of a holster on his uniform and shot Simmons in the chest, the noise echoing through the halls. Blood filled the front of the doctor's lab coat as he stumbled back and fell to the floor, dead. Vikki was horrified as she scuttled back against the wall with Adelina, who appeared to be in shock.

Krupp turned sharply toward them.

"Our men went to collect your partner in crime, Matt Grayson. He turned himself in. The other two traitors are dead." Adelina let out a shriek, which Krupp ignored. Vikki held her close.

She couldn't believe the two men she'd just faced so many dangers with—wild helicopter rides, harrowing jungle escapes, and terrifying dragon confrontations—were now gone. And now Krupp was after Matt. She still had her reservations about Matt, but she didn't want to see him in danger—not when he was finally starting to show signs of being the genuine person she'd originally met. She had to somehow put all that old baggage behind her. She tightened her fists, blood surging through her veins. She had to be strong for Matt and Adelina. As long as they were still alive, there was hope.

"It's over," said Krupp. "You can cooperate and come with me, and we can do this the official way. Or you can die right here like you deserve."

Vikki was trembling, but she nodded. This was the end of the line. She patted Adelina on the back. "Let's get up," she said. "We have to cooperate so they won't hurt us anymore."

She wished she believed it. She wondered: Was this really the end of this long ordeal, or just the beginning of something worse?

Chapter Twenty-Seven

Dragons and Copters

Smoke. Matt could smell it in the breeze as he stood there gazing at what was left of the soldier's body. He tossed the useless weapon on the ground. The wind was blowing in from the east, where no doubt Vikki and Adelina were being kept at Fort Majestic. He turned in that direction and immediately spotted the flames jutting up into the sky in the distance. Was it coming from a dragon? Was that really where Fort Majestic was situated? It had to be. It was also the direction the tire tracks he'd seen were headed.

Despite what he'd told Krupp about waiting, he needed to go toward the fires. What if Vikki was in trouble? What if he was already too late? He had to get there fast. Besides, if the guards were going to come and get him, they'd probably find him en route anyway—if the dragons didn't get to him first.

He took one last look at the dead guard. He grabbed the guard's tattered rucksack and opened it. Inside were some used snack wrappers, a first aid kit, a crushed compass, and an empty water canister. No other weapons or ammo. He took the bag with him, then headed toward the path he'd entered from. At least he wouldn't need his calabash bowl, which he'd left by the palm tree anyway.

He scanned the skies looking for any sign of the deadly dragons and didn't see any. At first, he was relieved, but then it dawned on him.

If they weren't in the skies, they were on the ground somewhere.

This felt like a suicide mission. Just the thought of those razor-toothed, fire-breathing predators lurking in the dark jungle sent chills down his spine. These things were literally death machines—military-trained experts at killing. He shook his head. No, he couldn't give up now. He had to do this.

He took a deep breath and then reentered the thick brush, wishing he still had his machete. The air was warm and muggy, and he was feeling dehydrated again. He wiped the sweat from his brow and pushed through, parting the branches and oversized leaves with his hands. An insect buzzed in his ear, and he swatted it with enough fury that he couldn't hear for a few seconds. He picked up his pace into a jog. He couldn't wait to get out of this God-forsaken jungle.

While he didn't consider himself out of shape, there was a difference between using a treadmill in the gym and trying to jog in a scorching hot jungle with bugs and branches hitting his face nonstop. Especially considering how hungry and thirsty he was. He pushed on with the determination of Hercules, but he wasn't sure how long he could last. His feet were already blistering, and his knees ached with each step.

Exhausted, he made his way up the familiar path as the acrid scent of smoke grew stronger. He slowed his pace to save his energy. He used the flames—still burning—as a visual marker, so at least he knew he was headed in the right direction.

As tough as it was, the journey back seemed shorter, possibly because he now had a clear destination. Still, he needed to tread quietly. Every step he took through the brush, twigs, and foliage echoed throughout the jungle. At least it felt that way. Around here it was like ringing the dinner bell.

A noise came from the left. A broken branch. He stopped in his tracks. The sound of crackling twigs grew louder, and so did his heartbeat. The rustling was getting closer. He gazed up into the trees, half expecting to see the familiar yellow eyes staring at him. But he saw nothing.

He remained as still as possible, barely daring to breathe as he strained to listen.

Another snap. It was close.

Just then, a small animal came running out of the trees, startling him. A brown mongoose with a white tail. It stopped, stared up at him and screeched, and then ran off.

"Yeah, screw you, too," he said to the little creature. "Almost gave me a damn heart attack."

He exhaled and started jogging again with a burst of adrenaline. But it didn't last. After about ten yards, he had to slow down.

He stumbled through the trail, delirious—pushing leaves aside and stepping on the occasional rock. Eventually, he reached the clearing where he'd seen Vikki's footprints and the tire tracks. If he could follow them, they'd lead him to Fort Majestic. That had been his plan last time, before the dragons scared him half to death. Now, he was back to square one.

He left the safety of the trees and stepped into the open, his eyes fixed on the distant smoke as he approached the tracks. The dirt road headed eastward. He glanced up at the sky, half hoping for rain—like the last time he was dying of thirst. Every fiber of his being screamed at him to stop, to rest, to give up. His vision blurred. How could he possibly make it to the fort?

A deep, resonant chittering echoed from behind him. He knew that sound. This time, it wasn't a mongoose.

The hair on his arms stood up. He turned slowly—and gasped.

Four enormous dragons stood side by side, silently watching him like wolves circling a helpless deer. They must have been there a while, or he would've heard them. Lucky for them—not so much for him—he'd wandered right into their path. Or maybe they knew he was coming. Maybe they were that smart. He thought to run, but the ground began to shake. Two more dragons emerged from the trees behind him, blocking the road to Fort Majestic.

He was in the same position Toro had been—right before he was torn apart. The grisly memory flooded his mind: the veteran's body ripped in half, the blood, the screams. Matt's heart raced, and he felt faint. If he passed out, he'd be an even easier target.

But maybe that was his only hope.

If he played dead, maybe the dragons would lose interest. It was a long shot, but he'd seen what happened to Toro and Reggie when they tried to run.

Slowly, he lowered himself into the mud, watching the dragons to his right and left. He reclined until he was flat on his back, eyes slitted just enough to see.

One dragon on the right lowered its massive head, glowing eyes fixed on him. Its sulfurous breath washed over him. The creature opened its jaws and screeched, alerting the others. Matt flinched, shivers racing down his spine. The dragon nudged closer. His legs shook uncontrollably. Sweat stung his eyes, but he didn't dare move.

He squeezed his eyes shut and tried to breathe slowly, praying the beasts would lose interest. Each breath might be his last.

A deep growl from the left rattled his bones. Then the ground rumbled with their movement. Forcing his eyes open, he saw the dragons closing in, their thunderous steps growing nearer as they blotted out the sun.

He trembled in shock as one beast dropped its enormous head and roared. Its breath blasted his face like a furnace, the sound rattling his skull. Drops of burning dragon saliva splattered his chest.

The others pressed closer, forming a canopy of death. The behemoths hovered just ten feet above. They could snatch him in an instant. All he could do was wait—and hope.

The terrifying growls came without warning. Their mouths opened as they roared, yellow flames forming in their throats.

He curled into a ball and braced himself. This was the end.

He waited for the blazing fire, the searing pain, the razor-sharp teeth tearing into his burning flesh.

But the growling stopped. He felt nothing.

Almost afraid to look, he glanced up.

The dragons were gazing skyward, mouths closed, as if listening to a silent call.

They all took off at once. The wind from their wings pressed him into the ground, stealing his breath. Their screeches echoed as they soared away, gusts swirling as they vanished in different directions.

Still in shock, he let his head fall back, completely drained. He'd survived, but it didn't feel like victory. He tried to will his body to move, but nothing happened. He needed a moment—just a moment—to gather his strength. Every second he lay there was a second lost, a second he could've spent getting to Vikki.

His respite didn't last. An Army copter was approaching—he could hear it in the distance. Krupp could just as easily kill him as help him. He wasn't about to find out. He hadn't survived the dragons just to be gunned down by his own side.

No matter what it took, he had to run for cover if he wanted any chance of helping Vikki. He couldn't gamble on Krupp's goodwill—not with both their lives at stake—and Adelina's. As the copter swept into view, he forced himself up and sprinted for the trees. The noisy chopper tracked him relentlessly.

He crashed through the undergrowth, branches slashing his face, oversized leaves blinding him. Soon he lost all sense of direction. The copter circled overhead, never letting him out of its sight.

He ran until his legs buckled. He staggered into a clearing, desperate for a glimpse of smoke—his only guide. As he paused to catch his breath, the copter swooped back. He tried to run but fell, his body too weak to obey. Hunger cramped his stomach. His mouth was parched. Even if he reached Vikki, he'd be useless like this.

He realized his only hope was to stop running. Maybe surrender would give him another chance. At this point, it felt like his only choice.

He dropped to his knees and waited.

The copter landed in a storm of noise and wind. Matt raised his hands in surrender as the pilot swung open the door. He wore a black helmet and black goggles, like an assassin. The pilot reached into the cabin—Matt braced for a gun.

But it was only gloves. Then the helmet came off. The goggles.

Matt's heart leapt. It was Reggie.

He let out a deep, hearty laugh as Reggie grinned and shouted over the roar, "Do you want to get out of here or not?"

***

"I thought you were dead," said Matt as he climbed into the Army copter's passenger seat. He strapped himself in and donned a headset. "I heard you screaming."

"Yeah, well you'd scream too if your ass was about to be lit on fire."

"I know the feeling. I nearly got eaten by six dragons just now. They all took off somewhere."

"Six? There were at least seven that we know of," said Reggie, lifting the copter off the ground. "Where's the other one?"

"I don't know and I don't care. I just know we have to get to Vikki."

"She's alive?"

"Krupp has her," said Matt, holding on as they rose. "That's all I know. Hey, what's that smell? It's like rotten feet in here."

"It's Stinking Toe Fruit."

"Seriously?" The stench was overwhelming.

"Dead serious. It's how I survived those dragons. Covered myself in it. Turns out their sense of smell and hearing is off the charts. Yessiree, Stinking Toe Fruit to the rescue."

The copter banked hard above the trees. Matt gripped his seat. "I don't even want to know what that is."

"It's everywhere around here. Smells like toes, looks like toes, and you can eat it. Want some?"

"That's a hard no," said Matt as the copter leveled out.

Reggie reached under his seat and produced a brown, toe-shaped fruit. "Here, try it. You gotta be hungry."

Matt hesitated, but his stomach growled. He'd eat anything at this point. He took it, bit into it, and instantly gagged. The putrid scent filled his nose, and he nearly vomited.

"Okay," said Reggie. "Want a Snickers instead?"

Matt shot him a look. "Very funny."

"No, really. Open that cooler." He pointed to a metal bin at Matt's feet. "We got water, too."

Matt opened it and stared in disbelief at the stash of snacks and drinks. He grabbed a water bottle and chugged it, nearly choking.

"Easy there, Speed Racer," said Reggie, laughing. "We got plenty more."

Matt reached for another bottle. "Thank the Lord. Where'd you get this chopper?"

"My luck, I spotted a couple soldiers not payin' attention and I just took it. They were busy looking at a dead body—uh, well half a body anyway. Don't worry, the guy was one of theirs. Saw the uniform."

Matt couldn't help but grin. "I know, I saw him."

"Ah, so you were in the neighborhood." Reggie took the copter lower, sending butterflies into Matt's stomach.

"Nice place to visit but I wouldn't want to live there." He took a sip of water.

"So, what's the plan?" said Reggie. "I mean, it's us against the Army. And I'm not ready to Thelma and Louise it—because—"

"Dragon!" said Matt, spitting out the water.

A massive dragon swooped in from the right at full speed, its mouth wide open.

"I see it."

The copter shot left as Reggie tried to avoid the beast. The dragon matched their climb, forcing Reggie to take them even higher.

"Can this thing go that high?"

"We'll find out," Reggie muttered, frantically working the controls.

"When!?"

The dragon surged ahead, leaving them behind—it must not have been after them; it was just passing through.

An alarm blared. The copter sputtered.

"Shit," said Reggie.

"What?" Matt's nerves were frayed. How many times could he cheat death in one day?

"Retreating blade stall. Air's too thin up here."

"Is that bad?" The copter dropped suddenly. "Okay, it's bad."

"It's not good."

Another alarm. "There goes the engine," Reggie said.

Matt scanned for a parachute. "We're going down fast." It felt like a refrigerator falling from the sky.

"That's what we want," said Reggie.

"I thought we *didn't* want that," Matt said, his stomach lurching.

"Gotta get it in autorotation."

"What's that?" The descent steepened.

"Manual mode. Wind turns the rotors."

"Can you do that?"

"We'll see. Brace yourself."

Matt didn't see anything to hold onto, so he ducked his head as if he were on a commercial flight. Reggie was all focus, hands flying over the controls.

The chopper rocked as Reggie angled it upward. Matt hugged his knees, bracing for impact.

"We're gliding now," said Reggie. "Wind's turning the rotors."

"Where are we gonna land?"

"That's the question, isn't it?"

The alarm kept blaring as they glided in a slow descent over the trees.

Matt lifted his head. They were headed straight for the treetops. He gripped his shoulder belt.

"This isn't good," he said. "We're gonna crash."

The trees rushed up to meet them. Another alarm beeped rapidly.

"Hold on," said Reggie.

As the copter approached the tops of the trees, Matt braced his legs. He could hear the rotor blades cutting against the branches. In seconds, the front window was pelted with leaves and sticks. The chopper jolted violently. In the dense foliage, the vehicle slid down until it came to a sudden stop, throwing him forward against his shoulder belt. Just as he turned to look at Reggie, the copter lurched and fell about fifteen feet to the ground, landing with a thud.

After a few seconds of shocked silence, they both started laughing at the same time.

"Welcome to Nibo Island," said Reggie, in a forced announcer voice. "The current temperature is hot as hell. Please check your seat for any personal belongings you may have brought on board and please use caution when opening any bins, as heavy articles may have shifted during the flight. On behalf of the US Army, I'd like to thank you for joining us on this trip and we're looking forward to seeing you on board again real soon." He pounded the dashboard in victory. "Damn right!"

Though it hurt to laugh, Matt couldn't help but smile, if only in relief that he was, once again, not dead.

"Let's *hope* it's real soon," he said. "We still have to get to Vikki. Good landing, by the way."

"Okay Thelma," said Reggie. "I guess it's time to get to work."

Matt forced a smile, but his thoughts were already racing ahead. Vikki was out there—and time was running out.

They climbed out of the copter and inspected the damage. Aside from scratches, dents, and dings, the fuselage looked to be salvageable. The mechanics were another story.

"Engine bay's up top, under the main rotor system," said Reggie. "Turboshaft."

"Whatever you say. How do you get up there, anyway?"

Reggie looked at him as if it was the dumbest question in the world. "Ladder," he said, "of course."

Reggie climbed into the copter and emerged a few minutes later with a service ladder, which Matt helped him set up. Then Reggie made his way to the top, carrying a small toolbox he found in the cabin.

As Reggie got to work, Matt watched.

"So, how's the dating search going?" Matt said, trying to bring some sense of normalcy. Nothing about this trip was normal.

"You know me," said Reggie, as he opened the engine panel. "All the wrong girls in all the wrong places. Had a girl in a bar ask me if I ever had a friend with benefits. I said no but I had an aunt with a huge 401(k)."

Matt chuckled.

"How about you?" said Reggie. "What's the story with you and Vikki?"

"You really wanna know?"

"I don't know," said Reggie, who appeared to be inspecting the engine compartment. "Do I?"

Just as Matt was contemplating how to begin, a distant, menacing roar cut through the jungle.

How many dragons were out there?

He glanced up at Reggie, a chill creeping up his spine. Whatever danger lurked on Nibo Island, it wasn't finished yet.

Chapter Twenty-Eight

Shadow on the Mountain

"You like pointing guns at kids?" Vikki peered up at Krupp, who hovered above her with his pistol drawn.

He shifted his aim squarely in her direction. "Better?" he said.

A smoldering pile of ash lay before them, spewing plumes of dark smoke and burnt embers toward her face, making it difficult to breathe. She was tempted to grab a handful and throw it in Krupp's eyes, but she didn't want to risk getting them both shot.

A bellowing roar came from the right, a good distance away. Alpha must've gotten loose.

Krupp turned. This was her chance.

As she rose with Adelina, she discreetly grabbed a pile of ash in her left hand. She winced as the scorching heat charred her palm.

"Faster," said Krupp, redirecting his attention toward them. He moved behind her and nudged her in the back with his pistol.

The burning ash was getting harder to hold. She had to decide quickly. Should she drop it and cast their fate to the wind? Or should she risk everything and use it?

She strode forward with Adelina, contemplating her next move.

Up ahead, a small sign hung over a cross-corridor. It had random section numbers on it that meant nothing to her.

"Go left," he said.

As soon as they rounded the corner, Vikki froze. A slew of blood-soaked bodies lay scattered across the floor. The blistering ash continued to burn in her palm, somehow getting even hotter. She'd have to drop it any second.

"Step over them," said Krupp.

"Ew," said Adelina.

As Vikki helped her over the bodies, she heard scuffling behind her. She turned around to see that one of the fallen soldiers had grabbed Krupp's leg. She wasn't sure if it was a reflex or a last desperate move on the part of the soldier, as the man still looked dead. As Krupp tried to catch his balance, his gun fell to the floor.

Vikki's heart was beating through her chest. It was now or never. The pain in her palm was unbearable. She glanced down to see smoke creeping out from between her fingers. Krupp spotted it, his eyes bulging as he tried to shake the soldier's hand off his leg.

Adelina noticed it, too.

"Do it," she said.

Without thinking any further, Vikki tossed the ash directly into Krupp's eyes.

He screamed and covered his face. She wanted to grab the gun, but she couldn't risk reaching through Krupp's legs to get it.

The adrenaline rushed through her veins. "Run!" she said, grabbing Adelina's hand.

The two of them darted up the corridor, slipping on the shiny floor. Vikki glanced back to see Krupp staggering to his feet, his hands still over his eyes.

"We have to move faster," she said, gasping for air. "Look for an exit."

Adelina grabbed a fire extinguisher from the wall.

"We don't have time," said Vikki.

"We may need it," Adelina insisted, tucking it under her arm.

Krupp's shout echoed behind them. "Get back here!" She glanced back. He was picking up his pistol.

A gunshot rang out. Vikki flinched. "Move fast!"

"Is he shooting at us!?" said Adelina.

"Just run."

They scrambled ahead, ducking low.

"In here!" Adelina darted into a doorway—it was a stairwell. Smart girl.

As soon as they entered, a shrill alarm blared from the speakers.

"To all personnel," Krupp's voice crackled. "Eyes on target. Tango one and tango two headed up B Wing stairwell."

They raced up the steps. Krupp burst in below.

"You can't go anywhere!" he shouted. "Your only exit is the top of the mountain."

They continued rushing up the steps. Adelina tripped; Vikki caught her shirt and yanked her up.

"We have to hurry," Vikki said as they made it past the third level. "Why aren't there any doors?"

If Krupp was right, the only way out was at the top. There was nowhere else to go.

She looked over the railing—Krupp was gaining.

Adelina pulled the pin on the extinguisher, held it over the railing, and squeezed the lever. A cloud of white powder blasted Krupp in the face. He recoiled, cursing, as she hurled the canister over the edge at him. It clanged hard, and he yelled out.

"Good job. Let's run!" said Vikki.

They bolted up the steps.

"There's a door!" Adelina pointed.

Vikki tried the handle. *Dammit. It was locked.*

"Wait," shouted Adelina. "There's another one up there!" Adelina raced ahead to a metal door at the top of the stairwell.

Krupp's footsteps thundered below.

Adelina struggled with the door. Not this one, too! Vikki rushed up to help her. After pulling with all her strength, it finally gave way.

A rush of cool air immediately hit Vikki's face. No wonder the door was hard to open. She stepped outside and froze—her stomach dropped. They were at least 5,000 feet up, with only a narrow path along the edge. The rainforest treetops stretched far below, the turquoise sea sparkling in the distance. One misstep and it was over.

She put an arm in front of Adelina. "Okay," she muttered as a head-spinning feeling of vertigo set in. "This is okay." She didn't know if she was trying to convince Adelina or herself.

There was nowhere to go but to the left along the treacherous path.

She dreaded heights. But the path had to end up somewhere or there wouldn't have been a path. Maybe it would lead to a trail down the mountain. Then they might at least have a shot at escaping. She didn't even want to think about the alternative if they were captured. Fear or not, she had to continue.

"Take my hand," she said. "Stay close."

She stood with her back to the stone wall as she made her way along the gravelly path. She was already getting dizzy and had to pause to gather herself. It was a long way down and the strong wind kept blowing her hair in her eyes.

Adelina shifted and accidentally kicked a stone. As it tumbled off the ledge, the curious girl leaned down to watch it fall.

"Don't lean," said Vikki, holding her back with her arm. "Please."

She was surprised Krupp hadn't come out yet.

Carefully, she stepped to the left, keeping her back to the wall, and continued around the perimeter. The wind nearly took her breath away. It occurred to her that one big gust could knock them off the ledge. She reached back and gripped Adelina's hand tightly.

The path began to grow wider, but not wanting to tempt fate, she kept close to the wall. Finally, she spotted a set of stone steps leading up to another level. The steps were part of the path, so going around them wasn't an option.

"Great, we get to go even higher," she said.

She let Adelina go ahead of her, just in case Krupp came from behind them.

Navigating the steps was trickier than she thought, as the stairs were narrow and there was no railing on the outside.

"Take it slow."

Adelina didn't seem to have any problem, but then again, she didn't have a fear of heights.

When they finally got to the top, she heard Adelina say, "Oh wow."

She followed her onto a vast, soil-covered plateau. The breathtaking vista around them was both beautiful and terrifying. Somehow, it made her feel free and trapped at the same time—perched like an eagle, but isolated from the rest of the world. The plateau itself was shrouded in cool, misty white fog, adding to its air of mystery.

A dome-shaped brick facility stood at the center, its entrance marked by a set of double doors. It must've led down to the labs.

"Are we in the clouds?" said Adelina, her silky mane of dark brown hair dancing in the breeze.

"Seems like it," said Vikki. "The question is where we go from here."

She looked at the doorway, wondering if it was an option.

"You can't go anywhere," said Krupp, stepping out from around the dome, gun raised. He lifted his radio with his other hand. "Krupp to Blue One. Tango one and tango two secured at Echo Summit. Request backup."

He smiled.

"Seems it's Groundhog Day."

***

As Vikki stood trapped with Adelina, her heart sank with the realization that there was nowhere left to run.

"I'll come with you," she said. "Just tell me Adelina will be okay. That you'll send her to my father. He'll make sure she's taken care of."

Krupp smiled. "You seem to think you're the one calling the shots here."

Vikki threw up her hands. "I just want to make sure she's safe."

He chuckled. "So you knocked out our power, left her with a loose dragon, and dragged her up here to a dead end. Seems to me she needs to be kept safe from you."

"I'd rather be with Gamma than you!" shouted Adelina. "You killed him."

"Well, if Vikki here tries anything, you may get your wish."

Vikki's face turned red. "You're threatening a twelve-year old."

Krupp smirked. "Ease up. We don't kill little girls around here. If you want to—"

He stopped mid-speech. The skies grew dark, and an ominous shadow descended over the plateau. It seemed a storm was rolling in. Krupp looked unusually concerned as his eyes darted around at the skies.

Vikki turned to gaze up at the darkening clouds behind her. Adelina took hold of her hand.

The young girl looked up at her. "Is that—"

A deafening roar came from above. Krupp backed up and aimed his pistol at the clouds.

Vikki grabbed Adelina. "Get down."

As they crouched to the ground, the dragon emerged through the clouds, the air pressure from its massive wings nearly blowing them off the plateau. Vikki's ears began to pop as she smelled a faint scent of sulfur.

"It's Alpha!" said Adelina.

Krupp fired several rounds at Alpha as the dragon lowered to the plateau and landed on its enormous talons. The huge beast lowered its neck to the ground as Krupp fired again.

Vikki squinted to get a better look. "I think he's hurt."

As she looked into Alpha's soulful left eye, the only one she could see from the side, she felt a certain pleading from the ancient creature. She interpreted it as a combination of fatigue and sorrow.

"No," said Adelina. "He's waiting for us."

"Waiting for us to what?"

Before she could process what that meant, Adelina charged toward the dragon.

As soon as Vikki realized what was going on, she wanted to protest. She wanted to stop her. But she didn't. She knew Adelina by now and trusted her judgment, especially when it came to reading animals. But she wasn't about to just watch her run into danger alone either.

Without hesitating, Vikki darted forward. She glanced back to see Krupp turning and running toward the entrance to the dome. She scrambled up the dragon's spiky neck and planted herself beside Adelina, gripping the jagged scales. It was like riding an elephant—something she'd done once in Thailand—but much scarier and far less comfortable.

Just as they settled in on top of Alpha's massive neck, Krupp came out of the dome holding one of those giant sonic weapons.

"Oh no," said Vikki.

"Alpha, go!" said Adelina.

As the dragon rose with a single thrust of its powerful wings, Vikki clung to its rough scales with one hand and grabbed the back of Adelina's shirt with the other. "This was a bad idea," she muttered through her gritted teeth. No saddles. No harnesses. No nothing. The wind threatened to tear them off at any moment, and the dragon's wild aerial maneuvers weren't helping. It was like riding a mechanical bull covered in spikes—except instead of falling onto a padded mat, you'd plunge into oblivion.

Below them, Krupp fired his weapon just as Alpha lifted rapidly with a deafening shriek. The dragon's massive wings beat against the air, propelling him higher into the atmosphere. Vikki dared only brief glances at the shrinking ground below; her stomach churned with every flap of his wings. She clenched her teeth, counting silently in her head to keep herself from screaming—or worse, fainting.

Alpha banked sharply to the right and dove without warning. Vikki's stomach lurched into her throat as she was thrown sideways, gripping Adelina even tighter. For such a massive creature, he moved with startling agility, twisting through the air like a predator closing in on its prey. As he dove again, her body was tossed upward, then slammed down hard. Then came a sharp pain—one of his jagged spikes had pierced her thigh. She winced but held on tighter. She couldn't let go.

"Hold on!" she yelled to Adelina. She prayed for the ride to be over.

Krupp fired again. Alpha veered sharply to the left, narrowly avoiding the blast. Vikki was thrown off balance—her body lifted off the dragon before slamming back onto his spiky neck. She gasped, her fingers clawing against his slick scales as she fought to hold on. Adelina let out a piercing scream.

Alpha pitched upward, then dipped suddenly with the wind. Vikki's stomach rose into her throat as she clung tighter. The cold wind whipped against her face, sending chills down her spine. Despite her terror, a brief feeling of exhilaration ran through her chest. "He knows how to fly," she told herself over and over, her grip slipping again. "He'll get through this. It's his turf."

Again, Krupp fired. Alpha looped sharply to the right, dodging just in time. Vikki's muscles clenched as she imagined what would happen if one of those blasts hit their mark—they'd all plummet thousands of feet to their deaths.

Alpha circled wide, flying away from the plateau before banking hard and heading straight toward Krupp.

"No!" Adelina screamed, her voice cracking with panic. "Alpha, don't!"

Krupp aimed his sonic weapon directly at Alpha's chest as they hurtled toward him head-on. Vikki felt a deep rumbling beneath Alpha's armor-like skin—a vibration that seemed to grow stronger with every second. The wind took her breath away as Alpha dove at terrifying speed, forcing her to grip his enormous spikes until her knuckles burned. She couldn't even think; survival was all that mattered now.

Krupp fired again. Alpha jolted deftly to the right, twisting his massive neck mid-flight as he opened his mouth wide. A torrent of fire erupted from his jaws, engulfing Krupp in an instant. The heat was overwhelming—Vikki felt it searing her skin even from above. Sulfur pummeled her nose like a physical blow. Below her, Krupp let out a bloodcurdling scream that echoed across the plateau before abruptly cutting off.

Alpha swooped up and circled once more before landing gracefully on the plateau with a heavy thud that sent tremors through Vikki's body. She was so relieved she nearly passed out on his back. Adelina leaned toward her with a nervous grin, her face pale but alive with excitement. Before either of them could speak, Alpha dipped his head low, scooped up Krupp's charred remains in his massive jaws, and—with one swift motion—flung the body over the edge of the plateau into the vista below.

"I wouldn't want to be on your bad side," said Vikki as she patted Alpha's back. The dragon gently lowered his neck. She knew what that meant. It was time to go.

Vikki climbed down and helped Adelina off. Everything was still spinning as she staggered onto solid ground.

As she turned to face the blood-soaked plateau, a strong gust came out of nowhere and nearly knocked her and Adelina over. She glanced up to see Alpha taking flight, heading into the thick clouds. The gust had been caused by the dragon's humongous wings.

The doors burst open, and Krupp's soldiers came running out of the dome. A decorated Army officer led the unit and marched in front like he owned the world. With his gray crew cut, fierce stare, and square jawline, he looked like a typical hardened commander right out of Central Casting.

"This is Colonel Curtis J. Adler with the United States Army," he said. "Hands up. Don't move."

She and Adelina held up their hands as the soldiers drew their weapons.

"We didn't kill the general," she said.

The skies grew dark again, this time from the far end of the plateau beyond the facility.

"You may as well have," said the colonel, scowling as his eyes scanned the charred soil and bits of human remains. "Your actions and the actions of your whole gang have caused our country irreparable harm. As for your dragon buddy . . ." He paused and smirked.

A whole flock of dragons emerged from the clouds behind him, getting into formation and hovering like giant sentinels of death. She noticed one of his men entering instructions into a tablet.

"We have ten of them," he said. "We'll get Alpha, too, soon enough."

Vikki's heart sank. There was nowhere left to run.

Chapter Twenty-Nine

National Security

"So you're going to kill us?" said Vikki. "Is that it?" She noticed Krupp's sonic weapon melted into the ground next to his scorched radio. The weapon would be useless anyway against all those dragons.

"Depends how you cooperate," said Adler.

"We have no intention of stopping you. We never did."

He sneered at her. "You just felt like causing a little chaos, I suppose. That it?"

"We didn't want to be brainwashed for no reason. I'm sure you can understand that. I'm a scientist, not some—"

"Right now, you're nothing but a huge impediment to this program."

"I don't want to argue," she said. "I'll come willingly. I just want to make sure Adelina is taken care of. That's what I told General Krupp, and he couldn't answer that simple question. Can you?"

Adler stomped toward her with a fury she hadn't even seen from Krupp. A few of the dragons began impatiently growling—their deep, resonant vocalizations echoing across the plateau. Vikki stepped back, her palms sweating.

"You listen to me," he said, his weather-beaten face about a foot from hers. "When you talk to me, you're talking to General Krupp, only meaner. He was my friend. You got that?"

She could feel her face growing red. "I am not the enemy," she huffed. "I had nothing against your general. And I'm not some schoolkid. I'm just trying to—"

Static came from a radio on the ground. Krupp's radio. She was surprised it still worked.

"General, pick up," said a male voice through the receiver.

Adler bent down and scooped up the blackened radio. "This is Colonel Curtis Adler. State your name, rank, and serial number."

"Where's Krupp?" said the voice.

"State your name, rank, and serial number."

"This is Asher P. Forsyth," said the impatient-sounding voice from the radio. "The Secretary of Defense. Now where is General Krupp?"

Adler shook his head and pursed his lips. "Mr. Secretary, we're still trying to assess that. It appears the general is MIA."

"Well, I'm here with Dr. Jim Barnes, who says you have his daughter."

Vikki tried to contain her emotions as Adelina glanced over, her eyes wide with delight. A wave of relief washed over her—thank God he was safe. Her hands trembled as she fought to keep her voice steady. She wanted to call out—to let her dad know she was here, but she waited to let the situation play out.

Adler paused, his poker face not letting on to any emotion one way or the other. He pressed the receiver.

"We'll look into that, sir."

The blood rushed to her face. That pompous—

"We're right here!" she shouted at the top of her lungs. "This is Vikki Barnes. They have us illegally. Dad, they have us!"

Adler nodded to his men and two of them swiftly came forward to cover her and Adelina's mouths with their hands.

"One other thing," said Forsythe. He must not have heard her desperate calls for help—Adler didn't have the *talk* button pressed. "I'm telling you the same thing I was gonna tell Krupp, and . . ."

Static crackled through the receiver, drowning out his words.

" . . . operation at Fort Majestic," continued Forsythe on the bad connection, "is unauthorized and unbudgeted, and . . . until it's formally reviewed, you are . . . secure your assets and cease all operations. Am I clear?"

More static.

"I said am I clear?"

"This is an unusual chain of command," said Adler. "Is this order authorized by my direct superiors?"

"Would you like me to have the Lieutenant General contact you? Or how about the Chair of the Joint Chiefs?" said Forsythe. "I'll tell them the same thing."

"No copy, Mr. Secretary," said Adler. "Please repeat." He turned and walked calmly to the edge of the plateau and threw the radio over the side.

Vikki took a deep breath as the soldier released his hand from her mouth. "Colonel," she said, "they know I'm here. If something happens to me, someone will have to answer for it."

"I don't know what you're talking about," he said.

"But the Secretary of—"

"This project isn't going anywhere!" he shouted, his temples flaring. He shook his head. "The secretary isn't the guy who's gonna defend this country. We're talking national security here, and *we* are the last line of defense. Not him, not the president, and not your dad." He reached in his holster. Her muscles froze. On instinct, she moved in front of Adelina to protect her. Her heart hammered as she braced for the worst. "Besides," Adler said, "there are things none of them know."

Instead of pulling out a gun, he lifted a radio to his mouth.

"Bluebird 405, this is Colonel Adler. I need you at Echo Summit. Need you to make a drop."

A broken voice came across the radio. "Roger."

"What exactly do you mean by a *drop*?" said Vikki. She hoped he didn't mean drop—as in drop them into the ocean.

"Why couldn't you just leave well enough alone?" said Adler, as the dragons began snarling again. "Would you rather have us send thousands of troops to die on some fool's mission overseas, or send *these* guys?" He motioned with his thumb to his army of dragons, menacingly hovering above—two of them snapping at one another.

"And what if someone launches a nuke?" she said. "Where does it end?"

"These assets can take out their nukes before the enemy even knows what happened. Undetected! Don't you get it?"

He seemed to be pleading with her, as if he owed her an explanation.

She nodded reluctantly. She understood the rationale, but their methods were reckless. To them, the end justified the means.

"I get it," she said. "I do. But your lack of respect for an ancient species is . . ." She fished for the right words. " . . .sobering, at best—and I think you're underestimating the risks."

"How 'bout you let me worry about that."

"But wait. Let's say I understand why you're doing it. What I don't understand is what's happening right here . . . right now. I'm a paleontologist. She's a kid."

"You think I don't know that?" he yelled. "I have a granddaughter her age!" His cheek muscles twitched as he clenched his jaw. Then he spat out, "Who the hell do you think I'm doing this for?"

Vikki shook her head. Krupp and his sons. Adler and his granddaughter. But no problem if some innocent people get in the way of their holy mission. Damn the torpedoes.

"Then you should know better!" she shouted back. "Are we just collateral damage? Jesus, the greater good doesn't have to be heartless. Is there no room for grace in there? At all? Or is it all just about winning?"

"Right now, it's about winning," he said, his tone somber, despite his cold stare.

The wind picked up, blowing her hair in her face. She was sick of her life being in someone else's hands—first Krupp's, now Adler's. Sick to death of it.

"If you're willing to do this to us," she said, her voice trembling, "what other lines will you cross?"

She clenched her fists. "What other lines!?" He ignored her and looked past her. The Krupps and Adlers of the world infuriated her, bulldozing their way through their agenda with their one-track minds, playing games with people's lives. People like her and Adelina—just pawns for the chess masters: corrupt politicians, corporate bigwigs, military goons. And now, they'd have an unspeakable weapon by exploiting yet another species. Those in control would stop at nothing to keep their power, no matter the cost.

"You don't deserve that kind of power!" she yelled, then instantly regretted it. All it would do was make him angrier. She remembered a Mark Twain quote her dad used to tell her: "Never argue with stupid people; they will drag you down to their level and then beat you with experience."

The whirring of a helicopter interrupted her thoughts.

"Here comes your ride," said Adler, his voice calm—though she sensed a flicker of regret. Maybe he just hated not winning the argument.

Vikki looked for the copter but saw nothing yet. She squeezed Adelina's hand.

"Where are they taking us?" Adelina asked, tugging at her arm.

Vikki shook her head. "I'm not sure."

Adelina turned to Adler, her face red with anger. "Would you do this to your granddaughter!?" she yelled.

Adler didn't answer, but for a moment, he looked shaken.

"*Would* you?" Adelina repeated.

Adler's face hardened as he spoke into his receiver. "Adler to Blue-bird 405. Tango one and tango two secured and ready. Drop zone eighteen-seventy-five. Is that clear?"

"What does that mean?" said Vikki.

"I said is that clear?" Adler repeated, frustration in his voice.

"Respectfully, sir," came the reply. "Piss off."

"What the—"

The helicopter's whirring grew louder as it rose to the plateau. Vikki turned to see Matt standing in the open side door.

"Run!" yelled Matt.

She grabbed Adelina's arm, and they sprinted toward the copter. Vikki glanced back—about twenty soldiers were aiming their weapons at them. Adler had his hand up, apparently waiting to give the order to fire.

"Hold your fire," Adler yelled. "Remember. Plausible deniability. We've got dragons."

"Go first!" Vikki shouted to Adelina, glancing back as the dragons began to snarl louder, their grumbles vibrating in her chest.

Adelina stepped back, then ran toward the edge of the plateau. The gap to the copter was about two feet, and it was shifting in the wind. Vikki's heart was in her mouth as Adelina leapt across the gap.

Matt caught the girl easily.

Vikki was about to jump, but the copter drifted away from the plateau.

"Jump, Vik!"

"I can't," she said. "Take Adelina." A gust of air hit her back—was it the dragons? A strong scent of sulfur stung her nose, but she didn't dare look back.

"I won't let you fall."

She hesitated. The gap looked impossible.

"You can do it," he said, horror suddenly flickering across his face as he glanced past her. Behind her, dragons growled, the sound sharp and close.

He met her eyes. "Trust me."

Springboarding off her left foot, she leapt into the void.

For a split second, she saw her mother falling from the mountain—helpless. That's how she felt now, as she realized she was going to fall short of the copter.

She wasn't going to make it.

Gravity pulled her down below the open door. As she fell, a vise-like grip closed on her right arm. She winced, swinging below the edge of the copter, her heart pounding. Matt strained to pull her up as the wind tossed her back and forth.

She was slipping. She grabbed his arm with her left hand, trying to lift herself. Matt gripped her tighter, but the chopper drifted farther from the plateau, the wind thrashing her.

Her strength was failing. Matt's arms had to be getting tired. As she swung in the wind, she saw a chance to reach the doorframe. She had to time it perfectly.

The next time the wind pushed her right, she stretched out—but missed the ledge, and her left arm slipped as well. Matt squeezed tighter, saving her.

"Try it again," he shouted.

She swung like a pendulum. This time, when the wind carried her right, she grabbed the ledge. With Matt's help, she hauled herself up and over.

"Let's go!" Matt yelled toward the cockpit. The copter darted forward, tossing Vikki to the floor.

She scrambled to her knees. Matt knelt beside her, staring out at the hovering dragons with his mouth open. The beasts had moved closer to the center of the plateau, but why hadn't they attacked yet?

"Quite a sight," she said, gazing at the shrinking plateau.

"Let's hope they stay there," said Matt.

Adler, some distance away, brought his hand down sharply. His men lowered their weapons. Even from afar, it looked like he was smiling, making a round 'em up gesture to his men with his hand. Did Adler have one more trick up his sleeve—was he about to test how fast his dragons were?

"Where's Krupp?" said Matt.

"He couldn't handle the heat," said Vikki.

A familiar voice rang out from the cockpit and shouted over the engine noise. "Told you about those secret Army projects. *Now* do you believe me?"

"You're alive!" she said, looking at the back of Reggie's head. She hadn't even noticed who was flying the copter. "They told us you were dead."

"Not yet," he yelled over the engine noise. "Better buckle up!"

Vikki rose carefully, the helicopter still shifting unsteadily in the wind. As soon as she was on her feet, Adelina rushed up and hugged her. As they embraced tightly, she thought of all they'd been through—more than most people experience in a lifetime.

Vikki let go as Matt placed a hand on Adelina's shoulder and guided her to a seat. Before joining them to find her own seat, she steadied herself with the handrail and took one last look out the side door.

She gasped.

Alpha had returned, hovering in mid-air, facing off against the ten dragons. That must be why they came forward—and it was also why they hadn't attacked yet. Below, Adler and the soldiers scurried like ants while the dragons grew more animated, perhaps preparing to strike.

Vikki didn't dare tell Adelina. The girl had been through enough heartache already. Brave Alpha had saved them before and would no doubt make a valiant effort once more. But she feared it wouldn't be enough. Not with ten dragons under military control.

Her heart sank. But now there was a bigger problem. Unless Reggie could put the helicopter in hyperdrive, she feared they would soon have visitors.

Outside, Alpha hovered, facing ten dragons alone.

Chapter Thirty

Homebound

Vikki strapped herself into the side bench of the helicopter's cabin, still trying to catch her breath. Adelina was already seated beside her. As the chopper turned, Matt sat across from them and pulled a headset out from under the seat. She and Adelina did the same.

"Where's Toro?" said Adelina, adjusting her headset. "Are we picking him up next?"

Matt looked at Vikki and then glanced down. Vikki knew immediately the news wasn't good.

He raised his head and leaned toward Adelina. "Toro saved all of us," he said. "He was the bravest man I ever knew, but even he couldn't take out a whole pack of dragons."

Vikki put her arm around Adelina's shoulders. The resilient young girl remained silent, her chin quivering as she clenched her jaw. Between that and a hardening expression of fury, it was about all the emotion Adelina would allow herself.

"So, he's gone," said Adelina, clearly trying to stay composed. "Just like that." She sighed. "I should've been there. He couldn't have beat them. Not those dragons. Not when they were trained."

"That didn't stop him from trying, though," said Matt. "He came damn close. Do you know he ran right up to those suckers and told us to go? 'Get out,' he said, 'I got this.' And he did, for a while. He saved Reggie. And he saved me. Because that's who he was."

"Immortal," said Vikki, remembering his snake tattoo.

Matt nodded. "Immortal." He glanced at her with a slight smile. His eyes grew moist, and he quickly looked away.

"He saved me, too," said Adelina, sniffling without tears.

"See, that's who Toro was," said Matt. "And I think he made all of us a little better."

Vikki wished this was the end of their worries—the well-deserved respite after all their ordeals, all their trauma—and that now the healing could begin. But she had a deep-seated fear they weren't out of the woods yet. Her mind drifted to Alpha and his showdown with his vicious genetic spawn. Her hands trembled as she thought about how long it would take the dragons until they began their pursuit. She wanted to tell the others. She *needed* to tell them. She contemplated how to bring it up without mentioning Alpha to Adelina.

Adelina reached up and put a hand over hers to comfort her.

"Don't worry," said Adelina. "The worst is over."

Vikki turned and smiled at her just as the copter began bobbing up and down erratically.

"Just a little turbulence," said Reggie. "Nothing to worry about."

"I'm more worried about those dragons," said Vikki, adjusting her headset. "Do you think they'll come after us?"

"They probably would have been here already," said Matt.

"Maybe we should go faster, just in case," she said.

"If those dragons decide to come and get us," said Reggie from the cockpit, "they're gonna get us. I've seen how fast they are. I'm just sayin'."

She glanced out the side door, checking for any sign of them.

"Can it hurt to go faster?" she said.

The copter lurched and dipped more strongly in the turbulent air, causing the cabin to rattle and groan. As squeaks and squeals rang out from the metal exterior, Vikki thought the chopper might burst apart any minute.

Her heart was in her mouth as she glanced around the cabin, the seats shaking violently. "Is this thing going to hold together?"

"It should," said Reggie. "I think we patched it up pretty good."

"Patched it up?"

Matt looked at her. "Long story."

After a few more bumps, Reggie brought the copter to a higher altitude and the ride grew considerably smoother.

Vikki took a deep breath. Maybe she was wrong. Maybe Adler wasn't sending the dragons. Was her luck turning?

The farther they got from the island, the more comfortable she began to feel. Still, she was worried about Alpha. It was possible Adler rounded them all up and poor Alpha was once again confined with the others. She'd never forget that sad look in his glass enclosure, or his determination to save them from Krupp—risking his life for their sake. What a majestic creature—far more worthy of the term *majestic* than that heartless compound.

She sighed and patted Adelina's shoulder to reassure her. Of course, who was she kidding? She was really trying to reassure herself.

She gazed out the window, though she wasn't just looking at the blue sky and sparkling ocean. She was looking at freedom. She thought about being back in the safety of the museum, and what discoveries she might make—possibly some that could even give hints as to Alpha's origins. Would the Army just give up on her—forget about her? Could it be that easy?

"By the way," said Matt, "I heard from your dad, sort of. He was on a dead soldier's radio trying to reach Krupp."

She couldn't imagine what her dad must've gone through, all the levels of hierarchy and communication channels. He always complained about navigating the labyrinth, even on a good day.

"He really didn't give up," she said. "He was just on the radio with the Secretary of Defense, too. They ordered the colonel to stand down."

Matt's eyes widened.

"The secretary! That would explain why those guys didn't chase us," he said. "What did he say? The colonel, I mean."

"He threw the receiver into the ocean," she said. "So, I'd say that was a no."

Matt frowned. "Scratch that about not chasing us then."

"More like he'd rather use the dragons. I heard him tell his men that."

"Then why didn't he?" said Matt.

"He still might."

"That's not good," said Reggie from the cockpit.

"No, it's not," she said. "Hey, can we radio my dad to let him know we're okay?" She couldn't get her dad's concerned voice out of her head from the last time he'd spoken to her. The thought made her chest tighten—he must've been worried sick if he made his way all the way to the Secretary of Defense.

"We sure can," said Reggie. "Just let me . . . no wait . . . damn."

He fiddled with the controls.

"What?" she said. This wasn't looking good.

"External comms are down. Been happening on and off ever since the crash."

"The crash? What kind of crash? Where?"

"We had a bit of a run-in with a dragon," said Matt. "We ended up in the trees."

"Damaged the antennas," said Reggie. "And a few other things."

"A few other things?"

"Don't worry," said Matt. "The important stuff works."

"I hope so," said Vikki. "I just want to get home and ice up these arm muscles." She tried massaging the pain out of her arms, but it wasn't helping. Even her hands ached.

"Gonna hurt worse, tomorrow," said Reggie.

"You're just full of good news," said Matt. "Let's be glad there'll be a tomorrow."

She reached across the cabin and gripped his hand; it was time to put the past behind them. A flash of surprise washed over his face. "Thanks to you and Reggie," said Vikki. She shook her head. "I really didn't think I'd ever see you again."

"Guess that made you happy," said Matt, smirking.

"Actually, no," she said, holding his hand tighter. "It didn't. I . . ." Her throat tightened. The truth was, she would've been beside herself if anything had happened to him. She let go of his hand. She didn't want him to get the wrong idea. Not yet, anyway.

Matt glanced down.

"This guy," said Reggie from up front, "was not gonna stop for anything until he got to you. I'm telling you, he was like a man possessed." He added in a silly falsetto, "I have to get to Vikki. We have to get back to Vikki." He paused. "No offense to you, Adelina, you're important, too. I think he mentioned you once or twice."

Adelina chuckled. It was the first time Vikki heard her laugh.

Vikki stared across at Matt and saw him in a new light—a true survivor who showed beyond a shadow of a doubt that he cared about her. "Thank you," she said. Though just two simple words, they spoke volumes to her. She hoped Matt would see it that way, too. But she couldn't read his face; he looked contemplative. His smirk was gone, replaced by an expression unlike the Matt she was used to. It was as if he was carrying the weight of the world on his shoulders.

"Vik," he said. "I have to get something off my chest and now is as good a time as any."

"I know what you're going to say, and you really don't have to. It's in the past."

She hoped she wasn't making a mistake minimizing his past actions, or how much they had hurt her. The moment they shared was genuine, but she couldn't help but think: Could he ever truly change? Long-term?

"Oh, I can guarantee you," said Reggie, "you *don't* know what he's gonna say. I heard the story, and it's a doozie."

"You told *him*?" she said, staring at Matt.

"I want to hear," said Adelina, suddenly lighting up.

"It was a silly misunderstanding," he said, smiling.

Now *there* was the old Matt.

She turned to Adelina. "Can you do me a big favor and take your headset off and hold your ears for a minute?"

"Can't I hear, too?" she said, her eyes widening.

"That would be a no."

Adelina, finally looking like a normal angsty pre-teen, reluctantly took off her headset and covered her ears. Once Vikki was satisfied Adelina wasn't listening, she looked directly at Matt.

"A naked girl was in your bed," she said, "half-wearing one of your shirts while you were in the shower." She threw her hands up in mock confusion. "You'll have to excuse me, but what exactly is it that's so hard to understand? Anyway, like I said, it doesn't matter. It was years ago."

"That's the thing," said Matt. "What you saw wasn't what happened?"

"What the hell does *that* mean? My eyes were wrong?"

"No, you're not getting it. She was my cousin. She—"

"Ew! And that's supposed to make it better!?" She could see his face was red with embarrassment, and rightfully so. How could he do that? With his cousin, no less.

"No, I'm not explaining it right."

"Ya think?" said Reggie.

Matt rolled his eyes. "She was just a fifteen-year-old kid. Danielle. She was—"

"Stop right there," she said, holding up a hand. "This is getting worse by the minute."

"Dude, get to the punch line!" said Reggie.

"Yeah, what *is* the punch line," she said, "because so far, I'm just nauseous, and it's not the helicopter ride. So, if it's a joke, I'm not getting it."

"Oh, you will," said Reggie.

Matt took a deep breath. "So, I'm about to grab a shower when the doorbell rings. Danielle's mom, *also* my cousin, drops Danielle off at my house because she just got an emergency call to go to work. Meanwhile, the kid just had her wisdom teeth out and couldn't be left alone."

Vikki couldn't help but think back to Dr. Simmons and the anesthesia he'd given her. She couldn't tell up from down. Was the girl drugged?

"Anyway, Beth—that's Danielle's mom—goes to work. Danielle's still half out of it, so I give her an orange soda to wake her up, which she tries to drink but then proceeds to dribble it all over her shirt. So, I give her one of my shirts, toss hers in the wash, and go to take my shower." He threw his hands up. "When I come out, she's passed out on the bed, clothes off, other than my shirt—sort of—and then I see your note on the table. The end. Finis. That was it. I can even introduce you to her."

Vikki was dumbfounded. Matt sat across from her with a serious expression on his face like someone had died. It was so far-fetched, and *so* not what she'd imagined all this time, that she didn't know if she wanted to slap him or burst out laughing at the ridiculousness of it all. Perhaps it was the stress requiring an outlet, but she had to admit it was quite the comedy of errors. Nobody could make that up. Not even Matt.

Finally, she shook her head and allowed herself to crack a smile. But then the true absurdity of the situation settled into her funny bone. She, Reggie, and even Adelina—who was wearing her headset and apparently listened to the whole thing—all burst out laughing at the same time.

"Why didn't you tell me this in the first place?" she said, once she could talk again.

"You never let me! I visited your house. I wrote letters."

"I never opened them. Did my dad know this story?"

"I tried to tell him, but he didn't want to hear it. Something about not wanting to have to take sides. He wanted *me* to tell you. And now . . . well, I guess I did. Are you still mad at me?"

She shook her head, smiling. "How could I be?" She wanted to get up and hug him and apologize for not listening to his side of the story sooner, but the copter began pitching again. She gripped the side of her seat.

"Speaking of your dad," he said, "there still is something you should probably be mad about."

She couldn't imagine what it was.

He looked at Adelina. "Hold your ears," he said.

"No way," she said.

"Just tell me," said Vikki.

"I was the one who insisted on bringing you on this mission. I figured it would be a good excuse to see you again. Once I told your dad my idea, he agreed it might give us a shot. He just wanted you to be happy. But he said his main reason was that he hoped it would be a way to sort of . . . how did he word it? Oh yes . . . to reignite your passion for research. So, basically, what I'm trying to say is that it was me who got you into this mess."

"We're not out of this mess yet," said Reggie, as he brought the chopper around sharply to the right and out to sea. "We got company."

This was the moment Vikki feared. She glanced out the opposing side door and her breath caught in her throat.

Adler's whole fleet of ten dragons was flying right toward them at rapid speed.

Her stomach churned as the copter dipped a few hundred feet with no warning.

"This time I'm goin' down instead of up," said Reggie.

"Good move," said Matt.

Vikki wasn't sure what they were talking about, but she was glad Reggie seemed to know what he was doing. Her heart raced at the thought of yet another brush with death. She should've known Adler was going to send his beasts. Poor Alpha.

As the helicopter dove dangerously close to the rippling sea, Vikki ducked her head to keep an eye on the dragons. They were approaching fast.

Matt jumped out of his seat to get a better look, holding on as he swung around to watch out the side doors.

"They're in attack mode," he said as they rose up to prepare for a dive.

Vikki wrapped her arm around Adelina, who seemed more riveted than afraid, intently watching the dragons.

"No, they're not," said Adelina. "Look." She pointed upward.

Vikki craned her neck to get a better look. Immediately, her gaze was drawn to what Adelina had spotted.

Just above the imposing fleet of dragons was Alpha, majestically soaring over them. The ancient beast called out, and at that moment, the flock of dragons ascended in perfect harmony to join his side.

"It's okay," said Adelina, as Alpha and the dragons soared over and past them.

Adelina jumped out of her seat to watch them out the left side with Matt. Vikki unbuckled her seatbelt and joined them.

"Alpha's leading them," said Adelina. "He's taking them home."

Vikki marveled at how elegant they looked.

"Yeah, but where's home?" said Vikki. They were flying westward, away from Fort Majestic.

Matt turned to face them with a puzzled look on his face. "Who's Alpha?"

Before she could answer, Adelina grabbed her arm and said, "Look what they're doing!"

Vikki turned to witness a stunning display as the dragons soared in synchronized arcs, as if on an invisible roller coaster. She gasped in wonder as Alpha suddenly led them upward in a breathtakingly choreographed formation. Then, with the graceful beauty of an Olympic water ballet, they plunged into the sea—together.

Chapter Thirty-One

Answers and Questions

Vikki sat in her office facing her dad, who was beaming from ear to ear. It was hard to believe it had been two weeks since her ordeal. In some ways it seemed like yesterday, yet it felt like a lifetime ago in another world.

"So, you're saying I'm in the clear," she said.

He slid a sheet of paper toward her.

"Fully executed non-disclosure agreement," he said.

She picked it up and studied it. "Wow, the Secretary of Defense himself."

"The president was busy," he said smiling. "Hope that'll do."

She placed the trusty dinosaur stress ball her mom gave her on her neatly stacked pile of papers.

"I think that'll work," she said. "And Adler?"

"Classified," he said. "Same with the project, though I can't imagine how it could continue with no dragons."

"Unless they kept DNA." She got a chill just thinking about that.

"We'll never know. At least I hope not."

Her muscles tensed, as they always did when she thought about humanity's disregard for nature—exploiting ancient creatures, wiping out species, polluting the seas, ignoring the planet's warnings. Earth had survived five mass extinctions, and only one of them was from an asteroid. The rest came from runaway greenhouse gases and falling oxygen. If only people saw the inevitability of a sixth mass extinction—this time, it would be of our own making.

"One question I have," said her dad, shaking her out of her mental doomscrolling. "If the dragons supposedly came from the sea . . ."

"Why would they have wings?" she said, finishing his sentence. "It's a puzzle. If something doesn't need to fly, then it probably won't develop wings. But if it used to fly and hadn't for years—or maybe even centuries—it would've lost that capability, right?"

"That's what I'm saying," he said.

"What do you know about vestigial traits?"

"Old remnants."

"Exactly. Species can retain traits they no longer need. It's why whales have leg bones. Or why we have an appendix, or wisdom teeth. But these kinds of things tend to get smaller or less functional over time without regular use. So that got me thinking."

Her dad leaned forward as if she was about to tell him who shot JFK.

"I'm thinking one of three things," she said. "One, what if they're not that ancient? Well, not in the sense that we think as ancient."

"I'm not following."

She stood and began pacing. It helped her think. "Alpha got lured when they were doing sonic testing. But maybe that wasn't his first time coming out of the ocean. Maybe he, and however many others there are, just fly where they're not likely to be seen? It's a big world out there."

He folded his arms and leaned back. "Remote areas of uncontrolled airspace. It would have to be pretty remote, since probably eighty percent of the planet is under satellite surveillance. It's possible. Unlikely, but possible. What's your next thought?"

She stopped and took a breath. "This is going to sound really woo-woo."

"Woo-woo away."

"What if there are wormholes down there? What if they live in some other dimension? Or even on another planet? Do not tell Reggie I said that, by the way."

He nodded. "Also a possibility. It'd be hard to prove one way or the other."

She returned to her seat behind her desk. "Okay then, let's come down to Earth a little. What if Alpha himself is very ancient?"

"Well, you did say he's really old."

"I mean really ancient. Like, he was around way back in the days when dragons existed, assuming there was such a time. Maybe he's one of the last survivors. Or even the last. And he just stayed hidden all this time. Like I told the students, in my field we're only dealing with a miniscule sampling of fossils, so it's possible they did exist at one time. He's living proof. It would explain . . ."

A wave of panic came over her. "What time is it?"

"Almost ten."

"The students!" She jumped out of her chair. "I have to get downstairs. Lecture at ten."

"Go," he said. "Don't let me hold you up."

***

As the group of middle-schoolers huddled around the portable iguana cage, Vikki gave her talk on the evolution of reptiles.

"Is he yours?" asked a young girl with blonde hair.

"He is," she said. "I brought him from home."

"What does he eat?" said the same girl.

"Iguanas are herbivores. Does anyone know what that means?" She looked around at the raised hands. "Just shout it out," she said.

"They eat veggies," said multiple kids at once.

"That's right," she said. "I'm impressed. I feed him mostly plants, veggies like broccoli, and a little bit of fruit. Berries. Bananas. Apples. He loves apples."

"Does he have a name?" said a Latino boy.

"I named him Gamma," she said. Every time she said the name, she thought of the hapless beast that bonded with Adelina. If people only realized that even the fiercest creatures have fears, pain, and distrust beneath their surface. They all deserved a chance.

"Wow, cool!" a boy in an Incredible Hulk shirt said. "Like the Gamma Rays that made Hulk!"

"Exactly like that." Vikki smiled.

"What do you like most about being a paleontologist?" asked a tall girl with braces and black-rimmed glasses.

Vikki didn't have to think. "I'd say it's the wonder of finding a new species—something no one else has ever seen." She scanned the eager faces. "That's every paleontologist's dream. In fact, more than anything else, the most important trait you can have . . . is curiosity."

She spotted her dad at the back, smiling and nodding. Adelina stood beside him, her dark hair tied in a bow.

"I lost that curiosity for a while," Vikki continued, "and it took my father to remind me."

A red-faced boy blurted out, "What do you think about that dragon video?"

Vikki chuckled. "Speaking of curious . . ." The kids giggled. She waited for the teasing to die down, then looked at the boy seriously.

"We're all fascinated by the mystical. Dragons are the most mystical of all—so much so that science can't explain them. The truth is, I don't know what it was . . . or is. But I'd love to find out. I bet everyone here would. No one's seen it since. But here's something to remember . . ."

The room went silent as she met the boy's eyes.

"Always stay curious," she said. "Because one day we're going to find out exactly what it was and where it came from. And maybe you'll be the one to do it."

***

After the kids applauded her presentation and dispersed, Adelina came running up to her.

"Mom!" said Adelina. Vikki would never tire of hearing that. Officially, the adoption was still in progress, but it was just a matter of time. Only a couple of months, according to the lawyer, given the unique situation. Usually, the process takes longer.

"Addy," she said. "Did you hear the whole thing?"

"It was perfect. I think Gamma liked it too."

"I'm sure he did. By the way, we have a little surprise for you."

Her eyes lit up. "What?"

Vikki nodded to her dad, who pulled a small, flat box out of his jacket pocket. He handed it to Adelina.

"We just got this from the government," said Vikki. She'd only had a few minutes to look at it herself an hour ago.

Adelina took off the lid to the box, and gasped. "Is this a medal?" she said.

"It's Toro's medal," said Vikki. "Not only a medal, but the United States Medal of Honor. Not many people get those. The president himself just awarded it to him for his bravery during the war. But between you and me, it was secretly for saving all of us, too. I know for a fact Toro would've wanted you to have it. Hold it up. Let's see it."

Adelina smiled through her tears as she held up the beautiful five-pointed gold star surrounded by a green laurel wreath. A gold bar ran across the top, inscribed with the word, VALOR. It separated the medal from the blue ribbon above it.

"Who's that in the center of the star?" said Adelina. "The Statue of Liberty?"

"It's Minerva," said Vikki's dad. "She was the Roman goddess of wisdom and justice."

"I'd say that's pretty fitting for Toro," said Vikki. "What's on the other side?"

Adelina flipped the medal over. The inscription on the reverse side bar read:

THE CONGRESS TO RAYMOND "TORO" CORTEZ

"I wish he could be here to see it," said Adelina.

"I think he is," said Vikki. She meant it. She always believed that lost loved ones could sense when they're being treasured by those who cared about them. She couldn't help but think of her mother. She would've loved Addy.

Adelina nodded, then looked up at her, blushing. "I have a surprise, too," she said.

Vikki had no idea what she was referring to. Adelina turned toward the adjacent hall and yelled, "Come on in, guys!"

Matt and Reggie came wandering in from the hall, each looking like the proverbial cat that ate the canary.

"Wow, this *is* a surprise," she said as she hugged them both. "The gang's all here. What's the big occasion?"

"Funny you should ask," said Matt, looking suddenly uncomfortable. "How do I put this?" He paused as if he was afraid to continue.

"Just say it," said Vikki. She was wondering why Adelina had a knowing grin on her face.

"I kind of need you to come to another island with me."

She almost fell over. Out of all the things he could've said, that wasn't one she was expecting. "This is a joke, right?"

She turned to her dad, who shrugged. "Tell me this is a joke."

"Before you say no," said Matt, "just read this." He held out a sheet of paper. "It's really not that bad."

She took the paper, her hands shaking, and read the words.

"Read it out loud," said her dad. Adelina was giggling, and now she knew why.

She tried not to laugh as she read it. "It says, 'You are hereby cordially invited to an all-expenses-paid trip for two to the Bahamas.'"

"That's three if you include the pilot," said Reggie.

"Seriously?" she said.

"Don't worry. I'm gonna be far away from you guys, having my own little vacation. I'll be on the beach, relaxing with my Bahama Mama and maybe a few other mamas. But if I see you, I'll be sure to wave."

"Well?" said Matt. "Do you accept?"

She rushed forward to hug him.

"I guess that's a yes," he said, embracing her.

She stood back and smiled, looking at him in a whole new light. "That's a yes," she said.

"I figured we could get a fresh start."

"I'd like that," she said.

"Can I go?" said Adelina. "I can hang with Reggie."

"Oh, that's not gonna fly," said Reggie.

"You have school starting next week, anyway," said Vikki. She looked at Matt. "Wait, who's going to stay with Addy?"

"It's already been arranged," said her dad. "I got this. Besides, Addy has to show me how to take care of Gamma."

Vikki's phone buzzed. As soon as she glanced at the message, her eyes lit up.

"Not to be rude," she said, "this visit was beyond amazing, but I do have to get back to work. We just got a new fossil shipment in from Bavaria, and I can't wait to find out what it is."

Her dad peeked over at Matt and smiled.

"What?" she said.

Her father shook his head, grinning.

"I'm just glad to have you back."

Acknowledgements

When I set out to write a fun, escapist book about a dragon attack in modern times, I wanted a story that fired the imagination the way *Jurassic Park* did when I first read it. But I also wanted it to feel scientifically believable—not an easy task when we're talking about dragons. So I reached out to noted paleontologist Ted Daeschler at the Academy of Natural Sciences in Philadelphia (the museum featured in this book). He was kind enough to meet with me in person, give me a behind-the-scenes museum tour, and share insights into a day in the life of a paleontologist.

From that meeting, I learned far more than I expected about Earth's history, the evolutionary tree, and the scientific and personal perspective of a working paleontologist—only a fraction of which found its way into the book. He even described how a paleontologist might approach the discovery of a new species. Of course, he also pointed out a few of the physics challenges of a creature that could navigate both land and sea—which turned out to be just as useful. I'm deeply grateful for Professor Daeschler's generosity of time and expertise. Many of the brilliant details are his. Any mistakes are mine alone.

I must, of course, acknowledge my indispensable dream team of beta readers: my dear friend and writing buddy Dawn Mahan, who never fails to provide great insights; my critique partner Veronica Wolff, a marvelous sci-fi writer in her own right; and my good friend, writing mentor, and former editor Paula Berinstein, now focused on her wonderful time travel series.

I'm also grateful to Ajia Saunders, Savy Guthrie, and Felicia Martin for their helpful feedback; to Eric Miller for his always-keen editing eye; and to my brother, Dr. Eric Manas, for his scientific insights.

My gratitude knows no bounds for my long-time cover designer, Kirk DouPonce, whose work never fails to amaze me. Thanks also to Diane and Rodrigo Vilches, Guy Dorian Jr. (my fellow writer on the COR graphic novel series), Ed Miller (my co-author on *The Kronos Interference* and *The One*), and Marvel legend Guy Dorian Sr. for their encouragement and support.

Immense thanks to my cadre of author friends from International Thriller Writers who meet each Tuesday to share progress, exchange feedback, and inspire one another: Christina Irene, Stephen Matsuba and Bex, Stephanie Scott-Snyder, Nancy Cottrell, M. Gamble See, Diane DeRuggiero, Monica DeZulueta, T.O Paine, and Sherry Barron. Special thanks to Christopher Graham and USA Today bestselling author Hank Phillippi Ryan for entrusting me with being the "notetaker" each year at ITW's Online Thriller School (this gives me an idea for a crime novel about an enigmatic character code-named "The Notetaker").

And, of course, as always, thanks to my wife Sharon and my daughter Elizabeth—who I'm sure are more than tired of hearing about dragons.

About the author

J. B. Manas is an award-winning American author of suspense thrillers, often blending elements of sci-fi, mystery, espionage, and the supernatural. He is the author of *The Mirror Man* (a 2022 BestThriller s.com award winner), which Kirkus Reviews touted as "a stylish and engaging crime tale," and co-author of *The Kronos Interference*, which Kirkus named to their Best of 2012, calling it "impressively original" and "[a] tour de force."

Manas is also Editor-in-Chief for Good Alien, an IP development firm, collaborating with legendary artists and creators from the world of comics and multimedia. He is a member of the Authors Guild, International Thriller Writers (ITW), Mystery Writers of America (MWA), and the Association of Former Intelligence Officers (AFIO), and is a popular speaker at comic con events.

In addition to his work in the world of fiction, Manas's bestselling nonfiction books (written as Jerry Manas) on leadership lessons from history, science, and the arts have been translated into eight languages and course-adopted in universities worldwide.

He writes out of his home in suburban Philadelphia, where he lives with his wife, daughter, and dog Max, a loveable mutt that looks like a cross between a King Charles Cavalier Spaniel and a Corgi, but in fact has the DNA of neither.

J.B. loves hearing from his readers and can be reached via email at jb@jbmanas.com. Visit his website at www.jbmanas.com.

Also by J.B. Manas

The Kronos Interference (with Edward Miller)

"... Impressively original ... [a] tour de force."
– *Kirkus Reviews* (Starred Review, Best of 2012)

An underwater discovery leads a scientist to travel back in time to kill Hitler, causing a ripple effect he must undo before humanity is erased from the Earth.

Atticus

"Fast-paced sci-fi fun with timely application."
– *AgentPalmer.com*

A rookie policewoman must protect a downed pilot who thinks it's 1944 and find out why they're both being hunted by government agents and a Nordic assassin with unearthly powers.

The Mirror Man

"A stylish and engaging crime tale."

– Kirkus Reviews | Winner: BestThrillers.com Award, 2022, *Best Sci-Fi Thriller*

A reclusive writer with the power to read memories is forced by a mysterious stranger to steal government secrets.

The One (with Edward Miller)

"... A sophisticated thriller that deftly explores the nature of belief, loss, and redemption within a highly entertaining package . . . an action-packed battle for the future of humanity."
- BestThrillers.com

When a malevolent alien posing as the Messiah plans a false rapture to abduct millions, a downtrodden former pastor is approached by a mysterious child to help save the world.